I turned to leave. But Lady Hadleigh had closed the door and stood with her back pressed against it. Her lips curled into a slight grin and her blue eyes danced with a strange delight.

'Have you taken my daughters yet?' she asked.

'No, my lady,' I replied.

'Before you take my daughters, as no doubt you will, it would be as well for you to take me,' she said. 'But you will have to be quick for they are due back soon.'

With that, she locked the door, raised her skirts and lay across the bed. She was naked beneath her petticoats, obviously having planned the moment of seduction well in advance. I could not believe my eyes, nor my ears. Was this really Lady Sarah Hadleigh lying before me, with stockinged legs wide and high in the air? Was it a dream?

'Hurry!' she ordered. 'I need you, now!'

Indeed, it was no dream . . .

Also by Ray Gordon in New English Library paperback

Arousal

House of Lust

Ray Gordon

NEW ENGLISH LIBRARY
Hodder and Stoughton

First published in 1995 by Hodder and Stoughton
A division of Hodder Headline PLC

A New English Library paperback

10 9 8 7 6 5 4 3

British Library Cataloguing in Publication Data

Gordon, Ray
House of Lust
I. Title
823 [F]

ISBN 0-340-63493-6

Typeset by
Letterpart Limited, Reigate, Surrey
Printed and bound in Great Britain by
Cox & Wyman Ltd, Reading, Berks

Hodder and Stoughton
A division of Hodder Headline PLC
338 Euston Road
London NW1 3BH

House of Lust

Chapter One

Being but a humble stable lad, it would not have been my place to relate stories concerning my mistress or her business. But such stories as I know cannot be laid to fallow. Such stories put a mockery to what I had always believed to be the great British aristocracy. And it is that mockery that I must now expose, if only to lighten the burden on my conscience. So, after much thought and deliberation, I will reveal all.

The day I lugged what few belongings I had up the winding lane to Royston Manor, my mind was unsettled. More than unsettled, in fact, as it was to be my first proper job.

I had worked previously, but it had not been akin to the physical work that lay forebodingly before me at the stables of the manor. My work, in London, had been for my father, an accountant. He had assumed, no, expected me to follow in his footsteps and, being his only son and heir, inherit the business upon his death.

My brain for mathematics being somewhat backward, not only was my father displeased at my ineptitude but he threw me out of the firm and the house in which I had grown up. My mother, being weak of mind and body, could do nothing to save me from my unknown fate in the outside world.

My childhood days were littered with visits to an old aunt who lived in the country. My father would pack me off to stay with her at every possible opportunity – more, I think, to be rid of me than for my benefit. Happy, happy days! Far away from London, the country always held a calling for me. And so it was that I found myself employment at Royston Manor.

I was met by Harry, the head man. The only man, in fact: he ran the stables and tended the grounds and did anything he was asked simply because he was fearful of losing his job – and his home. Old and decrepit in appearance, his body had seen better days – hence, his fear.

There could have been no-one better than Harry to work under, even had I had a choice. He was a good man with a sense of humour I found pleasing and most reassuring. He smoked a pipe and sported long white sideburns, thick grey hair and the rugged complexion of a man who had spent the best part of seventy years working outside in all weathers.

No sooner had I dumped my bag in the hayloft than Harry took me to his small cottage for tea. His wife was a kindly old lady who invited me in as one of her own. We ate and they talked and I listened for two hours or more. The conversation covered anything and everything but Lord and Lady Hadleigh, which eventually caused me to enquire after them. Harry looked first to me and then at his wife. I thought it out of character and most rude at the time when she suggested that I find myself employment elsewhere. Now, of course, I know why. She would not elaborate on her statement and Harry, obviously wanting to keep the peace, winked and gave me a knowing look.

It was not until later that evening that he explained his wife's apparent rudeness. Lady Sarah Hadleigh, he said, was not of the breeding one would expect of a lady of the manor. In fact, she had started her life as the illegitimate child of a chambermaid and, after herself becoming a maid, had somehow married into the aristocracy. Neither Harry, nor anyone else, he assured me, had the slightest idea as to how she had managed such a feat. But managed she had, and he charged me not to repeat his words to a living soul. You will presently discover why I had to repeat not only his words but the story in its entirety.

My first meeting with Lady Hadleigh was not at all as I had expected it to be. It was her wont to stroll around the grounds every Sunday afternoon, always taking it upon herself to visit the stables. My initial impression on seeing the Hadleighs from afar was how young she was and how old her husband. Ah! I thought, the secret of her marrying into the aristocracy is not really a secret after all. The old man had obviously taken more than a liking to the fair maid and married her for reasons of the flesh rather than because of her station in life.

I later put my surmise to Harry. He scolded me and told me to hold my tongue, save for the subject of work. He knew more than he let on, I was sure of that, but tell, he would not. Being a young lad of eighteen, I was intrigued and swore that, with or without Harry's help, I would discover the truth.

As I was saying, Lady Hadleigh made her customary visit to the stables, unaccompanied by her husband, as was also usual, as he tired easily and needed rest.

We, or rather, I, had mucked out, groomed, scrubbed and cleaned for the best part of the day – a chore that, according to Harry, would take me the best part of every Sunday in readiness for her ladyship's visits.

On her arrival, Harry introduced me as Tom, the new lad. I smiled and answered only yes or no in response to her questions, as he had instructed beforehand.

A maid she may have once been, but now she was a fine woman with a tight, curvaceous figure and the most exquisite face that I have laid eyes upon. Her features were large and sensuous – in particular her deep blue eyes, and her full, pouting lips which curled into the slightest hint of a smile and invited a kiss, I was sure. Her long fair hair cascaded over her shoulders and down, to partially cover the roundness of her breasts which also invited my caress.

But stable lads do not do such things to their mistresses as I had in mind. They *think* such things, perhaps, but that is all. I thought such things that night as I lay in the hayloft. In fact, I thought and dreamed of nothing other than such wicked things most every night after that.

My thoughts were diverted and my dreams shattered the following Sunday upon Lady Hadleigh visiting the stables. This time, she was accompanied by her two daughters who, although I would have never thought it possible, outshone their mother with their sheer beauty.

Noticing my admiring eye, she led her daughters to me and introduced them as Clara and Elizabeth. They were of the same age as I and home for the summer holidays. I could not avert my eyes from their angelic faces, their small, newly formed, firm breasts, and their young, oh, so young and pretty mouths. More than invite a kiss, I will swear they yearned for such.

Clara was the elder of the two, but only by a year, I would hazard. Her dark hair fell in ringlets over her graceful neck. Her black eyes shone with child-like innocence but I did detect an impish glimmer within. Dark as her mother was fair, they shared the same full ruby-red pouting lips.

Elizabeth, too, had inherited her mother's sensuous lips and eyes. Her hair was long and sun-kissed yellow, soft undulations suggesting that, like her sister's, it was once twisted into ringlets.

Leaving the girls with Harry, Lady Hadleigh took my arm and led me outside. I thought for a moment that she had detected more than admiration for her daughters in my eye. And she would not have been wrong for my eyes had seen the girls naked, their young, fresh bodies open to my every whim, my hardness deep within them, filling them with the fruits of my loins as they lay writhing in the hay.

'You are a fine lad,' asserted her ladyship, once we were in the yard. 'And I want you to keep an eye on my daughters, for they are mischievous at times. Their father is . . . Well, he is older than I and is unable to help as much as I would like with their upbringing.'

I answered yes or no as the questions demanded until she smiled and asked me of my sexual experience. My face reddened and my hands trembled. I knew not what answer to give for I had only had but one (lengthy and fulfilling, I may add) sexual encounter in my life.

At the tender age of fifteen, I had been initiated to the delights of sexual intercourse by an older cousin. Ah, the glorious times we had during her visits! Her father, also an accountant, would pay attention only to my father as they discussed their businesses. Her mother rarely accompanied them so we were not missed during our escapades in the garden. Oh, how sweet she was! How warm and wet between her legs! And how firm her breasts! As ripening plums, they stood out, enticing, waiting to be picked. Such was the sensitivity of the buds upon them that she would crumple and moan with pleasure as I suckled on them.

She loved to milk me, as she so aptly put it. Not with her hands, as one would imagine, but with her mouth as I, on all fours, lowered my cock over her face and buried my mouth in her sweet bush. Stroking my balls with her tiny hands, she would take my cock to the back of her throat and suck the fruits from my quivering body. How she loved to drink from me as I lapped at her well! Ah, never shall I forget those lustful, heady days of ecstasy! But I was not prepared to divulge such information to Lady Hadleigh.

'I have experience, my lady,' I confessed as she repeated her question for the third time.

'That is good, Tom,' she replied, to my surprise. 'For my daughters have not, and I would not wish them to be crudely taken by a fumbling lad who knows nothing. I would rather they remained virgins but, alas, that cannot be as they are to go to a finishing school in Switzerland this autumn and they will be taken there, by some young man, of that, I am sure.'

'But, my lady . . .' I stammered.

'There are no "buts," Tom. Losing their virginity to fumbling males is not my only concern. It is not unheard of for young girls to be lured into lesbian relationships at such schools and that I do not want. If they have experience with a male, they will turn from such relationships with females.'

'But I would never dream of . . .'

'Do not speak falsehoods! I cannot tolerate untruths!

You know as well as I that you have it in your mind to take them! I have nothing more to say on the matter.'

I stood aghast as my mistress summoned her daughters and ushered them from the yard. Harry wandered from the stables and asked what it was she had said that had obviously stunned me so. I could not tell him, of course. Although I had a suspicion that he knew some, if not all, of the words that had passed between our lips.

'Be careful, lad,' he admonished as he turned and made for his cottage to take tea. I did not reply but followed him from the yard wondering what he had had in mind when he had advised caution. I should add here that the arrangement was such that I ate with Harry and his wife every day. Harry's wage had been increased slightly to take into account the cost of extra food but I had decided to add a modest sum to that from my own wage for the inconvenience.

After our food, we sat beneath an apple tree and I asked Harry once more of his secret. Again, and not to my surprise, he declined to speak of the matter. But I did feel that the day would soon be upon us when he would tell. When the time was right and the mood took him, he would enlighten me.

I had cause to visit the village the following afternoon on an errand for Harry. Following his directions, I took the path across the field and through the wood. The day was hot and, once out of sight of the manor, I removed my shirt. The cool breeze in the wood refreshed me. My mind reeled with thoughts of Elizabeth and Clara, not to mention of Lady Hadleigh herself, thoughts that, I must confess, rather stimulated me.

7

I was in two minds as whether or not to relieve the hardness of my aching cock when I heard the echoes of twigs cracking under foot. It would have to wait, I thought. On the return journey, I would find a clearing where the grass had been cropped short and soft by rabbits, and strip naked. Under the summer sun, I would take my hard cock and disgorge my seed, spurting it over the grass until my head should be clear of its tantalising naked forms.

Suddenly, Clara and Elizabeth came bounding through the trees and stood before me in their pink, gingham frocks. The bulge in my breeches was all too obvious and did not go unnoticed.

'Did mother have a word with you?' Elizabeth asked of me innocently.

'About what, miss?' I returned.

'About us,' Clara rejoined, her gaze transfixed by the swelling below my leather belt.

'She mentioned neither you nor your sister,' I lied.

'Oh, but she did!' Clara insisted. 'She charged you to keep an eye on us!'

Lady Hadleigh's every word was etched in my memory. How could I forget what she had told me? And how could I defy her request?

'It is true,' I replied at length. 'Lady Hadleigh did, indeed, charge me to keep an eye on you.'

'And which of us would you prefer to keep an eye on?' Clara taunted, winding her dark ringlets around her fingers.

'Why, both of you, of course.'

'And which part of us would you like to keep an eye on?'

At that, I had to make my excuses and take my leave, for I knew only too well that otherwise I would take them both in turn. Not that that would have been against Lady Hadleigh's wishes. On the contrary, she had as good as told me to take her daughters. But in the state I was in, I would have taken them crudely, brutally indeed, for my own satisfaction rather than their enlightenment. And that was *not* her ladyship's wish!

On returning from the village, I was surprised to find Elizabeth waiting for me at the same spot in the wood.

'Where is your sister, miss?' I enquired, barely slowing my pace as I passed.

'She has gone home,' came the reply.

'You should not be here alone,' I scolded, now some ten yards on.

'Unless you come back now and kiss me, properly, I will tell my mother!' she called.

'Tell her what, miss?' I asked, walking towards her.

'That you have spoken ill of her.'

So, that was to be her game – do as she says or her mother would be told terrible lies about me. I was quite happily settled in my new employment and was not prepared to have my job held in the balance by two young girls. It seemed there was only one course of action left open to me.

Holding her head in my hands, I pressed my lips to hers. How sweet her taste as our tongues touched! Ah, such a heavenly child as she surely deserved more than a mere kiss! My cock rising, I pushed my tongue deep into her mouth and explored the hotness within. She pressed her heaving breasts against my chest, and I my hardness against the softness of her belly.

'I will not tell her now that you have kissed me so,' she breathed as our lips parted.

'You will never tell her such things that are untrue! And to assure myself that you do not, I must punish you.'

Holding her arms tight, I lay her over a fallen tree. Lifting her dress, I near tore the knickers from her wriggling body. As her screams and threats filled the wood, I wondered for a moment what had possessed me to do such a thing. But my straining cock and the sight of her pale bottom exposed to my hungry eyes drove me on.

Snapping a small branch from the tree, I landed a stinging blow squarely across her tightening buttocks. Ah, how she cried out! The birds took flight as I landed the second blow and I will swear the trees themselves shook as the third and fourth blows reddened her youthful flesh.

As she squirmed, I caught a fleeting glimpse of the downy bush nestling between her milk-white thighs. The need in my breeches was by then painful and I had only one thing in my mind – to sink my cock deep into her tight little hole and take her virginity.

But alas, it was not to be. Reluctantly relinquishing my weapon at the sound of voices calling in response to the girl's screams, I fled into the bushes. Crouching in the undergrowth, I heard whoever it was talking to Elizabeth.

'It was a snake,' she garbled. 'A great big snake!'

So, she had not taken it upon herself to tell of her plight as I thought she would. Why, I wondered, had she not told of her terrible ordeal? Why had she not said that the stable lad had torn the knickers from her trembling body and thrashed her buttocks until they glowed? Perhaps she had enjoyed it? I thought – I prayed! Or would she tell only her mother? That worried me greatly for her mother would surely not take kindly to my beating her daughter so!

Harry was sitting in the yard on my return. He looked

pale and worn. I knew then that unless he rested more, he would not be long for this world. Poor Harry – once retired, he would have no home as his cottage was tied. I swore to help him. I knew not how at that time, but I would see him all right.

I had done my duties, and Harry's, by the end of the day and eaten well with him and his wife. Would that my mother and father were more like them, I thought, as I made my way to the hayloft at dusk. I had heard nothing from them, of course. I had not expected my father to write as he had disowned me. But my mother, I was sure, would find it in herself to communicate, secretly.

To my surprise and great delight, I found Clara waiting for me in the hayloft. Clad in her nightgown, she had slipped through her bedroom window to come and see me.

Her small breasts and brown nipples were just visible in the flickering light of the oil lamp. She was a beauty, indeed! As she lay back in the hay, she asked what I had done to her sister. I said only that I had passed her on my return journey from the village.

'She was most distressed on her arrival home,' she whispered.

'Then you must ask her why,' I said.

'Tell me what you did to her or I will tell my mother!'

Ah, another hussy who requires a good beating, I decided. But I could not allow her to disturb the quiet of the night with her screams. My cock was now in dire need of attention so I lay beside her and pressed my hardness against the warmth of her body.

'I allowed her to touch me,' I whispered in her ear.

'And did she?' she asked, her huge dark eyes sparkling.

'Oh, yes. She took it in her hand and she even kissed it.'

'Then I must do the same for I am older than she,' came the unexpected but most welcome reply.

With that, Clara wrenched my swollen cock from my breeches and clasped it in her warm hand. Ah, what ecstasy! I thought that I would finish there and then as she fondled and explored its length, the loose skin, the hardness of the knob.

Moving her head down, she kissed the swollen knob. Softly, gently, she kissed it with her sweet, young lips. But then she made to move away. I would not be left in such a state – pray, what man would?

Pulling her head down again, I took my cock in my hand and pressed it firmly against her mouth. Still finding her unyielding, I pinched her nose. As she struggled and gasped for air, I entered the portal. What warmth I found against her tongue! What ecstasy did her hot throat yield!

Wiggling and squirming as she did only served to heighten my delight and I quickly filled her soft cheeks. Ah, sweet relief! Wrenching her head back and forth, I took her mouth as I would her pussy. There is a subtle difference, I find, between a maiden's mouth and her pussy. Although it is beyond my comprehension, as they are both hot and wet and feel much the same, I surmise that it has to do with the mind. But that is by the by.

I did not withdraw until the last drop had left my cock and she had savoured my bitter-sweet fruits. It was her first taste of a man's sperm, I was sure. And who was I to shorten her delightful if not awesome experience?

When I finally granted her freedom she choked and spluttered and cried as she crawled towards the ladder. In the affray, her nightgown had lifted, affording me a perfect view of her beautiful body. Her breasts were swollen, her nipples elongated, whilst her bush, sparse with black hair, allowed me sight of her vaginal crack as she swung her leg over the ladder.

As I lay in the hay, satisfied and happy in the knowledge that I had two beautiful young girls to occupy my spare time, a realisation came to me. I could play one against the other. What delights there were in store for me! And what better thought to sleep upon?

Chapter Two

I awakened to the sun streaming in through the cracks in the stable roof. I had slept long and well, dreaming of the girls – and their mother – crawling naked over my body, kissing and caressing my cock as I licked and sucked them in turn.

Harry was not in the stables to greet me as was usual when I descended the ladder. Neither was he in the yard, where I washed the sleep from my eyes in the horse trough.

I was late – it was six of the clock and I should have been up by five to prepare the horses for their morning gallop across the heath. I was not yet a competent rider but, with Harry's help, I was learning fast. This was to be the first day I took out Giant, a magnificent black stallion that inspired a potent mixture of fear and challenge within me.

As I wandered down to the cottage, I knew instinctively that something was wrong. Alas, I was right, for Harry was in his bed looking decidedly old and ill. His wife's tearful eyes met mine as she asked me to cover for her husband. I promised that I would, which left them with some peace of mind, at least.

By nine, I had caught up with my chores. Giant had been exceptionally good to me, throwing me only twice,

which left me in no doubt as to who was boss! I will swear
that as I rubbed him down he had a knowing look in his big
black eye. He missed Harry, that I knew. But, strangely, in
his wisdom, he had accepted me – almost.

Lady Hadleigh appeared at the stable door as I was
admiring my hard work. My heart raced in anticipation of
what she might say about the events of the previous day.
'You have done well, Tom,' she said with a smile that
reassured me. 'Where is Harry?'

'He had to go into the village, my lady,' I replied.

'If he required something from the village, why did he
not send you?'

I had to think quickly, but I was unaccustomed to lying.
'Today was my first time out on Giant and he threw me
twice,' I enlightened her ladyship, playing for time.

'And you ache, is that it?'

Before I could answer, Clara and Elizabeth appeared to
take their stand on either side of their mother. I was aware
of my blushes as I looked first at one and then at the other.

'Fancy sleeping in the hayloft!' Clara mocked wickedly.
'Only vagabonds and the like sleep in haylofts!' She was
trying to repay me for using her mouth so the night before.
But I did not mind that, for I knew that she had not told
her mother.

'Be quiet, girl!' Lady Hadleigh chided, to my great
delight.

'Are you riding today, Elizabeth?' she asked, turning to
the other girl.

'No, mother. Not today,' she replied meekly, her hands
moving to her bottom which, I discerned, was still stinging.

Turning my face to conceal a grin, I asked Lady
Hadleigh if that would be all. She said it would, and

hurried the girls from the stable. So, I had covered for Harry. But, I wondered, how long could I keep up the pretence? A day or two, yes. Three, maybe, but no more.

Mid-morning found me soaping the saddles in the yard. I had not had the time to visit Harry and my concern for him would not allow me to concentrate on the job. The girls had not been around, which pleased me, as my workload was hefty and I imagined myself working into the night.

The sound of a pony and trap trundling up the lane distracted my thoughts. The man who stepped from the trap as it drew up outside the manor house was surely a doctor, I surmised. Perhaps my exotic fruits had upset Clara's stomach, I speculated, as he wandered towards me.

'Would you water my horse, lad?' he asked on his approach.

I said that I would and then, as he turned towards the house, I brazenly asked if he was a physician.

'I am, indeed. Why, are you ill?'

'No, sir. But Harry, the head man, is.'

'Then I will speak with Lady Hadleigh.'

'I would rather you did not . . .' I began.

'Oh, and why is that? Are you going to pay my fee, then?'

'Yes, sir,' I blurted out, not having a clue as to the amount.

He walked away and I took it that he would not look at Harry. But I watered his horse, deliberately biding my time over the task. My plan paid off, as finding me still attending the animal on his return, the doctor agreed to see Harry.

Out of sight of the manor, I led him to the cottage. Harry was not a well man, I knew. But the physician's news was graver than I had expected. Harry, he informed me, was dying. Six months, perhaps a year, but certainly no longer. He had the foresight not to say such words in front of Harry's wife, and I thanked him for that. I expressed, too, my heartfelt appreciation for the waiving of his fee.

I was sorely shaken. So the man who, after only a short time, I had come to regard as my father, was not long for this world! I stood beneath the apple tree deep in thought. Harry's wife joined me, as I knew she would.

'It is not good, is it?' she asked.

'Harry will be fine!' I fibbed, the tear in my eye not going unnoticed.

'You do not have to keep it from me, I was listening.'

She had not been listening, I had made sure of that. But her ploy was clever and deserved the truth.

'Harry is dying,' I said gently, taking her shoulders. 'But you will not lose your home – or me.'

Taking solace in my words, she smiled. At least for a while she would feel secure, but her tears would come. Later that day or that night, I knew not when. The reality would hit her sooner or later.

While Harry's fate would not leave my thoughts, I had to continue with my work, and my lies, to cover for him. Later that afternoon, Lady Hadleigh came by and asked for Harry. Her husband was ill, it seemed, and she required Harry to rearrange the furniture in his bedroom.

'I will do it, my lady,' I assured her. 'Harry is in the field just now.'

'Then come with me,' she instructed, turning towards the house. I followed, watching her rounded bottom wiggle from side to side as she walked. I did not forget

Harry, but the sight of such a lovely bottom and tiny waist cheered me.

The manor house was huge – to this day, I have never seen such luxury. I was taken in through a rear door, of course, and led up the back stairs. Even so, I was amazed at the grandeur. A far cry from the hayloft!

Lord Hadleigh lay upon his bed, a more sorry sight even than Harry. I found myself wondering what Lady Hadleigh had taken up in place of sexual intercourse! Certainly, the old boy was in no condition to satisfy himself, let alone a woman.

I was to reset a table and a chest of drawers, which I did quickly, for I felt uncomfortable in my master's bedroom. I was then led to Lady Hadleigh's apartment, where she instructed me to move her dressing table.

Again, I complied speedily and turned to leave. But Lady Hadleigh had closed the door and stood with her back pressed against it, her lips curling into a slight grin, her blue eyes dancing with a strange delight.

'Have you taken my daughters yet?' she asked, ere long.

'No, my lady,' I replied, wondering if taking Clara's mouth could be thought of as equivalent to taking her pussy.

'Then you relieve yourself by hand?'

'No, my lady, I do not.'

'Oh, but come! Surely, you are concealing the truth? Tell me, what red-blooded young man can go for weeks on end without relief?'

None, I imagined. But I knew not how to answer. I did know, or, at any rate, I preferred to think, that she could not go for long without relief herself, either. I dared not ask if she pleasured herself by hand, of course. Although, again, I would have preferred to fancy that she did! Perhaps in the wood, on the downy grass, as her horse patiently nibbled at the hawthorn? I imagined her naked, her legs spread wide as she fingered herself and filled the air with squeals of delight.

'Before you take my daughters, as no doubt you will, it would be as well for you to take me,' she continued, bringing me quickly back to reality. 'But you will have to be quick for they are due back soon.'

With that, she locked the door, raised her skirts and lay across the bed. She was naked beneath her petticoats, obviously having planned the moment of seduction well in advance. I could not believe my eyes, nor my ears. Was this really Lady Sarah Hadleigh lying before me, with stockinged legs wide and high in the air? Was it a dream? A fantasy to savour as I lay in the hay relieving myself?

The gracious curves of her pale buttocks parted to reveal her smaller hole as she raised herself in readiness to receive me. The golden bush upon her mound shone in the sunlight streaming in through the windows. My balls fairly jiggled at the wondrous sight!

'Hurry!' she ordered, parting the soft, pink flesh of her vagina with her slender fingers. 'I need you inside me, now!' Indeed it was no dream! For I could feel my cock risen and straining against my breeches ready to dive into the golden fleece spread invitingly before me.

'I am not accustomed to waiting!' panted my ladyship.

'Then you shall wait not a moment longer, my lady!' I asserted, wondering if Lord Hadleigh was listening to our every word in the adjoining room.

Quickly, I slipped my breeches down, proudly displaying

my erection to her appreciative gaze before thrusting it deep into her wetness.

Oh, how she writhed and panted and gasped as I took her! How her hot cunt gripped and sucked on me!

'Take me harder!' she pleaded. 'You must be gentle with my daughters for it will be their first time, but not so with me!'

She cried out as I gave all I had. Harder, harder into her hot depths I rammed, until her cunt squeezed and sucked the sperm from my balls. Nearing the pinnacle of our union, she arched her back, her entire body shaking violently as she moaned her pleasure. 'Talk to me – tell me what you are doing to me!' she gasped.

'I am taking you, my lady.'

'Call me Sarah and tell me of your cock inside my body!'

Her face burned scarlet, her nostrils flared and the cords of her long neck stood proud as she flung her head back and attained her goal. At my last thrust, I drove my sperm into her womb, gasping all the while, 'I am fucking you!'

My ladyship grinned her obvious delight at my obscenity as I collapsed over the slight mound of her stomach, well and truly done. As her breathing settled and the colour faded from her cheeks, she manoeuvred her hips to relinquish my cock from her hole. Then, as if we had been up to nothing more than taking afternoon tea, she pushed me aside, arose, adjusted her attire and opened the door.

That was it. I had been used, yes. But oh, how I had used her! God, how I had used and abused her! And I knew, I prayed, that I would be required to service her again and again.

I found my own way out of the manor house and back to the stables where Giant seemed to have more than a knowing look in his eye. Poor beast, feeling as he must the urge to copulate as men do. I would allow him time with a mare, I promised him, and he seemed to smile.

By the end of that day I was truly hungry and made for the cottage with much haste. Harry seemed a little better, which pleased his wife. But they were concerned about the future. They knew, we knew, that the cottage would have to go. That is when I asked Harry to tell me the secret.

'I know no secret,' he rasped from his bed.

'But you do, Harry!' I insisted, to no avail. Although I found myself wondering whether he actually did know anything or not. After all, he had nothing to lose by telling me, for his wife had already informed him of the doctor's findings.

Eventually laying my head on the hay, I slept badly. Anxious about Harry, Alice, the cottage, my job, and still not having heard from my mother, I admit to a feeling of great despair and loneliness that night.

The following morning, Lady Hadleigh came to the stables in search of Harry. My nightmare was about to come true.

'I have not set eyes on Harry for two days,' she said. 'I will go to the cottage and speak with him.'

'Best not now, my lady. Harry is ill – dying,' I confessed.

'Then why was I not informed of this?'

'Because we . . . Harry and his wife, that is, do not want to lose the cottage.'

'But they have no choice in the matter. The cottage is tied to the job. If the job goes, then it follows that the cottage goes.'

I could scarce believe my ears! How could this woman,

this chambermaid masquerading as a lady, talk so of a dying man and his home?

'I will make *you* head man and *you* shall live in the cottage,' she continued.

'Then, my lady, I respectfully request that Harry and his wife live with me in the cottage.'

'No, that is not possible! I have no time to waste on such matters so you can tell them they will be receiving notice to quit in writing in due course.'

She left me no choice. I was shaking, I must admit, and my stomach churned, but I had no choice.

'I know of your background, my lady. I did not wish to reveal this knowledge to you but, in the circumstances . . .'

'My background?'

'Yes, my lady.'

'You know nothing! Absolutely nothing! What has possessed you to speak to me so?'

'I cannot reveal the source of my information, but . . .'

'You are dismissed! Collect your belongings and go – now!' she stormed and flounced from the stables.

'But I know that you were a chambermaid,' I called.

She stopped dead in her tracks but did not turn to face me. I cared not for myself what the outcome would be as she finally turned on her heels and walked slowly towards me. For Harry and his wife were my only concern and if they were to go, then I would follow.

Lady Hadleigh looked me hard in the eye. She was fuming but, at the same time, I detected that she was flummoxed.

'Do you honestly think I care one hoot what you do or do not know about me?' she asked.

'No, my lady. But I think you care what others might know.'

'Others? Do not speak in riddles, be explicit.'

'Friends, relatives, people in the village.'

Blackmail had not crossed my mind when Harry had told me of her ladyship's origin. But her attitude had riled me and I was not prepared to stand by and do nothing.

'There is no room for all three of you in the cottage. But if that is your wish, then so be it. How you will all survive on your wage alone is your problem. And in future, mind your tongue or you will have no employment, and none of you a roof over your head!'

With that, she lifted her skirts and turned to leave. But, having won that round, I ventured a step further. God only knows where I found the courage, but find it I did.

'May I be so bold as to ask that our agreement be put in writing, my lady?'

'You may not be so bold! You will not dare to be bold when talking to me! But, for my own protection, I will have the papers drawn up this afternoon. Six months, mind! After which time you, Harry and his wife will leave this place. Now, have you no work to do?'

To say I was elated would be an understatement. I was beside myself with joy! But I could not tell Harry and his wife of the good news until I had the papers in my hand. Bitch that she was, Lady Hadleigh may well have had cause to change her mind and that would have been too great a disappointment for Harry to bear.

It occurred to me then that Lady Hadleigh had agreed for reasons other than my threats – for reasons that suited her. Firstly, to dismiss me while Harry was laid up would leave her in quite a predicament. Secondly, Lord Hadleigh was ill and, judging by his age and pallor, he might well soon pass on. And last but not least, she would not wish to be rid of me, her stud!

I saw nothing of Clara and Elizabeth during that day and decided that their mother was deliberately keeping them from me. She would retaliate, I knew. But surely her vengeance would be more venomous than merely denying me her daughters' company once in a while?

As dusk fell, there being no sign of the papers, I began to fear the worst. Harry and Alice – the old woman had asked me to call her thus as we had talked beneath the apple tree – would be anxious as to my whereabouts.

I had just about given up all hope and was preparing to go to the cottage when Lady Hadleigh walked across the yard bearing an envelope in her hand. She was clearly not a happy woman. I can only describe the look in her eye as she opened the envelope and thrust the documents into my hand as vehement.

Taking her pen, I signed both copies of the agreement and handed one to her. No words passed between us, but I felt her eyes on my breeches. A bitch of the first order, yes. But also some woman of feeling beneath!

Harry and Alice were overjoyed at my news. In fact, Harry sat up in his bed looking better than I had seen him for some time. Alice cooked a fine meal of roast lamb and potatoes and even broke out a flagon of wine by way of celebration. I ate and drank far too much before making a move to leave.

'You will not be sleeping in the stables!' exclaimed Alice as I neared the door.

'That I will,' I returned. 'This is your home and it is too small for three. Besides, I like the stables.'

I did not explain my predilection for the stables, but the look in Harry's eye showed that he understood only too well. With three women to service, I needed my own home – albeit a hayloft!

Lady Hadleigh was waiting for me at the foot of the ladder when I returned to the stables. Judging by the smirk upon her pretty face, her mood had calmed somewhat. Either that, or she had devised a plan of revenge.

'You have told them of your good news?' she asked on my approach.

'Yes, my lady.'

'Then I shall tell you of mine.'

The glint in her eye was almost evil. Her good news, no doubt, would be bad news to me.

'Pray, what is your news?' I ventured.

'My news, Tom, is that you are only to be here for six weeks more. As our agreement is legally binding, you will leave, along with Harry and Alice, exactly six weeks from today!'

She was a shrewd woman, no less. I had not read the agreement properly, it seemed. My anger rising, I felt I had nothing to lose. Bold? I will swear I was never so bold in all my life! Grabbing her arm, I threw her to the ground, tearing the finery from her. The velvet dress and silk underclothes parted shamefully from her trembling flesh as I ripped my way to her body. Scream from the depths of her lungs though she did, still there was no holding me.

Taking a riding crop, I turned her over and beat her neat little buttocks until they positively glowed. Her threats rang out as I placed my knee in the small of her back and continued with the gruelling punishment.

Coming to my senses, I discarded the crop and rolled her

onto her back. Ah, how sweet is revenge! She knew full well what was coming to her next. Fight she did, but nothing could stop my stiff cock from entering the wetness of her pussy. Her muscles gripped my throbbing rod, in fear or sexual arousal I could not say. But I cared naught for her feelings at that time. I only had it in mind to satisfy my lust.

As I pumped her body with all the force I could muster, she cried out and wrapped her legs around me. She was enjoying her punishment and that would not do! Withdrawing my cock, I turned her once more and persisted with the beating. Ah, now she cried out with pain! After several stinging blows accompanied by her screams, it was time to relieve myself. Rolling her over like a rag doll I re-entered her and pumped her full of my sperm. Such a fuck, I will swear, I have never before experienced in my life!

She was tight – far more so than earlier – crushing, in fact. Even my sweet, virginal cousin had been slack in comparison. For a woman who had borne two children, Lady Hadleigh's cunt was uncannily constricted. I put it down to her great sexual arousal – and a little pain, of course!

Once I was done, I withdrew my cock from her used body and stood over her. She whimpered and cried and hurled expletives at me as she rose to her feet and covered her breasts with her small hands.

'You'll pay for this!' she screamed, retrieving the remnants of her torn clothing.

'I have no money with which to pay you,' I laughed.

'You will pay! As God is my witness – you will pay!'

I ascended the ladder for a well-deserved rest only to find Clara and Elizabeth awaiting me. Alas, they had seen everything, watching as their mother was stripped, beaten and fucked as never before.

'She deserved it,' I muttered by way of an excuse.

'She did that,' returned Clara, to my utter amazement.

'She will make you pay, though,' Elizabeth warned.

'No, she cannot. There is nothing she can do. I have nothing she can take – no money, no property – nothing.'

'She will still make you pay.'

I was in no mood for games. After a long day, and night, I was tired. I would have taken the girls there and then if it were not for my exhaustion. For I believe that after witnessing their mother's ordeal, that is what they craved.

Clara grabbed my cock through my breeches and began to knead the growing bulge, swaying my decision somewhat, I must confess. As she unbuttoned me and pulled it free, they both gasped with delight to see it yet wet from their mother's cunt. I, too, found some strange delight in the thought of taking first the mother and then her daughters.

Just as I was about to make my move, Lady Hadleigh screeched like a woman possessed. The girls quickly gathered their skirts and descended the ladder, leaving me with my cock standing stiff and proud with not a hand – other than my own – mouth or tight pussy in sight!

'Clara! Elizabeth!' The cries filled the night air, sending the sleeping birds from the trees as would a gunshot. Again and again she screamed into the darkness until, I surmised, the girls showed their presence.

Reclining in the hay, I put my hand to good use as I thought of Lady Hadleigh and her delectable daughters who, as yet, I had not had the pleasure of taking. But I would, I promised myself, as my sperm came in a fountain. I would take them in turn and deflower them – good and proper!

Chapter Three

I was awoken in the early hours by what I deemed to be a coach-and-four following the sweep of the drive to the manor. Aware of a disturbance, Giant had been uneasy all night. Neighing and kicking as he was, I had imagined he was dreaming of the mare I had promised him, and taken little notice.

Voices drifted from the direction of the house and, while reluctant to disturb my sweet dreams of the girls, I felt the matter warranted investigation.

Stealing across the yard, I spied through the bushes that concealed the stables from the house. Indeed, there was the coach-and-four, flanked ominously, I thought, by the doctor's pony and trap. Lady Hadleigh was standing on the steps of the house with her daughters.

Perhaps the old man has died, I speculated, remembering the aged and frail body lying on the bed. As I watched, the coach-and-four made haste down the lane, soon to be followed by the doctor.

When all and sundry had departed, I crept over to the house to take a look through the downstairs window. By the lamplight, I could see the girls sitting on a couch and Lady Hadleigh pacing the floor. Clara's dress was in affray and her hair a mess, as if she had been dragged through the wood and taken by force. Ah, how wonderful to tear her knickers from her body and part her milk-white thighs to the accompaniment of screams and protests! What joy to forcibly push my cock into her tight, wet pussy as she kicks and fights like an animal! Oh, sweet dreams! But not dreams for too much longer, I prayed.

All was glum and silent until Lady Hadleigh stood with her back to the hearth, tossing back her loose hair and flattening her dress over the contour of her belly.

'We are on our own now,' she uttered solemnly.

'We have Tom,' returned Clara.

'We do, indeed, Clara,' Lady Hadleigh smiled. 'But he is problematic, to say the least.'

The girls giggled at their mother's words for they were obviously remembering her ordeal under the riding crop.

'We will discuss this in the morning,' continued Lady Hadleigh. 'The two of you must be tired – especially you, Clara. Your journey through the wood to the doctor's house must have been most traumatic, to say the least. I thank God that you were not waylaid and . . . Anyway, off to bed!'

Again, the girls giggled, which I considered rather odd, seeing that they had just lost their father. Lady Hadleigh did not appear too distressed by the loss, either. The one most put out that eventful night I will swear was me! To think that young Clara had run through the wood in the middle of the night, her breasts heaving, her body wet with perspiration and her pussy . . . Alas, an opportunity missed!

Mystified by the girls' giggles and apparent lack of grief at their father's demise, I waited until they had retired to their beds and then lifted the sash window.

Not knowing for what I was looking, I had no idea where to begin as I stole through the window. I crept to the stairs but they creaked loudly, putting an end to my notion of searching the entire house – and finding the girls' bedrooms, I am sad to say.

Downstairs, I happened upon the study – as good a place as any to hunt for secrets. Daylight was dawning so I had some light by which to see as I opened the writing bureau. The old man had everything filed and labelled in his desk which made life somewhat easier. There was nothing of interest to be found amongst the assortment of documents but a locked drawer took my attention.

The small lock broke with ease as I pulled forcibly on the drawer. The action split the surrounding wood but I deemed it of no consequence – no-one would suspect me, I was sure.

My efforts proved worthwhile – to my great delight, Lady Hadleigh's copy of our agreement lay on top of the pile of papers. But the find threw me into a dilemma. Were I to take the paper, then she would know that it was I who had broken in. Again, I decided, no matter. With no proof, there would be nothing she could do. And with no agreement, Harry and Alice would be secure – for a while longer, at least.

What I next discovered amongst the papers I could scarce believe. Most of the document I could not comprehend, but the truth of it was plain. Lord Hadleigh was no more the father of Clara and Elizabeth than I!

So, I wondered as I made my hasty exit through the window, who was? It then occurred to me that indeed Lady Hadleigh might not be their natural mother. That was it, I decided – the girls were adopted! My conclusion also solved the mystery of the tightness of Lady Hadleigh's pussy!

Giant was improving by the day. He allowed me to take him across the heath and not once did he even attempt to throw me. But I felt that he, as I, had some uncanny notion that Lady Hadleigh would be awaiting our return. He seemed most reluctant to enter the yard, forcing me to dismount and lead him in.

Our intuition proved right, for standing by the stable door was Lady Hadleigh. Poor Giant reared on our cautious approach as if to show her who was boss! She moved, wisely, as I led him through the door.

'Tom, I want a word with you!' she called, not daring to enter the stable, probably in as much fear of my riding crop as of Giant.

'Yes, my lady,' I responded with a bright smile as I tethered the horse. I guessed the smile might throw her a little, as indeed it did.

'About last evening . . .' she began hesitantly, before tailing off. Following her gaze to my breeches, I observed with amusement that the jodhpurs had fallen into a crease, so giving the impression of an erection of impossible proportions.

'I am sorry to hear about your husband, my lady,' I ventured.

'And what do you know of that?' she asked quietly.

'I saw the coach and four – and the doctor.'

'Lord Hadleigh is no concern of yours – or mine now, thank God! I want to talk to you about your despicable behaviour last evening. Just who on earth do you think you are?' she bellowed.

'Who do you think *you* are?' I returned, immediately wishing I had not.

'I wish you to leave today. Now!'

'But, my lady, I know not only of your background, a secret which I assure you is safe with me, but also the history of your daughters.'

It had been a gamble but, happily, one that paid off. Without so much as a word, her ladyship turned on her heels and fair near ran to the house. I was winning round after round which worried me somewhat, for on the law of averages, luck eventually runs out.

During my visit to Harry, who was looking better than ever, I might add, I mentioned that I knew about the girls.

'I know naught of that,' he said. 'But that is not the secret that I . . .'

'Ah, so there *is* a secret!' I interrupted.

'Now you are putting words into my mouth, young man!' he laughed.

It was good to see the old man jovial and I began to wonder at the doctor's findings. Surely Harry was on the mend? According to Alice, he was eating well and had been asking for beer – a good sign if ever there was one. Alice, being Alice, would not allow him to partake of a drop of the stuff, so I took it upon myself to smuggle some in through the bedroom window that evening. As I later discovered, it was a move that was to rile Alice, much to my detriment!

Clara and Elizabeth were wandering aimlessly, it seemed, across the field as I made my way back to the yard. Perhaps the loss of their father was now taking its toll, I speculated. But no – catching sight of me, they came galloping over like wild horses.

'Tom! Tom!' they called in unison. I stopped by the gate to greet them.

'Has she sacked you?' Clara asked eagerly as she ran into me, her breasts heaving.

'No, she has not!' I returned indignantly.

'She will!' Elizabeth chipped in.

'She will not!' I replied confidently, adding in a softer tone, 'I am sorry to hear of your father's death.'

I *was* sorry, for selfish reasons, I am afraid. I had had it in my mind to take the girls that very afternoon as I knew that their mother was to visit a friend at a mansion across the heath. But Lord Hadleigh had rather upset the apple-cart with his untimely departure. I was unsure of the girls' future, to say the least. And it was with that in mind that I had decided to take them both as soon as the opportunity arose.

Lady Hadleigh's appearance some distance away sent the girls scurrying off in opposite directions like frightened rabbits. I walked back to the yard where, to my surprise, she was waiting for me. Her mood was difficult to interpret as she wore an odd smile – a smile that I knew from experience could mean any manner of evil. What was it this time? I wondered. Had she hatched a scheme to be rid of me once and for all? Or was she hot and ready for my body? Remembering the events of the previous evening, I rather thought not.

'Tom,' she said softly. I did not reply as, I must confess, I was rather bewildered by her tone. 'I must talk to you,' she continued, obviously finding some difficulty in being pleasant towards me. Still I said nothing, but with my cynicism waning, I proffered a smile. All the while she kept one eye on the stable door, just in case Giant should take a disliking to her manner and take it upon himself to save his master from a hostile woman, I surmised.

But hostile she was not – in fact, to the contrary, inviting me up to the house for tea. I was taken in through the rear door, of course, and led into a small room which I gauged was used by servants at one time. I must here add that, save my good self and the cook, whose acquaintance I had yet to make, there were no other staff.

The room was sparsely furnished, though pleasing to the eye. Having ordered tea, Lady Hadleigh sat me down in an armchair and proceeded to pace the floor by the hearth, as if planning her speech. I remained silent throughout, more out of curiosity than fear. Ere long, she turned to face me, flicking her hair back and smiling that queer smile.

'Tom,' she again intoned. This time I was obliged to reply for my curiosity was rising at an alarming rate and my patience wearing thin.

'Yes, my lady?' I answered firmly.

'Tom, we have had our differences, I know. What I do not know is how on earth we can have had such differences in the short space of time you have been at Royston Manor. It was probably my fault for seducing you in the first instance, but that is by-the-by.'

She was troubled of mind, that was clear. And I did not care for her manner one bit. After all, she was the queen of bitches and was not to be trusted. But I could not help but admire her slender hips, so tightly hugged by the velvet of her dress, and her pert bottom, so rounded and proud. Her ample cleavage was accentuated by some kind of uplifting brassiere, taking my notice not the least!

'You seem to know rather too much for my liking, Tom,' Lady Hadleigh continued. That was true enough, but still I was ignorant as to how she had persuaded a lord, no less, to marry her. 'You broke into my home and stole my copy of our agreement which was futile, as my solicitor also has a copy.'

Ah, I had slipped up there, I thought. But I thought also that I had the answer to that.

'There were no witnesses, my lady. So the six-week agreement is . . .'

'Null and void, Tom.'

'Exactly! Well, I think that clears that little matter up.'

'Indeed, it does.'

She was, indeed, a clever woman. What was it then she had in mind, I wondered, still gazing at the cleavage that so reminded me of a young girl's bottom – Elizabeth's bottom, in fact.

'I will come straight to the point,' she pursued. 'Should you tell my daughters what you believe to be the truth, it would upset them beyond all comprehension. You see, they adored their father, Lord Hadleigh, and to suggest that he was no more their father than a stranger would be terribly distressing for them.'

The fact that the girls obviously did not love the old man seemed to have slipped her memory but, at that point, I was not going to split hairs. My patience, to put it mildly, had all but gone.

'I am a very busy man, Lady Hadleigh, with enough work for three men on my hands,' I asserted.

'Yes, Tom. That is the point, or one of the points, that I was coming to. You see, my daughters have – how can I put it? – taken a liking to you. And, I must confess, in some self-destructive way, I too have an admiration for you. Although I cannot for the life of me think why!'

I was about to interrupt and tell her that her admiration was based on the fact that I had taken her to such sexual heights as she had never dreamed possible, but she raised her hand to silence me.

'You have no breeding . . . Well, in view of what you know, perhaps I should not have said that. However, I *am* the lady of this house, I own this house and all that goes with it, and I am not prepared to be blackmailed by a member of my staff – for that is all you are, Tom. A member of my staff.'

Again, that was true enough, but I still held all the aces. 'I must ask you to be brief,' I said with some authority, 'as I have no time for idle chat.' No sooner had I finished that clumsy sentence than I knew it to be a mistake.

'Your audacity riles me, Tom. I cannot stress that too much. However, as you have taken it upon yourself to be so blunt, then I shall follow suit. You have me cornered, I will admit. But little do you realise that you have cornered a lion! And believe you me, the day will come when I will fight like a lion! I confess that for the moment, I find myself at a loss as to my next move. That is why I have tried, unsuccessfully, it would appear, to conduct this discussion in a civil manner. We are both clever – too clever, perhaps. And if we cannot find a solution, then we are not worthy of such cleverness. Do you not agree?'

I did agree – I had to for she was actually cleverer than I, and I dared not risk losing such a battle, especially to a woman of such sexual charms!

'Pray, tell me the answer to our predicament,' I ventured, evenly.

'There is no answer, Tom, only compromise. And to that end I suggest that you move into the manor house as my butler. That will improve your appearance, for it leaves a lot to be desired, and raise your self-esteem, your function in life which, you must agree, is somewhat base, to say the least. I am doing all this for the simple reason that my daughters have lost their . . . They have lost Lord Hadleigh and, as I said, they have taken a liking to you.'

I had to turn my face to conceal the sentiments so obviously written in my expression. I could scarce believe that this so-called lady, this hussy who had seduced me, had the gall to deride me so.

Not once did she sit down during our conversation and I observed that she winced every time her hands cupped her buttocks. Oh, how I longed to see the weals criss-crossing her pale crescents! How I yearned to enter her once again! Later, I promised myself. Once installed as her butler, I would have greater opportunity to take all three beauties. But now, her harsh words would not leave me and I felt compelled to retaliate – subtly.

'Do you not care to sit down, my lady?' I asked innocently.

'I do not!' she thundered.

Save for referring to my behaviour of the previous evening as despicable, she had not elaborated on the matter, which I found peculiar. Surely, what could only be described as tantamount to rape demanded further mention? However, I preferred to think that she had enjoyed her punishment and would come back for more. But still, I had it in mind to score a further point, exchanging subtlety for bluntness.

'Are you sore, my lady? Shall I call on the doctor . . .?'

'You are impertinent beyond belief! How dare you speak to me so!'

'But, my lady, I was simply enquiring after your . . .'

'You *do* want the position as butler, do you not? Or would you rather I dismissed you here and now?'

'I am grateful for the position and I am sorry if I have distressed you in any way.'

'I do not get distressed, particularly when speaking with the likes of you! Let me warn you, you will rid yourself of your flippancy or pay the price!'

Ah, pay the price. Had not the girls said as much at the field gate? But what price had her ladyship in mind? Had I overlooked something? She had concealed a trick up her sleeve, I was sure. I was more than suspicious that it concerned Harry and Alice. The point was hers, I conceded.

Having resumed her composure, Lady Hadleigh informed me that I was to take up my new position forthwith. She showed me to my quarters at the rear of the house – a spacious, ground-floor apartment which was pleasantly furnished. I was to be measured for my new attire and trained by the lady herself.

It occurred to me that a new stable lad would be required to take my place. On raising the matter I was told curtly that it was no concern of mine. My wage was not mentioned and I dared not mention the subject for I felt that I was faring well and should not push my good fortune too far. No, I must be honest. The truth of the matter was that I was still strangely fearful of the lady. Why? I knew not exactly but suspected that it had to do with the point she had so admirably won.

I did not tell Harry and Alice of my news during lunch, for I felt that I was somehow betraying them. An odd feeling, I must confess. But it was as though I had taken

Lady Hadleigh's side in accepting her offer to move into the Manor House as butler.

In fact, as I collected my belongings from the hayloft, I was in two minds over the affair. My thoughts were swayed when it struck me that I would be under the same roof as Clara and Elizabeth. Moreover, from my quarters I would have access to the entire house – including their bedrooms.

Chapter Four

Having removed my belongings to the Manor House, I
wandered into the kitchen to introduce myself to the cook.
The aroma of freshly baked bread assailed my nostrils,
recalling memories of illustrious days at my aunt's country
home.

Upon my entrance, I encountered a portly, middle-aged
woman standing over a table, kneading pastry. Somewhat
fierce looking, she displayed little interest in me, barely
raising her head to acknowledge my presence. But, as I
turned to make my hasty exit, she deigned to mumble a
warning as grim as her demeanour. 'As with the others,
you will not last long 'ere.'

'What do you mean by that?' I asked.

'No-one lasts long in 'er 'ouse. I will give you a week, no
more, young man.'

'I will be here a good deal longer than a week, madam,' I
retorted, before taking my leave.

It was a disappointment to find the cook so, for I had
expected a kindly old woman who would spoil me with
fresh bread and cheese and cakes and pies. Neither Harry
nor Alice had mentioned her, and I made a mental note to
elicit some information during lunch.

On returning to my quarters, much to my surprise I

found Elizabeth awaiting me, seated at the foot of my bed.

'You have met the battle-axe?' she queried.

'If you mean the cook, then yes, I have met her,' I returned.

'She has many grouses. Mother makes her do not only the cooking, but the work of a maid, too.'

'Why does your mother not employ a maid?'

'Why should she? She has the battle-axe.'

'Then why does the woman not take her leave and find employment elsewhere?'

'She would never find other employment. Mother makes sure that whoever leaves her employ cannot find work elsewhere. She has friends, you see. So be careful or you may find yourself . . .'

'Where is your sister?' I interrupted, cutting short the whippet's futile threats.

'She is somewhere, I do not know where,' she replied nonchalantly. 'That reminds me, what did you do to her in the hayloft?'

Ah, so they had talked. But how much had each revealed? I wondered. The time had come, again, to play one against the other. Standing with my bulge well placed before Elizabeth's wide eyes, I smiled.

'Surely, it is not what *she* did to *me* that you should ask?'

'Then, what *did* she do to you?'

'She took me in her mouth.'

'I do not believe you! She would not do that!'

'Oh, but she did. Being that much older than you, she knows how to please a man – and herself.'

'Do you prefer her to me, Tom?'

'I prefer what she does to me.'

'Then I shall do the same – only better!'

Angelic little Elizabeth, being, as her mother, of fair hair and complexion, excited me more than Clara. I would employ a fair maiden's mouth any day to appease my hardness. Most fortunate it is that we are all of different taste! I detected Elizabeth's lips parted in readiness for my cock as, my own excitement mounting, she unbuttoned my breeches with her tiny fingers. Already straining, the beast sprang into the air as she freed it from its cage.

'Why, it is bigger than I remember!' she exclaimed upon intimate study of the weapon.

'And it will grow even bigger once inside the warmth of your mouth,' I assured the cherub.

Tease and tantalize as she did with her soft and gentle kisses, flicking the tip of her tongue over my engorged knob like an enticing butterfly, I found myself wondering if this was a girl of experience. But no – how could such a fledgling have tasted another's cock? How could she be wise to such things?

As these thoughts vied with the intensely pleasurable feelings stemming from my root, without warning, she opened her ruby red lips and sucked the swollen knob deep inside her hot mouth. Ah, sheer ecstasy! In and out I plunged, and round and round her tongue ran until it was all I could do to retain my cream. Sensing this, the young thing took fright. 'I do not wish for your seed in my mouth!' she whispered urgently, momentarily drawing away. 'You will promise to tell me when you are ready to be done?'

'Ah, yes, yes. I promise!' I moaned, without the slightest intention whatsoever of wasting my seed upon the floor.

Pulling on her golden hair and thrusting as if deep in her vagina, I filled her, all too quickly, I am afraid. But what great delight as she gripped me with her teeth, pain and pleasure mingling to heighten my ecstasy! She coughed and spluttered as I gripped her head tight to hold my cock, throbbing with pleasure, inside her throat. Only when I was sure she had swallowed the last drop of my seed did I withdraw, her sweet lips dribbling my sperm onto her chin as she cursed and spat and swore that I would pay.

'It seems that I have to pay for the pleasures I have afforded both you and your mother. Pray, how is it that I am to pay?'

'You will pay with your job!' screamed the lovely Elizabeth, wiping her mouth with her handkerchief as she fled the room.

Ah, how sweet the girls – and their mother! I will swear I had never been happier than at that moment. My days at Royston Manor were but young, and as I rebuttoned my breeches to recline dreamily upon my bed I looked forward to many, many more – her ladyship permitting.

'That was somewhat forceful, Tom!' Lady Hadleigh admonished, standing in the doorway. 'The door was ajar – I have witnessed your bungled attempt!'

I rose to my feet, cheeks aflame, hands trembling, but remained silent as she walked to the bed and picked up some items of my clothing. Discarding them contemptuously, she raised her head and locked her stare to mine. 'Do not overstep the mark!' she cautioned with an authority that required moderating, for I was by then the butler, not some mere stable lad.

'I was only carrying out your wishes, my lady.'

'No, you were not! That was lewd, and you know it!'

'Then tell me, how did Lord Hadleigh take pleasure from your mouth, my lady?' I ventured boldly.

'The pleasure gained from a union of that nature should be mutual. I do not believe that Elizabeth received one ounce of gratification!'

'No, my lady. I would say several ounces!'

'Your effrontery requires that I teach you a lesson! You have the audacity to enquire after the intimate relationship between Lord Hadleigh and myself. And you then make light of the awful plight you forced upon my daughter! You will come to my bedchamber at eight of the clock this evening, do you understand?'

Not only did I understand, but I looked forward to the appointed hour. For I imagined that Lady Hadleigh would instruct me as to how to take her beautiful mouth and pleasure not only myself, but her, too.

On her departure, I washed and tidied myself in readiness for lunch. Wandering through the yard, I became anxious, for the work in the stables was piling high. But, as Lady Hadleigh had said, it was no concern of mine. Far across the field, running and playing like two young children in the summer sun, I observed Clara and Elizabeth. What a wondrous thought that, only a short while previously, I had spurted my seed deep into Elizabeth's pretty mouth! My cock stiffened and my balls stirred at the delightful memory.

Sad to say, Harry had taken a turn for the worse. Alice was doing her utmost to keep his spirits up and had omitted to prepare lunch, for which she was most apologetic. I stayed a while, assuring her that I could miss lunch, but she and her husband should not. She promised she would eat something and try to give a little food to Harry during the course of the afternoon. Before leaving, I managed to brighten Harry's spirits by promising to bring him over a little beer later that evening. I told him, too, that Lady Hadleigh had asked after him, to which he grunted, 'You are a bad liar!'

Once in the garden with Alice, I took it upon myself to mention Lord Hadleigh's demise. Her reaction to the news was strange, to say the least.

'God help us!' she exclaimed. 'That is all we need!'

'Why do you react so?' I asked.

'You would not understand, Tom. I can only dread to think that our fate is sealed now that he has departed so.'

'What fate?' I persisted.

'It need not concern you. Go about your business, Tom. But mind you watch her!'

'You must tell me, Alice!' I insisted, but she returned to the house without another word. I dared not mention the cook just then, for Alice was in no mood for more questions.

Upon my walk back to the yard, I noticed the girls taking recreation in the field behind the stables. Their whispers were punctuated by giggles, and I could not resist the temptation to steal into the stables and listen to their conversation through the far wall. My ear pressed to a knothole, I could clearly hear every word that passed between their pretty young lips.

'Shall we watch mother suck Tom this evening?' Elizabeth asked of her sister.

'Are you sure that is what she intends to do?'

'Oh yes, I heard them talking. Eight of the clock, she said. Let us watch through the keyhole, as we did when she sucked father!'

'Would you like to suck Tom?' Clara asked softly.

'Certainly not! Would you?'

'Never!'

So, I had learned something that was to my advantage. Several things, in fact. The girls had not divulged to each other that they had both, indeed, sucked the seed from my cock. That was most welcome news as my game of playing one off against the other could continue unabated. Their mother was to follow suit in the sweet game that evening – oh, what heavenly pleasures lay before me! And she had drawn old Hadleigh's nectar! That, no doubt, was the only way she could entice an erection from his aged member.

I was about to take leave from my eavesdropping when I heard a somewhat strange moan emanate from behind the barn wall. 'Do I taste nice?' Clara asked eagerly, her breathing decidedly heavy.

'As nice as me, I hope,' came the whispered reply.

I could not, dared not, believe my ears! My eyes would not deceive me so, I knew. Yet, indeed, the knothole provided a spectacular view of the young sisters, mouthing with vigour between each other's open thighs.

'My God!' I breathed incredulously. 'What family is this, that they indulge in incestuous, lesbian activities?'

My head awhirl with wild imagination, I fled the stables to the faint whimpers of female ecstasy. Foolish was I to leave – I know not why I did so, for I surely missed a most wondrous sight at the pinnacle of that lustful union. Did their mother join them in their games? I wondered as I trod, stunned, across the yard.

My senses revived at the sight of Lady Hadleigh strutting towards me across the cobbles, her head high and mighty, her eyes wild.

'Where have you been?' she demanded of me loudly.

'Taking my lunch, Lady Sarah,' I replied.

'How dare you address me in such familiar terms! You will keep your place when . . .'

'But you said . . .'

'And how dare you cut me! Now, where are my daughters?'

Where indeed! Oh, how I would have delighted in showing her the games her girls played behind the stables! I was about to reply that I knew not of their whereabouts when, I will swear, the devil himself possessed me. 'I will show you, my lady, if you will follow me.' With that, I led the way to the field, my eyes wide with glee and my grin broad with mischief.

Clara and Elizabeth came into view as we turned the angle of the stables. Their dresses high, their knickers around their ankles, their mouths locked betwixt each other's milk-white thighs, they conjured a wonderful picture of gross indecency. Lady Sarah stood aghast at the sight as I turned my face, sniggering with delight at the plight of her daughters.

'Good God!' she exclaimed. 'What on earth . . .?'

The girls, scarlet-faced, wet mouths open, looked up to their audience. 'Go, Tom! I will speak with you later,' ordered their mother, grabbing Clara's arm and near wrenching it from its socket. With split-second thinking, I ran around the corner and into the stables where I spied and listened to the goings-on with child-like glee.

'What on earth do you think you are doing?' hissed Lady Sarah.

'We were just . . .' Elizabeth began.

'Being the elder, and supposedly more responsible, Clara will answer!' Lady Sarah thundered.

Clara's face was deep red – as red as an apple, I will swear! Her mouth hung open, but no words did she utter.

'Well?' her mother shouted, still gripping the girl's arm.

'We were playing, mother.'

Oh, how wonderful their shame! But, at the same time, how dastardly I felt for exposing them so. Guilt came upon me as Lady Sarah marched the girls from the field, fairly dragging her fledglings by the arms, towards the house.

Within minutes, I was summoned by Lady Sarah's shrieks. 'Come here this instant, Tom! Come here now!' I ran as fast as I could, diving through the bushes to behold my mistress standing by the rear door, her complexion flaming, her eyes wild. 'Follow me!' she bellowed as a woman possessed.

I was led upstairs where I found the girls cowering in Lady Sarah's bedroom. 'Remove your belt, Tom, and begin with Clara,' she ordered, pushing the girl over the end of the bed and raising her skirts high over her back. Ah, how the luscious sight of those pink, satin, lace-edged knickers provoked my cock to bursting point! To whiff their heady scent would surely have elicited my seed then and there! But there was work to do – my balls would have to hold my sperm, for the time being, at least.

Hurriedly, I slipped my belt from my breeches and moved towards the wonderful sight. 'Wait!' Lady Sarah demanded, wrenching the girl's knickers to her knees to expose her exquisitely tight buttocks. How sweet those pale orbs of young flesh! Parted slightly to reveal the tiny brown hole, they invited my tongue – if not my teeth!

'Do it, Tom!' Lady Sarah urged, standing back to give me room. And do it, I did! To Clara's blood-curdling squeals, I thrashed her young bottom until it glowed, leaving not one small patch of virgin flesh unblushed. The harsh action seemed quite to Lady Hadleigh's satisfaction.

'That is enough!' she interrupted. 'Now, you will whip Elizabeth!'

Poor Elizabeth – how the tears flowed to salt her pale cheeks as her mother pulled her over the bed. I could scarce bring myself to do the dirty deed – until her knickers were near torn off and her little rounded bottom came into view. But, as I raised my heavy leather belt, Lady Sarah put her arm out to halt me. 'What is this?' she asked, gently touching the weals across her daughter's pale crescents. My heart raced, my hands trembled. 'Who did this to you?' she cried.

Turning her tearful eyes to her mother, Elizabeth whimpered my name.

'What is the nature of this?' Lady Sarah asked of me.

'I had cause to punish the girl, my lady,' I replied, sheepishly.

'Then you will make a fine father some day – and husband,' pronounced Lady Hadleigh, to my complete astonishment. 'Now, pray, proceed.'

I was lenient with Elizabeth, strapping her only moderately, as the weals across her bottom were still red and very sore. Several times I looked to Lady Sarah for her signal to stop, but she only grinned and nodded for me to continue.

At last, she took my arm to put an end to the torture. The girl's buttocks shone rudely bright, and, upon closer observation, I discerned her young, downy bush nestling 'neath the stinging orbs. She was wet down there, as was the bed covering. Ah, how I would have taken her there and then, had not her mother been present!

'You may go, Tom,' came the instruction, to my great disappointment, as I fastened my belt.

Leaving the three to their own devices, I made my way

to my quarters, my mind swimming with images of those wonderful bottoms, my full balls swirling and my cock straining for relief. I would have taken myself in hand, but eight of the clock neared, so I stored my delicacy in anticipation of Lady Sarah's sweet, hot mouth.

Lying on my bed, wondering when my duties as butler would commence, I heard Giant neighing loudly and rushed out to the stables to investigate. A young girl I had not seen before was at the stable door looking somewhat agitated. 'I cannot still him!' she exclaimed upon seeing me, tugging on poor Giant's reins.

'And you will not by pulling him so!' I returned sternly, taking the reins and calming the beast. 'Pray, who are you and what is your business here?'

'I am here to see the lady of the manor,' she said, backing away from the stallion.

'On whose authority?'

'I have come about employment at the stables. Who are you?'

'I am Tom, the stable . . . the butler,' I enlightened her, forgetting my position momentarily. 'I will take you to her ladyship – follow me.'

The girl was no more than sixteen – far too young to run the yard. From her grubbiness and pallor, I surmised she had neither washed nor eaten for several days. Her thin face accentuated her huge brown eyes which were shrouded by scraggy brown hair. Her ample mouth seemed twisted with bitterness, as if never knowing how to smile or laugh.

Normally, I would have delighted at the prospect of a young girl taking my place in the stables – and the hayloft. But she, poor thing, did nothing to arouse my senses whatsoever. She had obviously heard of the position in the village, and was trying her luck which, I reckoned, was nil.

But take her I did to the rear door of the house and led her into the kitchen where I bade her wait for my return. The battle-axe – I refer to her as such for I knew not her name – was most displeased by what she called a waif being dumped in her kitchen. I told her to hush and leave the girl be, her expletives fading as I closed the door and went off in search of Lady Sarah.

Upon hearing her movements in the drawing room, I knocked and entered. 'Have you no manners whatsoever?' she greeted me.

'I did knock, my lady.'

'But you did not wait for my reply! What is it you want?'

'There is a young girl to see you, in the kitchen.'

'In the kitchen! Get her out of there, this instant!'

'But she has come about work in the . . .'

'Get her out!'

There and then, I promised myself to reduce the hussy to her station before the day was out. For behind the masquerade, she was no more than a maid, and that, I swore, in all her living days, I would never allow her to forget.

Presently, her ladyship stormed through the rear door to find me with the girl outside. She looked the waif up and down, her eyes full of disgust, before turning to me.

'You decide,' she declared. 'After all, she will be your responsibility.'

'*My* responsibility?' I queried.

'Yes. Did I not mention that, apart from butler, you are also head man?'

'No, you . . .'

'Well, I have mentioned it now. Throw her in the horse

trough, and then show her the hayloft. The stables are in dire need of mucking out.'

So, I was butler and head man. Were there any other duties of which I was ignorant? Most likely, I mused. Knowing her ladyship, I imagined that I would also be required to act as the maid! I put it to her that the girl was in need of food before starting work, but she dismissed me as she would a beggar.

We got down to the basics immediately, I spending some time teaching and helping the girl in the stables. I say teaching, but I knew very little myself, of course. Although, not wishing to appear green behind the ears, I did make out that I had been at the manor for some time. She was most grateful for my taking her on – and not dunking her in the horse trough! But I did suggest that she wash on completion of her work. She was an individual of few words, and had not even told me her name, but I put it down to nothing more than her tender age and shyness.

Happily, the appointed hour was almost upon me. Much to my surprise, the battle-axe showed her face at the stables and bade the girl go to the house to eat. Again, she did not acknowledge my presence, let alone invite me to partake of refreshment.

Having washed and tidied myself, I made my way up the back stairs and knocked on her ladyship's bedchamber door – careful to await her reply, of course, before entering. The door opened, slowly, and I wandered in to find Lady Sarah standing in nothing more than a pink chemise. Smiling slightly, she beckoned me with a finger, and I must confess to feeling somewhat afraid as I took one tentative step after another towards her.

Ray Gordon

Standing before the lady, I eagerly awaited her instructions. A rare beauty indeed! Her breasts heaved as she breathed heavily, her long nipples outlined against the fragile silk that stretched tightly between me and my goal. Licking her pouting lips, she stood perfectly still and silent, as if waiting for my move.

Dropping to my knees, I lifted the pink shroud to gaze longingly at the dark, triangular bush nestling between the tops of her slender thighs. On closer observation, I could just discern the dividing groove between the soft cushions of flesh. Clasping a tight buttock in each hand, I moved my head forward and pressed my face against the moist warmth. She quivered slightly as I brushed my mouth over her tight curls. But I had it in my mind to tease and tantalise her until she begged and cried for relief. I would reduce her to her station, as I had promised myself! And what finer way to bring the lady down than to humiliate her?

Pushing her hips forward, she whimpered and gasped, desperate for my tongue. I counteracted by moving back, my eager tongue not quite losing contact with her now wet valley. Each time she gasped, each time she pushed forward, I moved away, awaiting the magic words. But, save her whimpers and low moans, she remained silent, determined, I imagined, not to be beaten by having to plead with a mere member of staff.

Stroking the length of her groove with a finger, I watched her lips swell and part slightly in readiness for my cock. She was extremely aroused and becoming most wet, her juices beginning to seep from her body to trickle down the wrinkled pink flesh that now protruded well beyond the bounds of her bush.

54

Temptation is a powerful thing, and I must admit to nearly losing the battle as I watched the milky fluid seep from her orifice to hang in globules from the swollen flesh, awaiting my tongue. But, summoning all my reserves of strength, I somehow managed to restrain my desire to suck and drink from her hole, and give her the escape she so desperately craved.

Moving her feet further apart, she thrust forward once again. While she trembled as I breathed in her scent and brushed her wet curls, no more did she move. Her moans were now stifled – she was wise to the nature of my game. Whilst my cock was yet hard and impatient to sink into the hotness between her legs, still I managed to control myself.

Now her juices flowed in torrents down the smooth white skin of her inner thighs, and her breathing became low and noticeably heavier. Allowing her a little pleasure, I ran my tongue up the length of her groove and let it settle just near the top where, I knew, her bud throbbed somewhere beneath its protective cover. Down again I moved my tongue, to the centre of her quivering body, where I tasted the smallest drop of her sticky nectar. She responded only by gasping as I sucked gently on her pink protrusions, glued together like the folded wings of a butterfly.

At last, she could take no more torture and thrust her hands down, opening her lips with her fingers. Wide, stretched, they lay parted, exposing the little bud to my eyes. Further she opened herself – the pink flesh taut, ready to tear. How cruel of me not to release her from her torment! But how beautiful to behold her head back, face burning with desire, eyes rolling, mouth lolling open and dry from her gasps! But cruel I was, only permitting my tongue to lick and caress around the bud, not once coming into contact, for fear of losing the battle.

In her predicament, she was unaware of the girls' muffled giggles from behind the closed door as she lifted her chemise over her head and threw it to the floor. Teasing her entrance with a finger, I looked up at the wondrous sight of her nakedness. Her breasts pointed skyward, her nipples, elongated and erect, begged attention – attention that I steadfastly denied.

In the grip of desire, I sensed she was losing her composure. Running her hands over her smooth, flat stomach, she moved them upwards to cup her breasts, before squeezing each nipple. As she rolled them between her fingers, I pressed my face to her bush again and continued with my torture. Gyrating her hips, desperately trying to place her bud in my mouth, she was nearing her climax, even though she had not been touched there.

'Pleasure me!' she at last cried out, but I only continued my torturing caress. 'Now! Now!' she gasped as her pink flesh reddened and swelled and glistened with her juices. What, I wondered, were the girls thinking of their mother? Were they not disgusted by the spectacle? Or perchance they were gently fingering each other as they watched? Indeed, I dreamed so!

Holding her lips open with one hand, my lady finally surrendered to the violent demands of her body. Running two trembling fingers round and round her clitoris, she was soon panting like an excitable puppy. I had won! But more than that, I found myself gazing at Lady Sarah Hadleigh pleasuring herself – a delight I had never before in my life savoured. And such a delicacy! Her bud grew before my very eyes as she worked her fingers faster and faster around its base. It visibly pulsated like a tiny cock as she cried out in her moment of glory. Not wishing to deny myself some pleasure, I thrust three fingers deep into her dripping cunt. How hot and sticky and tight she was, near crushing me as she lowered herself to sink my digits deeper into her trembling body. Ah, how she came! How she gasped and shook as her fingers worked on and on, sustaining her climax for interminable minutes.

Presently, she collapsed to the floor, still panting and groaning with her thighs tightly closed, accompanied by faint whisperings from the hall. My hand trapped between her legs and my fingers still deep in the hotness of her cunt, I could feel her subsiding contractions, still causing her to twitch with bursts of pleasure. But, although clearly more than satisfied, she became agitated at my boorish behaviour.

'You think yourself clever, do you?' she gasped upon opening her legs and wrenching my fingers from her steaming body. I said nothing as I stood up, my bulge more than obvious. Kneeling before me, she slowly unbuttoned my breeches. Slipping her hand inside, she pulled out my cock and grinned wickedly. 'We will see who is clever!' she breathed as she opened her mouth and took half my length inside.

Muffled giggles came from the hall as Lady Sarah moved her head back and forth, bathing my hard shaft in her warm saliva. Oh, she certainly knew how to take a man in her mouth! Gripping the centre of my shaft, she pulled the skin back, hard against the root, exposing my purple fruit to her inquisitive tongue. Round and round she ran her soft snake, teasing, caressing, weakening my knees with every circular sweep.

As the first pumping sensation swelled my knob, I made to hold her head and use her mouth as a vagina, but she pulled away. Throbbing with imminent climax, my poor cock stood hard and proud in mid-air – untouched, desperate for the warmth of her accommodating mouth. But, most cruelly, the bitch sat back, cross-legged, to expose her open crack. Her hands on the floor behind her, her rounded breasts pushed forward, she wore, in her shameless nakedness, a huge triumphant grin. Opening her legs and raising them high in the air as she fell back upon the floor, she burst into laughter at my predicament.

On more than one count she had taken me beyond the point of no return, and she knew it. As the embryonic spunk glistened upon my aching knob, I took my beast in hand, vigorously chafing the skin over the bulbous end. Standing over her, my cream flew through the air like a white dove, homing in on her face, her hair, her breasts. Ah, what exquisite relief to loose my seed over Lady Sarah as she thrashed her head from side to side to protect herself from the shower! The girls giggled and she cursed as I finished myself, slowing the rhythm until the last pulse came and the sperm dribbled from my shrinking shaft to drip upon her stomach.

'You know not how to treat a lady!' she spat as she sat up and wiped the cream from her face.

'But you are no lady!' I whispered, aware of the girls.

'And you are no man! You are no better than an animal!'

Her anger aroused me greatly, and my cock rose in readiness to prove my manhood. Her eyes widened at the growing weapon hovering ominously above her. 'Go now,' she said decisively as she moved to rise.

'If you think that I am no better than an animal, then I shall behave as one,' I laughed, while pushing her back down to the floor.

Her delightful squeals filled the house as I rolled her over and pulled her hips up to expose her bottom. My cock, now once more bulging and rampant with desire, near burst as it sniffed out the gaping lips so beautifully spread beneath her bottom hole. Splaying her buttocks, I slowly pushed my shaft home, deep into the warmth of her cunt as she continued with her squealing. Grabbing her slender hips I began my fucking motions, slapping her buttocks hard against my belly with every thrust.

Resting on her elbows, she lifted her head, dropped her stomach and raised her bottom to deepen the penetration. This was not good enough for a woman such as she, I decided, pressing my thumb into her little brown hole. An animal, was I? Withdrawing my glistening shaft from nature's intended sheath I stabbed between her buttocks.

'No! What are you doing?' screamed Lady Hadleigh to the obvious delight of her daughters, who were by now panting and moaning with pleasure behind the door. Pressing my knob to the little hole, I splayed her buttocks further and, suddenly, I was in! Ah, what sanctum! What heavenly retreat!

'You filthy animal! You bastard! Stop! Stop!' On and on went her protests as I slowly sunk my cock into the uncharted depths of her bottom. Oh, how tight she was there! And how deep I pushed my shaft, right up to the root, where I let it linger to savour the grip of her lovely bottom. Wriggle as she did, she could do nothing to expel the hard intruder. 'Take it out!' she ordered, her muscles spasming as I began to undulate.

Placing my hand 'neath my balls, I located her cunt's gaping entrance and managed to insert four fingers within the wetness. She twitched and shook and screamed as I filled and stretched both holes to their limits.

'Animal!' she again yelled.

'Think of me as Giant, if it pleases you,' I laughed, ramming home yet again into the mysterious depths of her anus.

'Debased creature!' was her only cry, for I had painted the awesome picture in her mind and I knew she could not rid herself of the scene.

'Shall I neigh?' I asked as my cock shuddered with advance warning of coming ecstasy. 'Will that aid your fantasy, my lady?' Her expletives went unnoticed as my cock swelled and burst within her, filling her bowels with my fruits. 'Did Lord Hadleigh do this to you, my lady?' I gasped. 'Did he fuck you so?'

She was riled beyond belief, but, to my utter amazement, she began to tremble and shake and groan with delight. 'Do you come?' I asked, my shrinking cock imprisoned within her ring. She did not answer as I moved my hand up her valley and located her clitoris. 'Ah, so you *do* like it! You *do* enjoy being fucked so!' I cried, feeling the ripeness of her bud beneath my fingers.

'Bastard!' she screamed as her climax rocked her entire body and her bottom hole tightened painfully around my newly hardening cock. Only when she gasped and swore and sobbed and thrashed her head before collapsing to the floor did I slowly withdraw, watching her nether orifice close as my knob slid free of its hold. She neither spoke nor moved as she lay there, panting and shaking. Pleased with my efforts, I buttoned my breeches and moved towards the door. 'Rest now and I will see you on the morrow,' I bade her.

'Bastard!' was all she could summon the strength to whisper as she curled up on the rug like a ball.

The girls scurried off upon my turning the door handle. Fearful for the safety of their own bottom holes, I deduced, closing the door on the pitiful whimpering and sobbing of their mother. And fearful they damned well should be of every sweet orifice they had between them, I thought. For I will take them! Sooner or later, I will take them all!

Chapter Five

The new stable girl was up bright and early the following morning and I took it upon myself to assist her in her duties before Lady Sarah should arise to shout and yell, as I was now accustomed to her doing.

'I trust you slept well?' I asked of her, finding her already in the stables with Giant.

'I did,' she replied, adding curtly: 'And, for your information, I have washed and eaten.'

'Are you not happy that you have a place to sleep, that you have been fed, and that you have found work?' I enquired, somewhat mystified by her tone.

'I am not happy. Nevertheless, I am grateful to you. But I do not wish to find myself beholden to you from this day forward.'

'Nor will you find yourself so. Now, tell me, what is your name?'

'I am known only as Belle,' she replied, flicking her hair from her eyes as she looked up at me, for she was a good deal shorter than I.

'Ah, Belle. What a wonderful name! Have you yet met Clara and Elizabeth, Lady Hadleigh's daughters?'

'I have, indeed. They came to the hayloft late yester-evening and woke me up with their nonsense.'

'Nonsense?' I enquired, wondering if they had tried to interfere with the girl.

'Yes, they informed me that I am to be their personal maid, and that unless I carry out their demands – I know not yet what demands they will put upon me – then they will ensure that their mother is rid of me.'

Oh, Clara, Elizabeth! How could they treat the poor girl so? Obviously they carried their mother's nasty streak, and that would not do! I reassured the girl that she would have to do nothing for the little madams. She smiled, rather sweetly, I thought, as she tossed back her hair and looked up at me with her big brown eyes.

The devil was near to me, I will swear, for it came to me that perhaps I should put demands on the poor thing, in return for protecting her. With that in mind, I gazed down at her jodhpurs. They were tight, too tight, showing the contour of her full vaginal lips, and, I could scarce believe my eyes, the sharp outline of her sweet groove!

Was the devil himself really goading me? What was it that had possessed me so? What demon had inhabited my very being and increased my desire for lust one hundred-fold? I lifted my gaze to her breasts which were strangely small and, I imagined, most hard, like unripe plums. Would I ever see them, naked before my eyes, proudly standing from her slim frame? Would I have the opportunity to suck upon the little brown buds that topped them, as cherries upon cupcakes? Afire with perverse thoughts, my cock was risen and demanding relief once more. Observing, naturally, my wide, wandering eyes and my rampant bulge, the girl, without warning, spat at me. 'You would be better finding a friend in me, for I am a formidable foe!' I warned.

'Then cut your filthy thoughts!' she hissed.

Grabbing her arm, I threw her to the ground and pinned her there with my weight. 'You flatter yourself, my girl! For you are hardly worthy of my thoughts, filthy or otherwise!' I scorned.

'Then free me and be gone, for I have work to do!'

'When I am good and ready, I shall free you. Now stop your struggling, for the pain can only increase!'

'I should be surprised if any woman so much as looked at you, let alone . . .'

I cut her impertinence short with a good slap to the face. She was asking for a damned good beating, and, my God, had she come to the right place! Rolling her struggling frame over, I yanked her jodhpurs down to her thighs. How hard her buttocks – tight and puckered in anticipation of the beating to come! Using the palm of my hand, I thrashed the wondrous little orbs with all my might. Her screams would wake the household, I was sure, but I cared not, for she had a lesson to learn.

As the fight progressed, the girl's jodhpurs inched further down her skinny thighs to reveal sparse black hairs tucked neatly 'neath her bottom hole. 'If you hate me so, then I may as well give you something to hate me for,' I laughed wickedly, pushing her warm thighs apart and sinking two fingers into her very tight little cunny.

She squirmed and wriggled and swore to kill me as I massaged the sweet, soft flesh within her hole. Oh, how youthful her thighs, how firm her vaginal lips, how formed her little buttocks! I could not resist pressing my thumb into her bottom hole and, as I did so, her tight cunny juiced my fingers in readiness for penetration. But I was to arouse her the more ere taking her. Seeking her clitoris, I caressed the little nodule until it stiffened, hard as a button, 'neath my sticky fingers. She scarce let up with her futile struggling, but I fancied I did detect the odd gasp of desire betwixt her vile expletives. I was about to take her then and there, upon the stable floor, but footsteps sounded across the yard – no doubt in response to the girl's screams.

Hastily covering her crimson buttocks with her jodh-purs, I dragged her to her feet, standing her upright like a tailor's dummy before retreating some yards away. Lady Sarah appeared at the stable door, demanding to know the cause of the furore.

'It was but just a little fun, my lady,' I replied innocently.

'Is that right, girl?' she queried, her stare locked to Belle's tearful eyes. 'Was it but fun?'

Belle wiped her eyes and glanced at me. I frowned and shook my head threateningly, but she was determined to speak the truth.

'It was *not* but fun. He pulled my jodhpurs from me and . . .'

'And what?' Lady Sarah interrupted, flashing a knowing look in my direction. A look of arousal, I will swear!

'And . . . and he touched me!'

'I thrashed her for her impertinence, my lady,' I interjected.

'Then you have no complaint, girl! Get back to your work! And you, Tom – I wish to see you in the morning room the minute you finish here!' With that, Lady Sarah turned and took her leave.

Belle walked slowly towards me, her eyes fired with hatred, her mouth twisted. 'You will . . .'

'Do not tell me that I will pay, please!' I laughed. 'I am indebted to so many females as it is! Please, no more! And besides, I did feel your little clitty stiffen as I rubbed it! You delighted in every minute of my attention, be honest, now!'

'You will pay for violating me so! I swear, you will pay with your life – as the last man . . .'

'The last man? You killed a man?'

A tear trickled from her eye and rolled down her rosy cheek as she hung her head to face the ground. 'You killed a man?' I repeated.

'Yes, I had no choice.'

'Then, I am sorry, for I knew not of your plight. Please accept my apologies, Belle, for I am truly sorry.'

She wandered over to Giant and hugged his neck, whispering in his ear as she wiped her eyes. I said no more, for I felt I had done enough damage to the poor thing. Leaving her nuzzling Giant, I went out into the yard and washed.

My guilt rising, I returned to the stable to check on the girl's wellbeing, but stopped short at the door on hearing her talking to the animal. 'That fooled him,' she laughed. 'It always works, Giant. It always makes them find sorrow for me in their hearts – stupid men!'

Unnoticed by the girl, I entered the stable to give her not only the beating of her life, but the fucking of her life, too. The disagreeable bitch had, indeed, fooled me! As I walked slowly towards her, my hands raised to grab her, Clara and Elizabeth came running across the yard asking what the commotion had been about.

'Was it that little strumpet's screams that awoke us, Tom?' asked Clara.

'She needs a beating, Tom. Is that what you gave her?' Elizabeth squealed excitedly as Belle ran off.

'A beating I gave her, yes. And the both of you will get the same treatment if you pester her with your nonsense about her being your personal maid!'

'Oh, he wants the strumpet for himself!' Clara giggled.

'Have you taken her yet?' Elizabeth wheedled.

'Remember, both of you, that I have yet to take *you*! So, mind your manners and let her be, or, I swear, I will take you as a stallion takes a mare!'

'As you took mother!' they shrieked in unison as they lifted their skirts and ran across the yard. Leaning against the stable door, I watched their beautiful little bottoms wiggle below their tight waists, until they disappeared from view.

Being surrounded by the fair sex, as I was, caused my cock to rise habitually. My urge, whether driven by a demon or not, was growing insatiable, and I found myself planning one seduction after another as I wandered up to the house, breathing in the invigorating country air. Naturally, London held its share of beauties, but the countryside furnished a young stud far more opportunity, affording his prey the freedom to roam unhindered by chaperons.

Lady Sarah was sitting on the sofa in the morning room taking tea. I noted a second cup on the small table – presumably for me – and wondered which trick she had up her sleeve for me on this occasion. Being invited to take morning tea was not quite what I would have expected from the lady I had so brutally, and wonderfully, taken only the evening before.

'You may sit down, Tom,' she said, waving her hand

towards an armchair. 'It seems that we have these little talks rather too often, do you not agree?' I nodded my agreement and took the cup of tea she offered me. 'So, you beat that new girl, did you? And what, pray, had she done to warrant such? Or was it that you took it upon yourself to do so from sheer lust?'

'I beat her for her impertinence, my lady.'

'But, surely, are you yourself not the very definition of the word?'

'What you believe me to be does not affect the matter. I will not tolerate impertinence from a young girl such as she.'

'But you feel that I should tolerate it from such as you?'

What was her game? What evil trick had she conjured this time? 'Is it that you wish the girl for yourself, my lady?' I asked, imagining her wielding a whip above the girl's wonderful bottom.

'What do you mean by that?'

'Well, your daughters seem to derive great pleasure from each other, and I just wondered . . .'

'Do you really believe that I condone such behaviour between females? And do you honestly think that I would desire some common waif of a girl for myself?'

'Yes, my lady. It has crossed my mind.'

'Then you worry me, Tom. Your mind is riddled with perverse thoughts, is it not? Surely, you cannot believe me to have lesbian tendencies?'

'If my mind be riddled, then is not yours also riddled with such thoughts?'

Offering no reaction other than a faint smile, she sipped her tea as befitted a lady. Her hair shining in the early morning sun, her complexion glowing youthfully, she was, indeed, a very beautiful woman. A woman with whom, I was sure, I could do well to spend the rest of my life.

'Tell me, Tom. Have you seen Harry today?' she continued in a congenial tone.

'Why do you ask?'

'I am curious. Curious as to why you have taken it upon yourself to protect Harry and his wife. After all, they are nothing to you.'

'They are people. Good, kind people, my lady.'

'And am I not a good, kind person?'

'Will you please come to the point of our meeting this morning as I have a long day's work ahead?'

'The point of our meeting, Tom, is simple. I wish you to leave my employ, this house, and never return. I am willing to pay you a small sum of money, just enough to . . .'

'But I cannot leave . . .'

'I am not interested, Tom, in what you can or cannot do. I think your little game has gone far enough, and if you thought for one moment that you could somehow wheedle your way in here, to my house, or my heart, come to that, then you were sadly mistaken.'

Dismissal was the last thing I was expecting, and I was fair shocked. After the events of the previous evening, which I would have sworn her ladyship had enjoyed almost as much as I, I had indeed felt that I had my feet well and truly 'neath the Hadleigh table. But she was heartless, that was sorely clear!

'You have afforded me some pleasure, Tom, I must confess. But you were nothing more to me than a toy, a plaything, and now the novelty has worn thin. I could have tolerated you for a while longer, I suppose, but your behaviour last evening was the most vile, despicable, debased act imaginable. I lay awake all night long thinking of it, and to suggest that Giant . . . Well, quite simply, you have gone too far.'

'But your daughters, your background . . .'

'Your threats concern me not in the slightest, for I care nothing for the people in the village. Tell them all you know! Tell my daughters what you believe to be true about their father! I am sure they will laugh at you. You must do as you think fit – as must I. And, I am sorry to say, that includes removing the tenants from my cottage.'

It was not anger that I felt as I watched her leave the room. Nor was it sorrow, neither for myself nor Harry and Alice. The feeling that pervaded my being was strange to me. So strange, indeed, that it bothered me greatly. I had honestly thought that Lady Sarah and I . . . Well, as she had said, I was sadly wrong.

I mentioned nothing of my meeting with Lady Sarah upon visiting Harry and Alice that morning. But they both sensed that something was troubling me.

'What is it that plays on your mind?' Harry asked, the minute Alice had left the bedchamber.

'You are looking very well, Harry,' I said cheerfully.

'I am feeling very well. Now, will you answer my question?'

'It concerns the cottage,' I began.

'Then worry not, for I had a letter from a solicitor in London this morning, and, it seems, I have been bequeathed a small property in Hertfordshire. It will do nicely for Alice and me.'

'That is good news, Harry! I am so happy for you!'

'Will you now answer my question? What has happened to trouble you so?'

I could not tell Harry. I could not bring myself to burden him with my problems, especially as his news was so pleasing. 'You have done well, Tom, to stay here so long. Many have come and gone within days, but you, you have done well. Has the end now come for you, is that it? Has she told you to go?'

'Yes, I am afraid that is the case. Sadly, I am to leave.'

'Then, tell her ladyship that you know about Lord Hadleigh and she may well think twice about dismissing you.'

'What about him? What is your secret, Harry?'

'No, that should be enough. Now, be off with you and leave an old man in peace!'

I lost no time in running to the house in search of Lady Sarah. I had neither formulated a plan nor rehearsed my lines and had not the least idea of what I would say as I climbed the back stairs. My heart banging hard in my chest, I knocked on the morning-room door and waited. There came no reply, but I felt sure that she was there. Venturing to open the door, I discovered Lady Sarah standing by the window. She turned, as I thought, to scold me for entering without her invitation. But I had misread her. Smiling that strange smile of hers, she took a few paces towards me, and I was certain I did detect a tear in her eye. 'What is it, Tom?' she asked of me solemnly. I could scarce find the words – such a beauty was she that to resort to blackmail again seemed unfair. But had she not been more than unfair to me, to Harry – everyone?

'It is about . . .' I stammered, my hands trembling and my heart now like thunder.

'About what, Tom?'

'I know your secret.'

'Secret? What secret, pray?'

'Your secret, my lady, concerning . . .'

'What are you talking about?'

'Do not play games, my lady. You know only too well of what I speak!'

'I am afraid I know nothing of the sort! You come in here mumbling in riddles, and tell me not to play games. However, that aside, I have been thinking. You may stay, if you so wish, but there will be conditions. I have changed my mind for several reasons, none of which are your business, of course.'

'What are the conditions?'

'I will set them down on paper presently. Are you willing to stay?'

'Until I know the conditions, I can hardly . . .'

'One condition is that you will not again touch the new stable girl.'

'But I owe her a beating, my lady.'

'If she needs to be punished, then I will see to it. Besides, I believe you have more than a beating in mind! Now, will you stay? Yes or no, Tom? I need to know now!'

I was obliged to agree to stay, whatever her damned conditions. She appeared pleased, too pleased for my liking, and again, I began to wonder what she was about. She had dismissed my allusion to her secret in such a manner that I felt she genuinely knew nothing of what I was talking about. Perhaps Harry had reckoned that bluffing would bring results. Perchance if I had actually mentioned Lord Hadleigh by name she would have reacted in a different manner, but no matter. I was happy that, yet again, I did not have to resort to blackmail to secure my job.

I told her of Harry's good news, which brought some visible relief to her troubled expression, probably as it would save her the trouble of having him removed. She was a strange one, for sure. But, for the time being, I had a home and a job, and I did not intend to jeopardise my position by questioning her further, especially about Belle. I felt sure that on that score my instincts were correct – she wanted the girl for herself. Why else would she instruct me not to touch her? And why, perish the thought, had she taken it upon herself to administer the girl's punishment? Was it that the thought of beating her young, naked buttocks wettened her vaginal lips? Did her clitoris stir and send a tingle through her body at the image of those neat little buttocks bared before her? And of that fledgling, tight-lipped cunny?

I was happy – mystified about Lord Hadleigh but, nevertheless, happy. In such fine spirits, in fact, that I took it upon myself that afternoon to spend time in the field behind the stables, relaxing in the sunshine. The grounds were large and rambling, and I could have been working almost anywhere, so I knew that I would not be missed. And besides, if Lady Sarah were to screech my name from the house, then I would surely hear her, for she could wake the dead with her cries!

I had only just found a pleasant spot in the long grass and closed my eyes, when I heard voices. In a panic, I shot from my lair, in fear of being caught by Lady Sarah, but I quickly deduced that the voices were coming from the stable. Yet again, the knothole served me well – pressing my face to the warm wood, I saw Clara and Elizabeth in conversation with Belle. Blatantly defying my instructions, they were taunting her terribly.

'You will comb my hair this evening,' Clara told her.

'And you will comb mine, too,' Elizabeth instructed haughtily. 'When we come to the hayloft this evening, you will do as we say, do you understand?'

Belle said nothing as the girls prodded and poked her and finally pushed her to the ground. Like their mother, they were first-class bitches, and I was in two minds as to whether to beat them both that very instant. But the conversation, if it can be called such, continued, and I listened for a while longer.

'You will do everything we tell you!' Clara hissed.

'Everything!' Elizabeth echoed. 'We play games, you see. And you must join in our games – if you want to keep your job, that is. We will be here at eight of the clock, so ensure that you are ready – strumpet!'

I knew of their games only too well – Belle, obviously, did not! But who was I to intervene? Belle had not exactly taken a shine to me, and I had been instructed not to touch her, so were not my hands tied as to her fate? There was one thing I could do, though – spy on the threesome! The cracks in the stable roof would furnish ample scope for me to oversee the naughty games in the hayloft.

Whilst my cock shuddered at the prospect, one thing saddened me. What would I do for relief after witnessing such arousing scenes? Lady Sarah, I felt, would not entertain the idea of allowing me to pleasure her again! Ah well, I thought, if all else failed, I could always resort to my faithful old hand! But being spoilt for choice, as of late, for the real thing, it was not quite the same.

I was awoken from perverse dreams by Lady Sarah

screaming for me. Hot and sticky from the warm sun and, I must confess, my dreaming, I jumped from my lair and rushed around the angle of the barn, nearly knocking her clean off her feet. 'Where on God's earth have you been?' she yelled. 'It's six of the clock and I have called and called!'

'Working,' I returned sleepily.

'Here are the conditions I talked of. Abide by them, Tom, or you will regret it, I promise you!'

Transfixed by the burgundy velvet dress tightly hugging her breasts, I dropped the envelope as she passed it to me. Bending my knees to retrieve it, my eyes levelled with her belly. Thoughts of the previous evening filled my mind, and together with my recent sleep-state, it was as much as I could do to stop myself from lifting her skirts and burying my face betwixt her milk-white thighs. Wonderful images of her naked body writhing beneath me caused my cock to stir and nudge my clothing. As I rose and again stood before her, I noticed her eyes lower, to fix her gaze upon my breeches. But as I raised my hand to touch her long, fair hair, she turned and flounced off across the yard. A bitch, indeed! Knowing full well her cunt to be wet with desire, and my cock rampant with lust, she had absconded. Her loss, I speculated, not mine.

When she had gone from my view, I opened the envelope and read her so-called conditions. Most were nonsensical tripe relating to nothing more than my working duties, but the last few lines widened my eyes. 'You will not, under any circumstances, venture within the proximity of the new stable girl.' That, I knew already, of course. 'She will move into the cottage, as and when it becomes vacant, and you will not visit her there or trespass within one hundred yards of the cottage.'

To say I was shocked would be something of an under-statement. That waif, that stable girl who had only just arrived – from an orphanage, by the looks of it – move into the cottage? What had the bitch in mind? Nights of wanton lust with the girl? Nights of fingering her young pussy and ordering her to lick her ripened clitoris? Lady Sarah was, indeed, one strange woman. A woman of great and insatiable lust, undoubtedly!

However, there is more than one way to skin a cat, I told myself, and more than one way to get to Belle's wet little cunny, even though I might be obliged to share it with Sarah! I read on. 'You will come to my room when you are summoned, and only when you are summoned.' Interest-ing – now what would she want with me in her room? Perhaps she would like to suck Belle's cunny and then my cock, all in one evening? Or, would she have me fill her with my sperm, and then invoke Belle to suck it from her steaming hole? Oh wondrous thoughts!

'You will never take it upon yourself to touch me, unless I have instructed you to do so.' Ah, so I was right – she craved her stud, after all! The best condition yet, but one that I could never abide by, for I was not in the habit of touching ladies merely at their request. I would touch her as and when and where I so desired.

'You will treat me with respect at all times, and never cross me. In return, you will have employment and a place to live. I pray you will appreciate that I cannot allow you to continue with your futile blackmail attempts. If any of the above conditions are broken, needless to say, you will be dismissed instantly.'

Treat her with respect? But respect had to be earned, so

my father used to say. And how had Lady Sarah Hadleigh earned my respect? For sure, she had not – my admiration in some respects, yes, but never my respect.

The hours dragged on, lengthened by the prospect of viewing three young girls living out their fantasies – or, at least, two young girls forcing their fantasies upon the third! What wondrous delights awaited my hungry eyes! My cock ached with new rigidity, my stomach somersaulted with expectation, whilst my mind reeled with anticipation.

I would have taken my cock in hand and loosed my seed upon the grass, but I did not wish to quell my arousal. I have found that prolonging the moment serves to heighten the pleasure of the minute. My procrastination, my licking and nibbling everywhere but Lady Sarah's clitoris, had certainly heightened her moment. Ah, what pictures the mind conjures! Had she pleasured herself since that fateful evening? I wondered. Did she visualise my cock, stuck hard and deep in her bottom hole, as she lay on her bed with her legs spread and her fingers appeasing her bud? How often did she permit her fingers to pleasure her cunny? Once a week, once a day – or more? Perchance she pictured Belle, asquat upon her face, slit wide and wet, as she drank from her young body. Or Giant, God forbid!

Happy, happy dreams – but I had to make tracks, for the time was running on, and unless I diverted my reverie, my cock would surely loose its seed, without even the inter-vention of my eager hand! Thus I turned my thoughts to preparations for the big event – a ladder to give access to the stable roof, a blanket to ensure my comfort, and sandwiches, should the show be lengthy and render me peckish.

Chapter Six

I was comfortably settled on the stable roof by five and
twenty past seven. The evening sun was pleasantly warm-
ing and the view across the fields most pleasing to the eye.
But the view I awaited promised to be far more pleasing
than even the most lush rolling green fields and woodland!

A rather large gap in the roofing boards afforded a
perfect view of the hayloft – and young Belle, who, I
fancied, was looking decidedly anxious! Her big brown
eyes gazed up to the roof once or twice but, presumably,
she thought the noise came from the birds, which were
wont to gather on the stable roof in the early evening, ere
taking to the trees for the night.

Fortunately, I did not have a long wait. Clara and
Elizabeth ascended the ladder to the hayloft well before
the appointed hour. Giggling and chattering, they settled
in the hay next to Belle, who remained silent.

'We have brought you a gift,' Clara announced, opening
a large cloth bag. 'A dress!'

'For me?' Belle asked with surprise.

'Yes, you cannot wear jodhpurs all the while.'

It was a fine blue velvet dress, trimmed with lace, that
Clara held up to the girl. Surely she would not be imparting such a gift? It was a trick, I knew – the young

bitch would probably snatch the dress back to delight at the girl's disappointment.

'Take your clothes off and you may try it on,' Elizabeth ordered excitedly. Ah, so that was her ploy – naughty little Elizabeth! Belle appeared rather sheepish, but did, nevertheless, rise to her feet and slip off her jodhpurs. Unhappily, my vantage point did not permit me to see her legs, or, yet more wretchedly, betwixt them. But I did not fret, for I knew I was soon to be rewarded with an even greater spectacle.

No sooner had Belle removed her jodhpurs than Clara threw them down into the stable with an ear-piercing shriek of glee. The dress, too, met with the same fate, leaving the poor girl nothing with which to cover herself.

Pulling her down into the hay, the girls began to tug on Belle's underclothes. I must admit that for one of so small a frame, she put up quite a fight, crossing her legs tightly to bar access to the warm delights nestling betwixt her thighs.

'You will do as we ask, or we will tell mother that you stole the dress from the house,' Clara warned sternly.

'I will not!' returned the struggling girl.

'Then we will tell her this instant! Come, Elizabeth, let us put an immediate end to the strumpet's employ!'

That Clara, the spoilt little witch, was in dire need of a thrashing of all thrashings! Poor Belle knew not what to do as the girls descended the ladder. Had she not spat at me earlier, had she made even the slightest effort to be civil, I should not have beaten her, and rescued her from her predicament. But, alas, in the circumstances, there was naught I could do to save her.

'All right,' Belle called shakily, as the girls ran through the stable. Squealing with delight, they quickly scaled the ladder and took up their positions either side of their prey.

'Now, take your clothes off!' Clara commanded, almost beside herself.

'Not all of them, surely?' the poor girl sobbed.

'All of them!' echoed Elizabeth. 'Do not be shy, for we shall follow suit shortly.' Ah, please do, I prayed!

Much to my annoyance – for it blocked sight of the desired nether region – Belle rose to unbutton her blouse, the girls showing their eager participation by hitching the garment over her shoulders. She wore no brassiere, and I could plainly see why. Oh, how pointed were her breasts – more delectable, by far, than I had imagined! Small, no more than bumps upon her chest, but, oh, so pert, and crowned with the most delightful little brown buds.

Within seconds, the girl stood naked before her mistresses. 'Come on! Come on!' I urged in my excitement. 'Lie you down, and show me your full sweetness!' And lie down she did – as if in answer to my prayer, direct beneath my feasting eyes, she lay in all her nakedness. Her dark bush was sparse, hardly grown, and barely covered her tight groove. Hers were hips like a boy's, with no contours of womanhood, her legs with no trace of a curse. Was she of more tender years than I had imagined? At that moment, I knew not, and cared not, for the sight warranted appreciation, not analysis.

'There is nothing of you, girl!' Elizabeth resounded. 'How old are you?'

'I am of eighteen years.'

'You are not!'

'I am!'

'Touch yourself!' Clara interrupted. 'Open your legs and do it!' The girl refusing to comply, Elizabeth grabbed her tiny hand and placed it firmly between her legs, but she immediately moved it away. 'You do know how to pleasure yourself, do you not?' There came no answer but sobs. 'Unless you can show us that you know how to derive pleasure from your spot, we will have to teach you – and you do not want that, do you?'

Belle's hand moved slowly down over her soft belly to her little bush, where it lay upon her mound, motionless, until she was instructed to proceed. I watched with bated breath as she parted her pouting lips and tentatively fingered the pink flesh within. The girls gasped, as did I, as they pulled her legs apart and moved their pretty little faces nearer to the wondrous spectacle.

'You must harden your little spot until it brings you your pleasure,' Elizabeth ordered eagerly, but Belle, I could see, was not going to reach her climax merely by stroking her pinken lips. The girls perceived this, too, and warned that she would be attended to by their own fair hands if she did not immediately comply.

'Then carry out your threat,' breathed Belle, to my utter amazement. The girls, too, were stunned and, for a moment, looked at each other aghast. Belle permitted herself a smile, I will swear, as they argued over which one should 'touch the dirty little strumpet'.

'Neither am I dirty, nor a strumpet!' announced Belle firmly. 'And if you cannot decide, then why do you not execute your threat together?' Two hands reached out gingerly to touch the mound between the girl's childish thighs. No words were uttered as her now swollen lips were parted and her clitoris located by those young, slender fingers. My cock felt fit to burst, but I could not pleasure myself at that point for my eyes were transfixed on the glorious scenario. Besides, to move might have caused the roofing boards to creak and betray my presence.

'Do it properly!' Belle ordered, as she stretched her arms behind her head. What in God's name was I playing at, I asked myself, atop the roof? Why was I not down there in the hayloft 'doing it properly' to the young beauty? Her needs were not to be found at the inept fingers of Clara and Elizabeth – her young body begged *my* expertise, *my* rampant hardness to split asunder her tight little crack, swelling her with its girth and filling her with its hot, bubbling seed.

As my father was wont to say, the tables always turn, and, indeed, they had surely turned for poor Clara and Elizabeth, for there they were, heeding their plaything's instructions. Much to my delight, their plan had gone terribly wrong. Would the tables turn, too, for me? I thought not, for from my precarious vantage, my cock and balls were tied, so to speak. I would have to content myself with the solace later to come, when, recalling each graphic detail of the wondrous scenario from my memory, I should take myself in hand.

'Do you not know how to give a girl pleasure?' Belle demanded of her playmates. That was invitation enough for Clara to sink a finger into the young thing's tight little pussy, as Elizabeth worked with fury on her clitoris. Ah, to watch the threesome was pure heaven, Belle gasping, Clara taking her hole as though her sopping finger were a hardened cock, and Elizabeth enticing the little bud to grow, ready to burst! I watched transfixed as, writhing and panting, Belle twisted on her tiny nipples, invoking the girls all the while not to cease their activities.

And cease they did not – on and on Clara thrust, and

Elizabeth rubbed, until, arching her back and gasping with pleasure, little Belle brought her knees up to her chin, crying out her appreciation as her bud did, indeed, explode. 'You have a lot to learn,' Belle gasped, though obviously satisfied, as she sat upright.

'It seems we have,' Clara returned. 'Tell me, what experience have you with men?'

'Men? Why, none! I have no need of men and their presumption to give pleasure when I may be afforded the ultimate union with girls such as you! And now, I think it should be your turn, Elizabeth, for you are obviously the younger, and should be the first.' Looking to her sister for help, Elizabeth received only encouragement. 'Yes, I agree,' connived Clara. 'Take off your dress and allow Belle and me to do it to you.'

Within minutes, two maidens lay naked in the hay 'neath my hideout, which truly afforded me a bird's eye view. Elizabeth, obviously suffering some embarrassment, begged Clara to remove her clothing, too – and so she did! I could scarce believe what I was seeing! Three young unbridled fillies, with their wonderful manes in varying degrees of growth and hue, cavorting together in the hay. Touching – tentatively, softly – caressing nipples, bellies, exploring each other's grooves, they entwined in an orgy of wanton lust that, I must confess, caused me to loose my seed in my breeches!

Though appearing little more than a child against the two curvaceous young women, Belle was the initiator. Licking, mouthing and sucking between the girls' legs, she brought first one to a climax, and then the other. More fingers in more hot cunnies than I had ever dreamed I would witness! More tongues finding their way betwixt more wet valleys than I had imagined in my wildest fantasies!

And then it happened – just as the girls were reaching their pinnacle together. I had released my cock from my wet breeches and was happily fondling the hard end in anticipation of another gush of sperm when I fell clean through the roofing boards, to land betwixt the three writhing bodies. How they shrieked! And how I laughed, for I was unhurt. Cock still standing proud, I lay upon my back, gazing up at six hard breasts, six delicious nipples, and three profoundly wet grooves. And, I might add, three most astonished faces!

'A gift from heaven!' Clara squealed excitedly, when she had recovered from her shock.

'And a most timely gift,' Elizabeth rejoined, eyeing my cock. Only Belle remained silent amidst the giggles. She was upset, I surmised, by the presence of a male. After all, she had been in control, the teacher, and now I had put an end to it. All eyes were now on my hard extension rather than her wet slit, lovely though it was.

'So, which lucky maiden is going to be the first to receive my fine cock?' I asked, taking my chance to break in all three in one fell swoop. Belle covered the hard bumps on her chest and turned her face in a deliberate effort to snub me. Clara looked decidedly anxious, whilst Elizabeth, sweet Elizabeth, gazed at me, her long fair hair all fallen in disarray over her wide, blue eyes, and smiled.

'So, you are to be the first, Elizabeth, my sweet,' I said. 'Tell me, my three pretty young ladies, has any one of you before been taken by a man?'

'Never!' came Belle's indignant reply.

'Oh, Tom, you naughty boy! You know only too well that

Clara and I have never been taken by a man!'

'So, Elizabeth, will you be the first to experience the delights of a man's cock betwixt your cunny lips?'

Clara became most excited at the prospect of watching her sister being taken, and egged her on with great fervour. Elizabeth conceded, as I knew she would, lying back in the hay with her legs open and her soft mound proud below her smooth, flat belly. What a beauteous sight! Losing not a moment lest she change her mind I moved, cock in hand, betwixt her lovely thighs and sunk it into her young body. She gasped and cried for me to take it out, but it was too late. Oh, so tight, she was! Tight, hot and sticky from the mouthing she had received from her playmates.

'Oh, Tom!' she cried. ''Tis but my maiden voyage! Pray, not so hard!' But thrust hard I did, and deep, for I was lost in a wild sea of emotion. To the accompaniment of sweet Elizabeth's beseechments and Clara's squeals of delight, I let loose my cream, all too soon, I am sorry to say, filling her hot little cunny tube to the brim. Poor Elizabeth, how she writhed as her climax came! I thought that time had run out for her to attain her goal, for I was almost spent. But, come she did, my ever-shrinking cock thrusting on and on until, at its timely "death," she was done.

Belle remained ever silent, still covering her breast bumps as she cowered in the corner of the loft. But Clara, by this time, had moved behind me in an attempt to see my cock shafting her sister's hole. Whether she had a good view, I knew not, but from her hand cupping my balls and the other gripping my shaft as she gasped, I deduced that she was enjoying herself almost as much as I.

All done, I slipped my cock from Elizabeth's broken-in

cunny and reclined in the hay. Her breasts heaved as she panted and gasped something to the effect that she was now a fully-fledged woman. 'You are no longer a virgin!' I announced, stating the obvious, rather for my own pleasure than for her enlightenment. Clara was watching my sperm ooze from her sister's hole and delighting in giving a running commentary.

'It's all white and it's running down to your bottom hole, Elizabeth! Oh, look how it seeps from you! Squeeze your cunny, I want to see the cream flow!' From Clara's joyful squeal, I did surmise that Elizabeth did her sister's bidding.

Still Belle was silent, and, I guessed, in terror of her imminent encounter. But she would have to bear with her insecurity for a while longer, I decided, for young Clara was sorely eager to join her sister in womanhood.

'Come, Tom!' she entreated me, lying with her young legs splayed high in the air. 'You must take me now!' My poor cock hung sadly limp but soon revived as I took the liberty of tasting the sweet groove displayed before me. Oh, nectar! Hot, wet, sticky, with a hint of brine, I drank until I was hard and risen and she, pleading.

Thus, to her warm, soft, virginal entrance, I offered my cock. And then, in! Deep, deeper into her very womb I sank my shaft, to the music of her screams and cries. Was she hurting? Did she bleed? Perchance, but the pain would pass, I reasoned hazily – as with all virgins. Elizabeth was the exception, of course, for she was a horse rider and had proffered no blood at the surrender of her virginity. I vouch that straddling Giant's broad back had prepared her groove most admirably to take a man's cock! The pity, I thought, that Clara had not taken to riding the stallion, but it mattered not.

'You must permit yourself to enjoy it,' Elizabeth submitted, pulling apart her sister's legs to aid deeper penetration.

'It hurts less now,' she gasped. 'Do it slowly, Tom!'

I did, for a time, at least. But I was soon anxious to loose from my knob another flow of sperm into a young girl's womb. Her dark complexion growing ever darker, her nostrils flaring as she wrapped her legs around me to pull me deep inside, her pain turned patently to pleasure as she neared the pinnacle of our union, her strong little cunt crushing me with its grip of ecstasy as I filled her with what little sperm that remained.

'Ah, Tom, it is hot and hard! Oh, God, how deep you are within my hole! Ah, such pleasure and pain, mingling betwixt my thighs that I cannot . . . Ah!' Shuddering and gasping, sighing and panting, she had finally relaxed – a woman!

Elizabeth had invigilated the proceedings whilst cradling Clara's head in her arms. Looking down over her sister's heaving belly, upon which I rose and fell, she had a fine sighting of my cock sliding in and out between the splayed vermilion lips. The instant it slipped from its sheath, she asked, nay, begged, that it again tend her.

'No!' I gasped, barely able to catch my breath. 'For it is young Belle's turn next.' The waif moved away, her dainty hands still guarding her bumps as if they were precious stones. I thought that I would not be able to manage another girl so soon, but her boyish lines intrigued me, and behold, my cock rose yet again.

It fell to dear Clara and Elizabeth to hold the girl down, for she fought and struggled as a cornered animal. 'You will like it!' Clara remonstrated. Elizabeth seconded her sister's assurance, but Belle would have none of it.

'I would fain have a girl than a man!' she screeched.

'Then I must correct your wicked ways,' I admonished, moving between her legs, which were by now held asunder by my most able assistants.

'You should have no preference,' Clara remarked. 'We girls like each other, of course, but we enjoy Tom, too. Why not draw pleasure from both?'

'I do not want a man – I hate men!'

Spurred on by the compliment, I thence did my duty as a stud, and slipped my cock into her cunt. It was the tightest cunt I have ever had the pleasure of entering, and that is no word of a lie, for I was barely able to sink the knob betwixt her folds. But I could not, I would not retire. In and out I moved the knob, gaining a little more ground with each gentle push. Belle still fought, of course, but she was fast losing her energy and would soon cease her futile struggle. The knob now fully inserted, I pressed hard, and slowly my shaft sank, inch by inch, deeper and deeper into the virginal tube as she contorted her face and buried her fingers in the hay.

I will not pretend that she enjoyed the experience. But I did detect that she found a little pleasure as my body became rigid and my cock swelled within her hole. She was near split open by the sheer girth of my pumping cock, and I must confess to being intent on taking my own pleasure rather than minding her pain. As I rammed into her cunny harder than I had into all the other cunts I had rammed that evening, her squeals filled the stable, sending poor Giant into a fit of neighing and kicking such that I was sure would summon Lady Sarah from the house.

But, again without word of a lie, she did attain her

summit of pleasure, and in such a manner that I feared she would die! Her face reddening to a deep crimson, her neck tightening so that its veins stood out, she flung back her head and moaned a low, interminable sound of ecstasy.

Suddenly, she fell limp – again, I feared her time had come, being then ignorant of the female *petit mort*. But her breathing was heavy and the smile upon her face depicted naught but complete and utter gratification. Quickly, I slid my cock from her perspiring body and buttoned my breeches. Her swollen lips lay open, as if I were still inside her, dribbling a cocktail of juice, sperm and maiden's blood. I knew enough seed had been left in my balls to complete the job properly. Belle, like the other girls, was a woman!

She said nothing as she rose to her feet and betook her slender frame down the ladder. The girls watched, as did I, as she picked up the velvet dress and slipped it on. A well-found transformation indeed!

'You, too, are a fully fledged woman!' I informed her, wondering as to her reaction, upon her return to the hayloft.

'And you arc a bastard!' she hissed, as I had half expected, to the squeals of Clara and Elizabeth. 'But I thank you, all the same.'

'Thank me?' I queried. What was she about, that she thanked me?

'You have unleashed something within me that I thought was not there,' she confessed, unabashed.

The girls looked puzzled, but I smiled at Belle and took her hand. 'You are a fine girl, and that dress unleashes something in you that *I* thought was not there,' I retorted, gently kissing her sweet mouth.

Suddenly, the still night air was filled with the horrific shrieks of Lady Sarah. Her two naked daughters jumped and grabbed their dresses, making an unholy mess of trying to slip into them. 'More haste, less speed,' I whispered. 'Leave her to me – I will detain her whilst you dress properly and arrange your hair. I must say, you both look as if you have been well and truly fucked in a hayloft!'

In the yard, Lady Sarah was standing by the horse trough, shouting and screaming for her girls. 'Where are they?' she demanded on my approach.

'Why, I do believe they are talking to Belle,' I said innocently.

'Then why did they not come when I called? Bring them to me, now!'

No sooner had she spoken than the girls came scurrying over. 'Sorry, mother, we were with Belle,' Clara appeased her, tugging down her dress.

'Tom was not with Belle, was he?'

'No, mother,' came the most welcome reply.

'Good. Now, both be off to bed, it is getting late.'

I watched the girls – the women, should I say – run across the yard. Lady Sarah had been awaiting their departure to speak with me, I knew, and I smiled expectantly the moment her daughters disappeared from view.

'Will you take a little wine with me, Tom?' she asked.

'Why, yes, my lady, I would love to,' I replied, doing my utmost to comply with her list of conditions and treat her with respect. All conditions save one, that is – staying clear of Belle!

'Then please join me in the study in half an hour,' she said, smiling sweetly as she turned and left.

A thought struck me as I watched her rounded bottom

fade from view – a terrible thought! Forsooth, would I be of a constitution to service her? Would she expect my cock to be hard and ready to enter her? After her daughters, and Belle, it was quite flaccid, and would surely remain so until the morrow. Besides, I was still sticky with the juices of three virgins!

Being a warm summer night, a dunk in the horse trough refreshed not only my body, but my senses, a change of clothes also reviving my vigour. I felt elated and, I must say, somewhat proud of my conquests. To take three virgins! But to have a mother, too? Yes, I was now up to the task – thrice, if necessary! Lady Sarah would demand that I penetrate her, I knew, and I was confident that I had every chance of granting her wish, for did not the brute in my pants stir already at the mere thought?

The appointed time nigh, I knocked on the study door and waited. As the door inched open, I expected to see Lady Sarah resplendent in her chemise, but I was sadly disappointed. She had on the same dress she had worn in the yard half an hour previously – a pleasing dress though, by any score, following faithfully as it did the sensuous contours of her breasts and hips. Beneath the slight curve of her belly, from whence the velvet billowed, I could but only imagine the lines! But her chemise – where was it? Why was she not attired for love?

She bade me sit in the armchair facing hers, by which a glass of wine stood on a small table. As we sipped our wine and smiled at each other, I felt it best and only right to wait for her to commence the conversation.

'My daughters, Tom. They are behaving well?' she asked.

'Oh yes, my lady, very well indeed!' I replied, a trifle too zealously.

'That is good. And the new girl – you have stayed away?'

'But of course, my lady!'

'Good. So you have read the conditions and agree to abide by them, I take it?'

'Yes, my lady.'

What I had envisaged to be another night of lust was developing into nothing more than polite chit-chat, it seemed. However, I had taken more than my fair fill of fillies that evening, and, strangely, the prospect of a rest didn't bother me too much.

After discussing my duties which, apparently, no longer required me to act as butler, I asked her the reason for my having to distance myself from Belle. She did not reply, and I took it that I had been correct in my earlier assumption – she wanted the girl for herself.

'Rather than act as butler, Tom, I wish you to act as – how shall I put it? As you know, Lord Hadleigh is no longer with us and . . . Well, I would like you to act as the man about the manor. Please do not for one minute mistake my meaning! You are *not* to replace my husband, of course, but merely help in the general running of the manor. Now that my husband has gone, I intend to hire more staff, and I will require you to oversee them.'

'If that be my duty, my lady, then surely I must have contact with Belle during the course of that duty?' I ventured, determined to prove that the girl was to be used for her ladyship's sexual pleasure.

'You have a point, Tom. Yes, obviously you may converse with her. But only in relation to work, nothing more.'

'May I, again, venture to ask why?'

'You may not! Now, finish your wine and come hither.

My dress is tight and hot, kindly loosen the clasps.'

I moved to the back of her chair and she leaned forward to allow me to unfasten her dress. Holding up her golden hair. I parted the velvet of her dress to expose her gracious spine, continuing to undo each clasp until I neared the middle. There, frustratingly, she bade me stop.

'Now, sit at my feet and remove my shoes, Tom. The night is hotter than I can bear.' She collected up her skirts as I sat upon the floor, and placed her foot in my hand. Her long, curvaceous legs were visible only to her knees, but that was enough to rouse my cock. As I undid her laces, she raised her skirts, inch by inch. She knew only too well what she was doing but her manner was nonchalant and I made no point of staring as her knees came into view.

Biding my time with her laces, for her skirts were still slowly rising, I asked if she would be visiting Belle once she was installed in the cottage. She made it quite plain that it was not my business but, as I pointed out, the track to the cottage was in full view of the yard and stables, so visitors would not go unnoticed. She did not reply – had she, I would have paid not the slightest attention, for her skirts were now almost to the tops of her shapely thighs.

She had been leaning forward, watching my hands work, but now she relaxed and, seemingly careless, allowed her skirts to clear her thighs and expose her bush. It is evident from this narrative that she wore nothing beneath her skirts and, as with my first sexual encounter with the lady, the seduction was obviously well planned.

'Do massage my feet and my calves, Tom, for they ache so,' she requested, once her shoes were removed. They were delicate, neat little feet and I worked first on one and then the other, all the while keeping an eager eye on her groove which was just visible beneath her tight curls.

So, I wondered, how was she going to instruct me? 'Take me, Tom!' No, I thought not. 'Kiss betwixt my thighs!' No, she was more subtle than that. She had made it clear that I was to follow her instructions only, so I dared not take the liberty of touching her uninvited. That is, unless she made me wait too long, for my cock nurtured a need.

As she reclined in the chair enjoying my relaxing massage she allowed her hand to fall between her thighs and, seemingly oblivious as to my presence, began to twist her dark curls around her fingers. A droplet of milky fluid appeared on her pink inner lips as she parted her legs and let her head fall back. Her fingers now moved slowly up and down the length of her opening valley, affording a wondrous view of her entrance. Oh, to penetrate her as she reposed, serene, as if sleeping! Will she continue this torture until I am obliged to break the conditions and forcibly take her? I asked myself. Or will she arouse herself to such a degree that she pleads for my cock to plunge deep within her plumbing?

Slipping down in the chair, the curvature of her buttocks hung beautifully over the cushion, exposing the smaller hole of the two that I had entered and filled so recently. My cock, alerted to the warmth, the wetness, though having loosed four measures of sperm already that very evening, was sorely in need of draining yet again.

'You may kiss my legs,' came her request, not before time. I complied immediately by nibbling her inner thighs, breathing in the heady scent of her bush as I did so. My hands, all the while, massaged her firm calves. She began to squirm a little as my tongue neared its goal, but I was determined not to overstep the mark. 'A little higher, please!' As high as your ladyship wishes, I thought, moving my hungry mouth ever closer to her nest.

For some time I kissed and gently bit on the soft flesh of her inner thighs as they opened as imperceptibly as moves the minute hand against the clock face. Her soft, pinken pads were swelling, opening, too. Less perceptibly so than her thighs, but opening they were, to reveal the hot, wet centre of her being.

'A little higher, please!' she repeated, sliding forward a trifle more. Now only but a fraction of an inch from her open groove, I felt the softness of her hair against my face as I inhaled heavily, filling my nostrils with her aphrodisiacal scent. My cock pressed uncomfortably against my breeches and, whilst aware I had not been so permitted, I released it, allowing it the freedom to stretch and swell further. For, whilst her body may not have been as youthful and fresh as those of my earlier conquests, she had other qualities that were undeniably titillating. Unlike the girls' tight folds, her pinker inner lips protruded invitingly, well beyond the groove. Moreover, her fleshy outer lips swelled to far greater proportions, so accentuating her slit, which I found most aesthetically pleasing.

My face becoming wet as I inadvertently touched against a moist, pink petal, she breathed again the magic word, 'Higher!' There was nowhere higher to go, other than to her cunt. Now, I took the liberty of using my tongue to explore her groove, its warm juice bathing my chin as I lapped between her ladyship's legs. It was hot, wet and sticky, as were Clara's fruits, but the heavenly taste was perceptibly different. The same tang, yes, but a subtle difference which I could only attribute to maturity. Both were wonderfully nectarous, of course, and I drank from her ladyship's cunt until she was dry.

'Move your attention further down,' she commanded, her legs now almost at right angles to her body, which lay horizontal in the chair.

'Down?' I enquired through a mouthful of hot flesh. She did not instruct me further, assuming, no doubt, that I would understand her meaning, which I quickly did! Below the entrance to her womb I licked the small, tight bridge of skin, and then, down further to the orifice, so tiny that I wondered how I had ever managed to penetrate it, and with such ease! Initially, the acrid flavour bit my taste buds, but as I ran my tongue round and round the exotic little ring, the taste mellowed. Her smooth, flat belly undulated with her every gasp as I teased and tantalised the exciting little hole.

Moving her hands beneath her legs, she pulled open her buttocks, just enough to allow my tongue entrance. Again, the bitterness stung my taste buds as I tried, desperately, to invade her sanctum of sanctums. But I did get the tip inside and licked her there for some moments.

'Now up! Quickly, up to the top!' Ah, her clitoris, at long last! Enlarged to an incredible size, and as hard as rock, the bud was most gratefully engulfed in the warmth of my mouth. Round and round the tip of my tongue ran to the rasped instructions of her ladyship. 'Harder! Up slightly! That is it! That is it!'

Crushing my head betwixt her thighs she cried out and writhed, moving her hips back and forth, working her bud harder into my mouth until she shuddered violently, pushing my head away. Satisfied with my work she truly was, rewarding me by reaching down for my cock, which was more than ready to fill her cunt and burst!

Through the hot wetness it slid with ease, sucked into the very root by her wild contractions. Kneeling before her open legs I took a tight hold of her buttocks, lifting her pelvis clear of the chair to meet my thrusts. Having little or no sperm left in my swinging balls it was a timely opportunity to enjoy her thus, with no fear of an early finish.

But presently she cried out as her body shook with ecstasy. Her head swaying, her eyes rolling with euphoria, she begged me to stop. But no – the bitch deserved to be taken, long and hard, good and proper. On and on I thrust until she cried out yet again, sobbing with the sensations her clitoris fired throughout her trembling body. As if intoxicated, her pleas for mercy disintegrated to drool, becoming almost unintelligible.

She must have one more taste of paradise, I told myself, and then my turn will come. And one more she had! Her cunt squeezing my cock, almost to strangling point, she at last, again, hit her heaven, as I spurted what could have been only a teaspoonful of my fruits deep into her body. She was dry as I gave her my last few thrusts – tight, dry and thoroughly taken!

Dragging my cock from her body, I sat back on my heels and gazed at the gaping crack betwixt her twitching thighs. Aflame and crimsoned, she was in need of my wet, soothing tongue. Slowly, gently, I licked her valley from the bottom to the top until her breathing calmed and the colour left her cheeks and she fell into a deep sleep.

Closing the door quietly, I left her in that most unlady-like position – legs asunder, swollen lips gaping, the entrance to her cunt wide open. I will swear I have never been so exhausted in my entire life! Falling onto my bed, I had no time even to wash or remove my clothing before sleep took me.

Chapter Seven

It had rained heavily throughout the night, and, as a consequence of the evening's adventure, poor Belle had been obliged to take refuge in the stable with Giant. I arose somewhat later than was usual, but not too late, thank God, to interrupt Lady Sarah's interrogation of Belle.

'The roofing boards have been in need of replacing for some time, according to Harry, my lady,' I lied as I wandered, seemingly nonchalant and bleary-eyed, into the stables.

'Then is it not high time something was done about it? Poor Belle was woken with her clothing drenched.'

'I will attend to it straight away, my lady,' I promised, searching her eye for a hint of acknowledgment of our intimate time together. But, as I should have expected, there was none. As usual, she was cold and indifferent.

I was hungry and had instructed the battle-axe to supply me with breakfast as I passed the kitchen, to which she had retorted, 'I only take orders from 'er ladyship.' Not for long, I had thought, eyeing the fresh eggs and bacon upon the table. Belle had eaten, of course, and took great delight in telling me so. Lady Sarah heard Belle's jibes upon taking her leave, as I hoped she would, but said nothing. A bitch of the calibre to love a man by night and watch him die of hunger come the morn, I was sure.

Belle seemed different – happier, perhaps, on account of experiencing the pleasure of my cock deep within her womb. Ah, yes, I had tamed her! Shown her what her cunt was for and how to use it! But, I must be honest, I felt that her mellowing had more to do with the friendship, if I may call it so, that she had found in the girls and I. This time, as she caught my gaze upon the sweet groove so prominent beneath her jodhpurs, she actually smiled rather than spat!

Hunger called from the depths of my stomach and there was only one thing for it – Alice! I made my way to the cottage with much haste, whence the finest breakfast of eggs, bacon, sausages and toast I have ever in my life taken set me up for the day. Sweet Alice! How I would miss her when she had gone – and Harry, who, compared to me after my night of wanton lust, appeared the epitome of health.

He informed me that there was plenty of wood in the barn left over from the wainscotting that had been replaced in the manor house. 'Ideal for the stable roof. Not that it should have required attention for many years,' he added, regarding me strangely. Had he, in more carefree days, also fallen through the roof? I wondered. I suspected that old Harry could tell a story or two concerning the young girls of his youth!

However, thanking my hosts for their hospitality, I set to without further ado to repair the stable roof. I was in half a mind to leave a spyhole above the hayloft for my future enjoyment, but decided against it. For Belle was to move into the cottage ere long, and besides, she was now a fully fledged member of my harem.

Ruminating upon these delights as I made good the roof, I presently spotted Lady Sarah and the girls leaving in a carriage. Whence they were bound, I had not a clue. But their departure afforded me the ideal opportunity for another rummage through Lord Hadleigh's writing bureau. I know not what prompted such a notion, but I deemed it worthwhile.

The battle-axe ignored me as I passed the kitchen and made my way through the house to the study. Closing the door quietly, I stole across the thick carpeting, settled myself in the huge leather chair and opened the desk. Luck was not with me, for by the look of it, Lady Sarah had already ransacked the various files. I knew not precisely what I sought, but whatever could have been of interest to me would no longer be in the desk, I was sure.

So where, then? I wondered. Her bedchamber? As good a place as any, I surmised – and I was right! For beneath her bed I discovered a large wooden chest containing reams of paper – documents, files, lists, accounts, receipts and the like. Where to start? I pondered, opting for the least obvious place, at the bottom.

It seemed a thankless task, and I had little time, but ere long, Lord Hadleigh's yellowed certificate of birth caught my eye. I noted that he had been born to Henry Clarence Hadleigh and Eliza Susan Hadleigh, of little significance until I observed the title column – Mr and Mrs! So, at long last, I had uncovered Harry's secret, I thought. Lord Hadleigh – like his wife – was a mere commoner!

In a state of confusion, I carefully replaced the document and beat a hasty retreat. Curiosity had driven me to my search, but I had not anticipated stumbling upon a hornet's nest! Now a battery of questions set my poor mind reeling. First and foremost, how the blazes had old Hadleigh, of no bluer blood than I, attained the lordship of the manor?

Ascending the ladder to the stable roof, I regretted neglecting to have searched the chest further. But, as it happened, I was relieved that I had not spent a moment longer in Lady Sarah's bedchamber, for she returned within minutes. Stepping from the carriage, unaccompanied by the girls, which I deemed odd, she disappeared inside the house.

I was more than puzzled. I could have accepted that Lady Sarah, though a mere maid, had somehow managed to marry into the aristocracy. But my discovery showed this not to be the case. Old man Hadleigh was a fraud too, as was his wife. How had this deceit come to be?

Harry was no help whatsoever, declining even to speak of the subject and warning me to search no further for the truth. Once out of the old man's earshot, I took the liberty of questioning Alice, but she knew nothing, or feigned so. There was no alternative but to search the chest yet again – at the earliest possible opportunity, I resolved. When that would be, I knew not, but the opportunity would arise, sooner or later, and my questions would be answered.

The sun hot in the clear blue sky, I was happy to spend the best part of the day dozing upon the stable roof. Lady Sarah did not scream or shout my name or appear even once, to my great relief, for I was in dire need of rest! But, curious as to the whereabouts of the girls, and her ladyship, I descended the ladder around four of the clock. The house was quiet, save for the droning complaints from the battle-axe, who seemed to be preparing enough food to feed an army.

'She's bin after you,' she informed me, without so much as raising her eyes from her work.

'I have been working,' I replied.

'Do not tell me of your excuses, save 'em for 'er!'

'You do not like me, do you?' I ventured.

'It don't pay to like no-one,' she moaned.

Leaving the old bat to wallow in her misery, I went off in search of Lady Sarah, carefully rehearsing my lines all the while, for I sensed another scolding coming. I located her in the dining room, setting the table herself, would you believe!

'Where on God's earth have you been all day? I have had Belle searching high and low for you!' she complained.

'Working on the stable roof, repairing the fences in the field, tending the . . .'

'No matter, you are here now. Wash, shave, and go to the morning room where you will find something suitable to wear for this evening. I am having guests for dinner.'

'Ah, and I am to be butler?'

'No, I have arranged for a temporary butler. You are to be a guest.'

'A guest! Your guest?'

'Yes, now pay attention. You are not to converse with anyone unless I am present. I will try and allay any awkward questions, of course, and . . .'

'But who do I say I am, my lady?'

'A friend of mine, from London – no more, no less.'

To say I was intrigued – and apprehensive – would be an understatement. But, at the same time, I must confess to feeling rather excited at the prospect of joining Lady Sarah and her company for dinner.

'May I ask why you invite me when, only hours previously, you . . .'

'I have my reasons, and they are my business. Oh, one thing more, Tom. I will be introducing you as Thomas – rather more fitting, I think you will agree. And on this occasion, and this occasion only, you will address me as Sarah.'

Ah, Sarah! What a magnificent name – an epithet oozing sensuality and femininity. Sarah! Does it not slip languorously from the tongue? Does it not conjure a picture of an exquisitely attractive, curvaceous lady? After speaking her sweet name for the duration of the evening I should be pained to revert to the formal title of Lady Hadleigh – or not so formal title, I hasten to add!

'Will your daughters be dining with us, Sarah?' I asked, wearing the grin of an excited schoolboy.

'Lady Hadleigh, for the time being. And, no, they will not. Now, hurry, you have little time to prepare, for my guests are due at seven and you will be in the parlour by six.'

Making my toilet, I contemplated the situation. No matter how sweet, how sensual I found her, I could not ignore the fact that it was the bitch of bitches who invited me as her dinner guest. Lady Sarah Hadleigh could change with the wind and that I deemed dangerous. I knew her intimately, yet I knew her not at all. She was as two people, of two minds, and there was no knowing, from one hour to the next, which character she would portray. Discarding me in one breath and inviting me to dine with her in the next only served to unnerve me. Not knowing where I stood from one hour to another, I knew not whether to love or hate her – in truth, I did both.

As I contemplated thus, my first thoughts were that she

was using me somehow. I knew not how, for her mind worked in mysterious ways, but I was sure that she intended to use me, one way or another, to her own end. I could not for the life of me fathom what she had in mind – ridicule, maybe? Parading me before her friends, she would treat me as the court jester. That could well be her evil plan, I decided.

However, I was indeed in the parlour by six. Clad in my new suit, I cut rather a dashing figure, though I say so myself. Sarah joined me at half-the-hour, looking more stunning than I could have imagined. Her dress of crimson velvet, laced with gold braid, clung, oh, so tightly to her slender body, to her pert breasts, that she surely epitomised feminine beauty. Oh, how I could have taken her there and then – lain her across the sofa, raised her skirts, spread her legs and taken the beautiful creature to heaven!

'You will not let me down, Thomas.'

'Sarah! I would not let you down in a million years! I would sooner rot eternally in hell than fail you.'

'You may have to if you do not meet my expectations of you this evening.'

'I would pluck the stars from the night sky and bring them to you on a silver platter, if you would only be mine!'

'I will never be yours, so you need not bother yourself with the stars! And I want to hear no such nonsense from you before my guests, do you understand? You are to be a friend, not a . . .'

'Lover, Sarah? Was not that the word hanging upon your sweet lips?'

'Compose yourself, Thomas! Your pants are already too tight, pray do not tax them further by entertaining such thoughts!'

Her assertion was correct, for my caged cock was, indeed, straining against the tight material in an effort to escape and roost beneath her skirts. Not a little embarrassed, I adjusted my attire and composed myself as best I could whilst in the presence of such a goddess of sexuality. Her arrogance enthralled me, her mystery intrigued me, her sheer beauty aroused me – but her cruel, dismissive manner pained me deeply.

I mentioned the word *dangerous* for that, I understood, is what she was. One false move during the course of the evening and the consequence, I knew, could be dire. I would have to be extremely careful lest I vex her. Whether to hide in the corners awaiting introduction to the other guests, or to mingle and converse, I knew not. But I was fully aware that by the evening's end I should either be Sarah's friend, or foe.

The guests trickled in – Lord and Lady this, Lord and Lady that. In the main, they were old, but some were accompanied by their delectable daughters, some with big eyes, some with small, some with long hair, some with short. But all with breasts, I cannily perceived! And, 'neath their flowing skirts and petticoats, all with fresh little cunnies, ready for the taking!

Her ladyship – Sarah – introduced me to one or two people, but I detected that she would rather I kept myself to myself. Imparting only that I was an old friend, and scarce allowing me acknowledgement, she would whisk me away ere I could strike up conversation.

So it was that, shortly before we were to dine, I found myself standing by the window looking out to the gardens when a youthful, black-haired girl by the name of Amy took her place at my side. We had been introduced earlier but had had little time to exchange pleasantries – Sarah had made sure of that! With a complexion of golden honey and dark eyes set back beneath a black fringe, I found the girl reminiscent of young Clara. And indeed, the more I looked for the similarity, the more apparent it became.

Amy, without doubt, was a most desirable young thing. Curvaceous, slim, though not lacking in proportion, I could not help but picture – I cannot for the life of me think why! – her callow cunt, hot and wet beneath her knickers. What colour her bush? How thick, or sparse? I imagined too, her nipples, teasing her tight brassiere. Were they long, hard, erect and ready to be suckled? Doubtless they were, for are not all young girls' nipples such? Whilst I had erstwhile preferred the fair-haired, blue-eyed Elizabeth to her sister, I was, of late, harbouring an attraction to the darker breed. I do believe it was young Belle, with her big brown eyes, that swung my favour. Sarah, of course, was fair, but in truth, a dark horse, with far more than mere beauty to offer!

The sweet tones of Amy tore me away from my wonderfully wicked thoughts. She lived some miles away with her parents who, she inferred, were the strictest beasts ever. 'My father will join us ere long, you see if I am not right,' she warned, and no sooner had her pretty mouth closed than he appeared at her side to take her arm. Sarah was keeping an eye on me, as she had most of the while, and quickly came to join us.

'Lord Miles, you have met Thomas, have you not?' she asked with a huge smile that displayed a perfect row of white teeth.

'I have, indeed. And I do not care for the way he eyes my

daughter so!' It was clear that Amy had not been exaggerating in the least – the poor thing was all of three years my senior, yet she plainly enjoyed less freedom than a prisoner.

Not short in diplomacy, I took my leave to find a corner in which to do nothing more harmful than spectate. Sarah's eye remained upon me as she talked to the old man, as my eye rested upon Amy. The butler kept me supplied with wine as I filled my head with wishful thinking and then, lapsing, imagined all the ladies naked. All of them – each and every one – possessed little cunny holes covered with bushes of varying colour and density. Such was my musing as Amy joined me once again.

'Take no notice of my father,' she smiled sweetly.

'No,' I replied inattentively, for I was anxious as to the whereabouts of the old man – and Sarah, who, though lost in the sea of people, would surely have me in her sights, ready to pounce should I make one wrong move.

'It is all right, you need not fear him, for he has gone through into the drawing room to discuss business with an acquaintance,' Amy enlightened me, with endearing perception.

'It is not only your father that I fear, I am sorry to say.'

'Then, who else?'

'Never mind. Tell me, Amy. For how long have your parents been acquainted with Lady Sarah?'

'I do not know that. This is my first time here, but I believe my mother has visited on several occasions. For how long have your parents been acquainted?'

'They do not . . . I mean, they are not present this evening.'

'Do you live with them?'

'No, I live . . . in London, but I have my own apartment.'

'London! Then you are staying over, surely?'

'Yes, yes. I am staying over, and travelling back tomorrow. Sarah has kindly offered me accommodation for the night.'

'I only wish I could stay over. I absolutely despise travelling home at night.'

Ah, how I, too, only wished she could stay over – in my bed! What a delightful young lady she was – being that little older than Clara and Elizabeth, she carried an air of maturity that quite took my fancy.

I felt guilty at misleading Amy, but it was my mistress's orders, after all. Masquerading was far easier than I had imagined, and I found myself yearning to become a genuine member of the aristocracy. Sarah, naturally, played the part of a lady extremely well, but she was well practised in the art.

Wearing that strange smile of hers, she wandered over to Amy and myself. 'You are getting on well with Amy,' she observed.

'I am, Sarah, for she is delightful company,' I replied.

'Delightful she is, but you must not keep her to yourself, Thomas. Come, both of you, it is time to eat.'

I was fortunate enough to be seated betwixt Amy and another fine looking young lady. Sarah, of course, sat at the head of the table and watched me like a hawk. I was happy, though, for I liked to imagine that she was jealous.

The occasion, her speech enlightened me, was in remembrance of Lord Hadleigh, her 'much loved and missed husband'. The funeral had already taken place – I could not for the life of me think when, and made a mental note to be more vigilant in the future, for I liked to miss nothing!

As the evening wore on and the wine loosed tongues, I learned that the Hadleigh girls were staying with Lord and Lady Cranfield who lived on the other side of the hill to the north of Royston Manor. Why they had been despatched so, I knew not, but suspected that it had something to do with Sarah requiring my presence at the dinner.

'Lord and Lady!' Amy whispered, for she had also heard Sarah's words concerning the girls' whereabouts.

'What do you mean?' I asked.

'They are no more . . . Oh, it matters not, Thomas.'

'Pray, do tell me, for I believe that I have guessed.'

'They are no more Lord and Lady than are our butler and maid,' she giggled.

'How do you know this? And how can that possibly be?' I enquired softly with great interest, and Sarah's eyes upon me all the while.

'I am not to talk of the matter. Mother is watching and she has charged me to rid the fact from my mind.'

I did not pressure Amy, particularly as Sarah was making peculiar facial expressions in my direction. Following the fine dinner, the gentlemen retired to the drawing room with their cigars and brandy, whilst the ladies occupied the parlour. Sarah, wanting to keep her eye on me, was at a loss as to what to do with me. 'You can hardly sit with us,' she whispered discreetly. 'And I do not want you open to questioning from the gentlemen.'

'Then, shall I take my leave?' I proffered.

'No, no. Wait in the study. Help yourself to a drink – one, mind, and I will call in on you from time to time.'

'Would it not be better if I . . .'

'I need to know where you are, Tom. Belle, no doubt, is in the hayloft and, as you know, I want you to stay away from her.'

'You do not trust me?'

'I do not.'

Having helped myself to several drinks I was becoming a trifle restless, mainly on account of images of young Belle alone in the hayloft, in dire need of my company. To calm my nerves, I paced the floor, awaiting Sarah's first visit, hoping that she might reward me for my good behaviour by allowing me to pleasure her later that evening.

I could not for the life of me understand her reasoning. Surely, she had not invited me to dine with her and her guests simply to keep watch over me? Did Belle really mean that much to her? And if so, then why had she not invited the girl to the occasion, rather than me? I could make no sense of the situation.

Before too long, Sarah slipped into the room, quietly closing the door behind her. 'You are all right, I trust?' she enquired of me, her smile sweet upon her soft lips.

'I am perfectly all right, but for one thing,' I replied.

'Pray, what is that?'

'I have so many unanswered questions, and . . .'

'And they will remain unanswered,' she returned in a whisper.

'I have taken a liking to your way of life. These clothes, the food, the manor house – all suit me admirably,' I expounded.

'But you are nothing more than an employee! Your station is . . .'

'My station is no more, or less, than yours.'

'We have had this conversation before, Tom, and I am not . . .'

'Or Lord Hadleigh's station.'

Had it not been for the alcohol, I would not have spoken so. Sarah moved nearer and looked deep into my eyes. 'There was a time when you thought you had me cornered. There was absolutely no truth in your allegations, of course, but, for my own good reasons, one of which was that I rather enjoyed your little games, I as good as admitted as much. However, this time, I will not. Lord Hadleigh . . .'

'Lord Hadleigh was no more a lord than is Lord Cranfield!'

For the first time, I did detect fear in Sarah's expression and, whilst I had only glimpsed at Lord Hadleigh's certificate of birth, and the question of Lord Cranfield's title was merely hearsay, I knew that I had hit the nail squarely upon the head. She poured herself a drink and paced the floor for some minutes, glancing at me nervously now and then, as if about to speak. Finally, she composed herself and turned to me.

'I have guests to attend! Wait here, and, when the last has gone, we will talk. But, no matter what your threats, my mind is made up – you are to go from this house, never to return!'

'You see, you invite me as your dinner guest, and then tell me to leave and never return! I do not understand you!'

'We will talk later!' she spat, closing the door firmly behind her.

Talk, that was good, for she obviously had something to talk about. Were she simply going to dismiss me, then there would be no talk. I was happy that I had enlightened her as to the thoughts in my mind, but, at the same time, I was still strangely fearful of her.

I drank, far too much, whilst I waited, I must confess. I suppose the excess was to face Sarah's vehemence, for I knew it only too well, and I hoped to find courage from alcohol. She kept me waiting deliberately, I know, for I observed her last guest leaving a good half-hour before she burst into the room and slumped onto the sofa like a spoilt child who, for the first time in its life, could not get its own way.

'I wish to make one or two points clear,' she began. 'Firstly, I am not keeping you away from Belle for the reason you think.'

'Then you do not want her for yourself?'

'Of course I do not want her for myself!'

'Then why on earth install her in the cottage if she is no more than a stable girl?'

'I have my reasons!'

'I can only conclude that you are jealous.'

'Do not be ridiculous!'

'That is the reason! You think I will take the girl and . . .'

'Have you taken her?'

'I do not take every female with whom I come into contact!'

'You surprise me!'

'Had I taken her, and you harbour no jealousy, then what concern is it of yours?'

'She is in my employ, and therefore she is my concern.'

'Since when, pray, has anyone in your employ been of concern to you? You discarded Harry and Alice as if they were nothing more than gipsies who had moved onto your land! The loss of your husband came as a relief, you said as much yourself. So do not talk to me of concern, for you know not the meaning of the word!'

I had silenced her, for a while, at least, and poured myself another drink. She indicated that she wished to partake in a little wine so I poured her a good measure, knowing that it would either bring out the fire in her, or quell her. Or, possibly, loose her tongue and enable her to reveal her true thoughts.

'I like you, Tom,' she said presently, rolling her glass betwixt her palms. 'But I cannot have you treat me so. You cannot speak to me as if I am your equal. Yes, I know that my background intrigues you, and that you believe I was once a maid. That, as I have told you, although it is none of your business, is not true. Lord Hadleigh was the son of Lord and Lady Henry Clarence Hadleigh. I am the daughter of . . .'

'He was the son of Mr and Mrs Henry Clarence Hadleigh – I have seen his certificate of birth.'

'You have searched my house? You have the audacity, the impudence to . . . Have you not heard of gentlemen becoming peers? A man does not have to be *born* a lord!'

Ah, first she says he was the son of a lord and lady, and then she changes her tune! I was not familiar with peerages, I must confess, but I knew that she was lying. So I took it upon myself to bluff her. 'I have also seen references to your being a maid. I can even tell you where you served.'

'You think you are clever, Tom. But you have seen no such references, for none exist. If you care to wait here, I will show you conclusive proof that I am who I say I am. Although, I do not for the life of me know why I should prove it to the likes of you – or anyone else, for that matter!'

So vociferating, she disappeared, to return presently with her certificate of birth. Thrusting it into my hand, she stood back triumphantly. I could scarce believe my eyes – Harry was wrong, very wrong! For the document plainly showed that the lady was born of Lord and Lady Hammond – she was, indeed, of true blue blood.

'Does that satisfy you?' she asked haughtily as I raised my eyes to meet hers. I confess that I found even greater beauty in the creature standing before me, knowing now, as I did, that she was of the aristocracy. But I was still perplexed as to why she had allowed me to blackmail her.

'No, it does not satisfy me,' I asserted. 'For if you are truly a member of the aristocracy, and I have no cause to doubt you now, then why did you allow Harry and Alice to stay in the cottage when I threatened to tell all and sundry of your background?'

'Ah, you are not so clever! I do not wish all and sundry, as you put it, to be fed a pack of falsehoods concerning my identity! Besides, I took a liking to you, and hoped, rather foolishly it seems, that you would become a reliable member of my staff.'

'Is that why you as good as asked me to break in your daughters? Is that a usual request from a lady to a potentially reliable member of her staff?'

'You have some breeding, some education, Tom. Your father owns a successful firm of accountants and . . .'

'How do you know such?'

'Two letters arrived, from your mother.'

'Addressed to me?'

'Yes, I took the liberty of . . .'

'You opened my letters!'

'They were of no consequence. Anyway, you searched my house!'

Beautiful though her gown was, I tore it from her body and flung her over the sofa. She had riled me beyond endurance, and she would pay! Her delicate underclothes fell away in my hands as she struggled and screamed which, although I had only in mind to beat her, hardened my cock wonderfully.

Naked, save a few strands of torn clothing, she wiggled and squirmed as I thrashed her buttocks with the palm of my hand until both glowed as crimson as the remnants of the dress upon the floor. She cursed me and cried of the conditions she had laid down, which only fuelled my anger.

Settled on the sofa, I dragged her across my knee and continued with the beating. Hotter and hotter my hand became, stinging the more with every blow until I could barely feel the slaps. I only wished I had had my leather belt to hand! Her long legs kicked and thrashed, affording fleeting glimpses of her swollen pads of flesh, the dividing groove parting spasmodically to expose her seeping entrance.

Coming to my senses, I rolled her from my knee and sat her upright. 'Let that be a lesson to you!' I yelled, standing before her, my prominent bulge level with her eyes.

'Get out! Get out of my house or . . .'

'Ah, you have not learned your lesson!' I laughed. Her legs had fallen apart to reveal her dark bush as she flopped back on the sofa, and I could think of nothing other than the delightful experience of taking her in the chair the previous night.

Dropping to my knees, I dragged forward her hips,

splayed her legs and began to lick at her wet groove, she beating my head with her fists and pulling upon my hair all the while. Her lips being partially open, inviting entrance to the wondrous portal, I released my cock to satisfy, and, I hoped, calm her. But still she fought like a lion!

As the battle raged, I spied, with sudden inspiration, a fair weapon – her neat little bottom hole, hiding 'neath her cunt. By way of punishment, for she had not erstwhile enjoyed the experience, and because it quite took my fancy, I decided to relieve myself in that bitter-sweet closet.

Entering first her cunt, all the while taking blows to the face, chest and arms, I rammed her womb until she calmed and relaxed, closing her eyes to permit herself the pleasure she so craved. Moving her hand down betwixt her outstretched thighs she stiffened her bud as I thrust on and on, making her ever the wetter. To heighten her pleasure, I took each of her nipples and squeezed and twisted until she threw her head back and gripped my cock within her burning cunt.

The usual expletives left her lips as she writhed and worked her hips to meet mine. Her belly jerked with every breathtaking convulsion, and her nipples hardened between my fingers as she reached her heaven. Mouth open and panting, eyes closed, breasts heaving, body rigid, she cried from the top of her lungs as her clitoris transported her very being to ecstasy.

Having saved my seed for the moment, I withdrew and pulled her buttocks up and apart, to display her tiny hole. Well oiled with her juices, my knob pressed hard against the stubborn aperture until it yielded to allow the head in. Ah, what joy her bottom hole! Her fists were flying again, punching me wheresoever they could, but I only smiled and forged ahead with my work. Inch by inch I sank my cock into her warmth, slipping in with ease, deeper and deeper into her bowels, filling and stretching the very depths of her body until I was there, my length buried to the root.

'Take it out, you bastard!' she screamed as I began to thrust in and out of her oh so tight little hole. Holding her legs wide and high in the air, I watched her juices pumping from her gaping cunt with every thrust. Dreaming wild dreams and picturing impossible things, oh, how I fantasised! Not one, but two cocks had I, opening, stretching and taking both holes in unison as my tongue licked feverishly at her clitoris. Oh what joy to be a contortionist with two cocks!

'Now do you picture Giant?' I laughed. Her small hole was beautifully stretched, tightly encompassing my girth as I pushed my shaft in to the root, ready to fill the bowels of her body with my sperm.

'You are vile, debased, perverse, and completely insane!' she cried. 'Please stop!'

Giving her no mercy, for females being fucked thus neither wish it nor deserve it, I emptied my full balls into her bottom. As I pumped and squirted the cream deep inside her bowels, I was amazed to feel her tighten around me. Her body quivered and began to shake violently as she gripped even the more on my granite-hard shaft. Was she actually enjoying the very act she had so despised? Did she picture Giant as she reclined and allowed the sensations to engulf her very being? Was that the source of her ecstasy?

'If I be perverse, debased, or whatever, then you be, too!' I gasped.

Her eyes rolling, her breasts swelling and her hands splaying her lips to satisfy her spot, she let out a long, deep moan and wrapped her legs around my back. She was done! We were both done as never before, and I collapsed, my cock still buried deep within her bottom hole, across the warmth of her heaving belly.

'You will never, never do that again!' she gasped, still caressing her bud as her climax subsided and brought her down to earth. Her bottom hole twitched delightfully, squeezing and sucking out the remnants of my fruits. Gazing at the spent beauty before me, I could not help but feel love for her. Oh, Sarah! Whatever she may have been, she was indeed, for me, a lady.

Slipping my spent cock from her bottom, I sat on the floor at her feet and gazed into her eyes. Would she now not admit that she could never live without me? Would she not invite me to her bedchamber to sleep peacefully, sated, limbs entwined? Could she yet deny the pleasure our union had brought her?

'Go now,' she breathed, cupping her glowing buttocks in her tiny hands. 'I cannot allow you to treat me so.'

'I will go now, Sarah. But we will love again on the morrow,' I whispered as I took her head in my hands and kissed her full lips.

'Love? You call this love? Beating me, using me, defiling me? Is that what you do in the name of love?'

'I bring you great pleasure in the name of love, Sarah, you cannot deny it. And I will do so again and again.'

'You will do nothing of the sort! Respect, I said! You know not the meaning of the word!'

I did not delay to argue, for she was exhausted, as was I, and yearned for her bed. The morning would, no doubt, bring with it her abuse, her foul language, her rage, her renewed hatred for me. But, for now, I sensed a closeness between us, a bond. Friend or foe? I knew not at that point, neither did I want to know, for I was happy with my hopes, my dreams.

She closed her eyes, her face serene with an expression of complete and utter satisfaction. Why, oh, why would she not admit her love for me? Why would that other Sarah, that monster within her beautiful body, rear its ugly head by the morrow, seeking to destroy me?

Resting my head on my pillow, I was happy in the knowledge that I was suppressing the darker Sarah, and, slowly but surely, allowing her love to shine through, unabated.

Chapter Eight

Upon rising, to my amazement I found Amy in the morning room, enjoying a huge breakfast. Her luscious lips curled into a beautiful smile on seeing me, and she leaped from her chair in greeting.

From what I gathered from the battle-axe's mumblings, she had spent the night in Clara's bedroom, on account of feeling ill and not wishing to travel home. To think that Amy had been ensconced so close to my bed, and I, all the while, oblivious to her sweet presence! What a waste! I chided myself. Clearly that was the reason Sarah had delayed in joining me in the study after her guests had departed.

The battle-axe passed the door and disappeared upstairs with Sarah's breakfast. I remained silent until she was out of earshot, fearing that she would inform her ladyship should she find me alone with her young guest.

'I trust you are feeling well, now, Amy?' I enquired.

'I was not ill, silly!' she laughed. 'I could think of no other way to be rid of my parents and . . . Well, I was rather hoping to talk with you, but I knew not of your whereabouts.'

'I was in my quarters. I mean, the room at the back of the house.'

'I searched for you, Thomas. You were not on the ground floor, obviously. In which room were you?'

'At the rear . . . No matter, for, sadly, it is too late.'

Disaster! A maiden, 'neath the same roof, and plainly desiring more than to talk with me! A rare opportunity, indeed, and I had missed it. But, I consoled myself. I had more than enjoyed my time with Sarah and, eventually, I *would* take the young Amy.

'Why are you dressed so?' she enquired, gazing at my old breeches and ragged shirt. Why, indeed? Even had I known I should encounter Amy thus I should have had little choice of garb, for my fine suit of clothes had gone with the night. The confounded Lady Sarah had surely taken it upon herself to reclaim them – I might have guessed the witch should not grant me even the vestige of a dream.

'It is a long story,' I began, desperately seeking some concoction to hide my embarrassment. 'I am to spend a few days with Lady Sarah and . . . Well, I enjoy gardening. It makes a pleasant change from London!'

Oh, how I longed to be more than a mere employee, as Sarah constantly reminded me I was. The role of master of the manor would have suited me admirably, and, no doubt, afforded me ample occasion to take lady after lady, daughter after daughter!

'Do you ride?' Amy asked.

'Oh, yes, most mornings. When I am in the country, that is.'

'Then let us meet on the heath! I often ride across the heath to the top of the hill where I can see Royston Manor. Why do we not arrange to meet there?'

What delight, to meet young Amy on the heath, far from the prying eyes of Sarah! My cock was now well risen and my stomach somersaulting at the prospect of taking her under the blue summer sky. Her dark eyes sparkled, wide with anticipation, as she awaited my answer.

'That is a marvellous idea,' I said, enticing a huge grin to her sweet little face. Will we meet at seven of the clock tomorrow morning?'

'I will be there!' she replied, as an excited child. How wonderful, life!

In a breath of sobriety, I raised the subject of Lord and Lady Cranfield, but Amy did not wish to discuss the matter. She remained strangely tight-lipped, too, upon my enquiring of the other guests. To know nothing of her parents' friends and neighbours struck me as odd, and I must admit to sensing that she was hiding the truth. But I would discover all she knew, in time. And all she hid beneath her skirts!

'My mother has arranged to collect me later this morning,' she enlightened me.

'Then, how will you while away the time?' I queried.

'I would be delighted if you would walk with me in the grounds,' she said. 'The sun is already hot in the sky, and I do not wish to stay in the house.'

Not so delighted as I! Sensing its chance forthwith, my already hard cock near flew in my breeches. Perhaps I would not have to wait till the morrow to take the young filly, after all. The grounds were rambling, with many a nook and cranny most well suited for hiding the secrets of young lovers!

Sarah was blessed, or cursed, with an uncanny sixth sense, it seemed. For the moment we were about to depart, she came bounding down the stairs calling for Amy. Most likely, having found her bed empty, she had deduced that I would be attempting to seduce the girl. She was right, of course, curse her!

As she neared the morning room, I hurriedly took my leave, explaining to Amy that I would return shortly. No sooner had I dashed through the rear door than I heard Sarah calling, not for Amy, but for me. Evidently not stopping to wish her guest good morning, she flew outside like a demon, screeching for me. The old Sarah, I reflected as I hid amongst the bushes and observed her complexion turn from pallid to a fiery red.

Belle gave me the fright of my life as she crept up behind me and grabbed my arm. 'Upon what mischief are you bent, hiding in the bushes?' she asked.

'I am doing exactly that,' I whispered. 'Hiding!'

'But why? From whom?'

Sarah's screams afforded the answer forthwith. For a moment, I was tempted to take Belle's whispered advice and hide in the hayloft. But, no, why should I run? Despatching Belle back to work, I emerged from the bushes to face Sarah, for I knew, sooner or later, I should be obliged to.

'You were calling for me, Sarah?' I asked cheerily.

'Do not address me . . .'

'Good morning,' came Amy's opportune, sweet voice.

'Good morning, Amy,' Sarah conceded, offering a smile most blatantly contrived.

'I will talk with you presently, Sarah,' I proffered, emphasising her lovely name, much to her displeasure, for her face was wrought with pent-up anger.

Finding Belle in the stables, I chatted easily with her, knowing that Sarah was safely in the company of Amy. Belle had eaten and completed most of her chores and asked if she might be allowed to take a walk through the wood to the village. I would have preferred that she stayed, to save me the trouble of covering for her should Sarah enquire as to her whereabouts. But she had worked well and deserved some reward for her efforts.

'Do not be too long,' I warned. 'For, as you are well aware, Lady Sarah is not in the best of moods this fine morning!'

'I will not be long – should I not lose my path in the wood!' she answered with a curious smile that, I will swear, beckoned me to join her on the cropped grass in the clearing.

'You will not, for there are but two paths and they both lead to the field behind the stables,' I assured her. Nearing the stable door, she turned, and again afforded me that curious little smile. 'See you later, then,' she said softly. God, I was determined to take once more that little beauty!

I had wished to speak with Harry concerning Sarah Hadleigh and the certificate of birth I had seen with my own eyes, but instead I was obliged to spend the best part of the morning playing hide-and-seek with the lady. The outcome of our game was inevitable – believing her to have returned to the house, I slipped into the stables, hoping Belle had returned from the village.

'We meet at last,' intoned Sarah as the huge door slammed shut behind her, causing me to turn on my heels. She was slapping the palm of her hand with a riding crop and walking slowly towards me.

'We do, indeed,' I replied, wondering at her strange smile.

Revenge was her panacea, I perceived, and deemed it

wise to afford her such, for no other way was there to calm
her. As she neared, I backed into the corner and pressed
myself against the wall, her smile already broadening with
the taste of vengeance.

Raising the crop, she brought it down and whacked my
arm. Though it pained not in the least, I feigned such, to
appease her. On and on she beat me, venting her anger
until her wrist ached and she was obliged to discard the
crop in favour of the use of her mouth. Swear and spit and
claw and beat my chest she did, until I restrained her,
pulling her close to my body. Turning her head, she tried
to escape my kiss, but conceded within seconds of my
mouth locking upon hers. I explored her tongue with mine,
savouring her warm, sweet juices, until she surrendered
and clung desperately to me, her eyes closed, breathing
heavily through her nostrils as she drowned in a sea of
desire.

'You wished to say something to me?' I asked as our lips
parted. Pulling me forward, she kissed me again, hard,
biting at my lips, pushing her tongue into my mouth.

'You are a bastard!' she breathed as she finally pulled
away. Her blue eyes were wide and deep with passion and
I would have taken her against the stable wall had it not
been for the girls calling for her.

Oh, would that they had known what a moment they
had destroyed! I would beat them for it later, and take
them in turn by way of punishment, filling their bottom
holes with my sperm, for they had not experienced such a
pleasure, yet.

'Come to my bedchamber in one hour!' Sarah demanded
fervidly, her passion high and, I imagined, her cunt hot,
wet and swollen.

'I will be there,' I promised. 'I will always be there for you, my Sarah.'

Composing herself as best she could, she opened the stable door to be greeted by her girls, who giggled uncontrollably, for their mother's face was afire, her eyes alive with passion and her hair in a fine state of disarray.

'You have had a good time, mother?' Clara asked impishly.

'The evening went well enough, thank you,' she replied to shrieks of laughter from Elizabeth.

'And your night away from home – I trust all was well?'

With an exhilarating mixture of lust and affection, I watched the girls chatter and giggle as they accompanied their mother across the yard, each clinging to an arm as they told of their adventures.

My reverie was broken as Belle wandered into the stable looking decidedly forlorn, and I asked what troubled her.

'I walked slowly in the wood, round and round in circles, until I became tired,' she groused.

'The village – did you not go to the village?'

'No, no. I had it in my mind that you would follow me and . . . Well, foolishly, it seems, I was mistaken.'

So my instincts had been correct – she *had* wanted me! 'I did, indeed, follow you, Belle!' I lied. 'I followed nigh after your leaving, but I surely took the wrong path. Where were you, my angel?'

Her brown eyes widened and her lips turned up in a huge smile. 'Did you really, Tom? Did you follow me? I wished as much! But I thought that you would join me in the hayloft yesterevening, and you did not. So I know not what to believe.'

'I could not join you in the hayloft during the evening,'

for I was working in the house. But I did look in on you in the course of the night – so sweet, you appeared, curled up fast asleep, that I had not the heart to disturb you.'

'Oh Tom! Would it be more than a dream, that you wished to waken me so?'

'Indeed, more than a dream, my love, but it was not to be, for you were sleeping soundly. Your workload is heavy, and I burden your thoughts. I cannot drain you by night as I do by day. A gift as precious as you I would not wish to wear thin, lest it fade into the very dream.'

'I would give you my all, Tom, if I believed that, in my heart of hearts, you speak the truth. But I cannot, for you are a man among men, and men are, by their very nature, deceitful.'

'But are not women equally riddled with deceit? Do not women, knowing what they have betwixt their thighs, play on deceit?'

'I am but young, Tom, but I have learned much, and many things. For I know that men, and women besides, not only lie, but kill, for what I possess. That certain configuration, that arrangement of skin and flesh betwixt my thighs, has power, greater than all other power, over not only men, but women, too. My bosom, though barely formed, aches as those fully bloomed. My heart, though young, yearns as a heart of experience. And my cunt, though yet tight, desires fulfilment! For whatever I may appear to you, Tom, I am a woman.'

'And I am a man, my love, and I desire you not only for your body, for your beauty, but the soul within you. I love you, Belle!'

Part truths and part untruths, I admit. But I had made her happy and, I might add, laid the way open to take her that evening. Should, of course, I not be otherwise entwined in the arms of the lovely Sarah – or Clara or Elizabeth!

I was, indeed, the most fortunate of men, I reflected, as I sauntered out into the sunshine to breathe in the fresh, country air. But I knew there was no room for complacency, being, as I was, ever aware that Lady Luck runs dry. The flame of passion, too, I knew, unkindles eventually. And when that day came, as surely it would, I had to ensure that my place at the manor was secure. My father had always advised me to plan for the future, and that is exactly what I had in mind. Not the future he had envisaged for me, I might add, for he was an upright man of strict morals. Poor mother – had she been a maid, perchance she would have discovered the delights of fiery passion and glorious nights of wanton lust!

The girls, I was sure, sought nothing more than fun and lust. Belle harboured an infatuation – as did Amy, I surmised. But Sarah – an enigma! – I knew not. She hated me, and yet she loved me, or so I thought at times. She had succumbed to blackmail, for she had little or no choice. But, I discerned, she had also fallen prey to something else. Love? But no – she was shrewd beyond belief and not to be trusted an inch. Her passion, the yearning desire in her blue eyes, was probably nothing more than lies and trickery. It was easy – had I not lied to and tricked Belle? With Amy, too, had I not proved the simplicity of deceit? And the girls – were they not both at my every beck and call, to satisfy my every whim and fancy? Not quite, maybe, but definitely there for the taking! Were we all, perchance, employing lies and trickery to our own ends?

Plan for the future, yes – but how? Secure my position at

the manor, of course, but by what means? Blackmail was my only weapon to hand, and I swore to use it to the full. But in a subtle manner, for I did not wish to rile Sarah and dash my chances of entertaining her cunny, as and when it took my fancy – or hers!

The voluptuous Sarah awaited my arrival in her bedchamber at the appointed hour. She was under the covers of her bed – naked, I prayed – as she beckoned me to join her. Closing the door, I turned the key and swiftly removed my clothes to reveal my erection, which stood proudly before her expectant eyes.

Her queen-sized bed was soft and warm – a far cry from the hayloft and the cold, hard, single bed to which I had grown accustomed! No words passed between us as I moved nearer to her and ran my hands over her body which was, in answer to my prayers, quite naked.

Kissing her mouth and then her long, gracious neck, I moved my attention down to her breasts. Long hard sucks to each nipple in turn caused them to elongate and stand proud from the dark skin surrounding them. She moaned deeply and spread her limbs wide as I kissed and nibbled the warm flesh of her slightly curved belly. Down and down I moved, ever nearer to the swelling mounds either side of her valley.

She could wait no longer than I, and pushed my head down deep betwixt her thighs, manoeuvring her hips to press my lips to hers. Digging her nails into my scalp, ever harder she pulled on me, grinding her cunt into my open mouth, suffocating me with her folds, drowning me with her juices of love.

Clearly in dire need of relief, the beginning of her climax was born quickly. As it swelled from the depths of her womb, she twisted and pulled on my head to grind my mouth, my tongue, deeper into her body. Rolling onto my back, I pulled her astride me to present my cock to her mouth as I drank the nectar from her hole. She took its length fully, raising her buttocks to allow me to lick the entire length of her slit. From her clitoris to her bottom hole, I licked and sucked, pausing momentarily to allow my tongue to enter and taste each orifice. Her cunt lips hung open, wet and glistening, stroking my cheeks as I moved my mouth back and forth.

Moving back slightly, I paused to gaze at the wondrous sight spread before me. She took me deep into her mouth, her throat, as she moved her opening down for me to continue my mouthing. And then we reached the wondrous heights of ecstasy – together we shuddered, pumping, squirming, biting, pouring forth the products of our union, filling mouths with cream and sticky juices. Her cunt opened wide for me and my cock swelled for her until we were both drained of every last drop of love.

My cock against her mouth, her cunt pressed to mine, we lay panting, gasping, filling our senses with the sweet perfumes of our spent bodies. Both kissing, nibbling, tasting the droplets that formed on her pink lips, on my soft knob, we rested, satisfied, entwined as one. Sarah, older than I, than all the delectable girls, held the key of experience that is only attained with maturity. How sweet her mouth, her breasts, her cunny! What warmth and security she offered when entwined thus!

We were almost sleeping in that wonderful position upon her bed when the girls knocked and hammered upon the door. 'Amy's mother is here to collect her!' Clara called. Sarah leaped from my body, her flushed breasts bouncing as she fought to disentangle her limbs from mine.

'But I believed she had already left!' she cried in a fluster, snatching up her dress.

'She cannot have done, for her mother would not now be here!'

'Have you seen her, Tom?' whispered Sarah, easing her dress up over her lovely breasts.

'I have not,' I replied. 'Not since I left her with you this morning.'

'Then where in God's name is she?'

Leaving me thus in the warmth of her bed, she fled the room, ensuring she closed the door firmly behind her. Amy was surely somewhere in the grounds for she had asked me to walk with her and would surely have searched for me, I reflected.

Lying dreamily in that cherished bed, the realisation suddenly struck me that the fateful wooden chest lay only inches beneath me. I was about to dress and search the chest when Elizabeth appeared at the door. 'Here, I found this,' she said, bearing a letter in her sweet little hand. 'I do believe that it is from Amy. You have not been up to your naughtiness again, Tom, have you?' she giggled.

It was, indeed, from Amy. Being 'without companionship', the poor thing had taken it upon herself to walk home. But evidently bearing me no malice, she indicated that she was greatly looking forward to our rendezvous on the morrow – and would I be sure to come alone? Yes, indeed! Unless – the wicked notion hit me as I admired Elizabeth's fair tresses – we could *all* meet upon the heath and writhe in naked ecstasy!

'You are getting along well with mother, I take it?' Elizabeth smiled as she sat on the bed by my side.

'Well enough,' I replied. 'Now, be off with you, else we shall both be in trouble!'

To drag Elizabeth into the bed and pleasure her betwixt the sheets, yet warm from her mother's body, would have pleased me greatly. But Sarah might have returned at any minute, and I doubt such a sight would have met with her favour! Elizabeth took her leave, but not without flashing me a loving smile ere she closed the door behind her. How sweet the young girl! My cock did rise, just to lay my eyes upon her pretty face.

Once dressed, I found my way into the yard, and a commotion concerning the whereabouts of young Amy. Not being at liberty to tell of the note she had written me, I decided to make myself scarce. Stealing round the back of the stables, I made my way to the cottage to enlighten Harry of his mistake concerning Lady Hadleigh's breeding.

'I have seen Lady Sarah's certificate of birth, Harry,' I whispered, the minute Alice had left the room.

'You are persistent, I will give you that,' he rasped. 'And to reward your grit, I will tell you of my secret. The certificate of birth you saw is, no doubt, Lady Sarah Hadleigh's. Had you searched long enough, I am sure that you would have found also a certificate of marriage.'

'Then all is legal and above board. So, pray, why did you say that Lady Sarah was no more than the illegitimate child of a chambermaid, and once a maid herself? What is the secret?'

'After your long wait, it is this, Tom. Many years ago, Lord Hadleigh's young wife, Lady Sarah Hadleigh, a recluse of an unbalanced mind, disappeared. Ere too long, a maid, named Mary, of roughly the same age as Lady

Sarah, stepped into the lady's shoes – as the wife of Lord Hadleigh.'

I could scarce believe what I was hearing. A maid at Royston Manor was now Lady Sarah! 'Surely people – friends, relatives and the like – asked questions when they registered the change?' I enquired.

'No, they did not. For the genuine lady, being a recluse, rarely, if ever, saw anyone. She had no visitors and never left the house. Her parents had died, leaving her the manor and, as far as I am aware, she had no other relatives. Only I knew the truth, and, in fear of losing my income and my home, I held my tongue.'

'What became of the real Lady Sarah?'

'Dead, most likely. It would not surprise me in the least if she were buried somewhere in the grounds. You see, Lord Hadleigh always craved offspring, but his wife could not grant his wish, for she was unable to bear children. The maid, by that time calling herself Lady Hadleigh, bore two daughters, Clara and Elizabeth. When I urged you to ask Lady Hadleigh about her husband, that is what I had in mind. I hoped she would believe that you knew some, if not all the story, and . . .'

'But when I once mentioned that Lord Hadleigh was not the girls' father, you told me that you knew nothing of it.'

'Indeed, I felt that you knew too much for your own good, Tom. As far as I know, one was born of a farm worker of foreign extraction, the other of a local farm-hand. Upon Lord Hadleigh discovering that the girls were not his daughters, his love for them turned to hatred.'

'I am sure that the girls know he was not their father for they were not in the least distressed by his death.'

'To this day, the girls know not of their real fathers.

They did not like old Hadleigh for the simple reason that he hated them so.'

I could understand Harry's reason for not revealing the truth earlier, fearing as he did, quite rightly, that I would run to Sarah with my blackmail threats. Harry alone knowing such things, the source of my information would be clear to her. For years, she had wanted to be rid of Harry and his dangerous knowledge and his illness had afforded her the ideal opportunity.

'If you see fit to use this information to your advantage, as no doubt you will, I would be obliged if you would wait until Alice and I have moved from the cottage,' Harry asked of me. I agreed, of course, but felt that he knew far more of the Hadleighs than he let on.

Making my way towards the stables, I imagined the expression on Sarah's face as I told her of all I knew. I could scarce contain my excitement and prayed that I would find the strength to restrain myself until Harry had moved, for it would only be fair. But come the day following the old couple's departure – that would be another story! Poor Harry and Alice had little money, and the small amount I gave each week only just kept them in food. It would have been rather nice if they had a small sum upon which to live when settled in their new home, and I promised myself that indeed they would. Sarah would happily send them one hundred pounds or so – once I had spoken with her, of course!

I was gathering information quickly, and becoming hungry for more. I had set out in the first instance to ensure that Harry and Alice remained in their home, but, it seemed, I was now driven by a strange need to blackmail Sarah. I knew not of my aims or goals at that point, only that I felt compelled to apply pressure to Sarah. Pressure to win her love, possibly? To have me live in her house with her? I was well aware that blackmail is no way to gain love, but I knew of no other way.

Amy's comments concerning Lord and Lady Cranfield had intrigued me. The girls, having spent the night at their home, obviously knew them well, and so it was to them that I decided to direct my questions. I swore to discover all there was to know, not only concerning Sarah, but about all with whom she came into contact.

Unfortunately, young Belle had set eyes on neither Sarah nor the girls. My search of the house proved fruitless, and I could only assume that all had gone off in pursuit of Amy. Belle disappeared during the course of the morning, leaving me alone, save for the battle-axe – the ideal opportunity to take another look in the wooden chest, I decided. But Sarah's bedchamber door was locked. On second thoughts, there was little point in trying to gain entry anyway, for she would have surely removed any further evidence.

Relaxing under the hot sun behind the stables, I reflected on my findings. The real Lady Hadleigh could well be buried somewhere in the grounds. But where? The discovery of her grave would certainly arm me with the evidence I needed to blackmail Sarah. Had Lord Hadleigh murdered her? Or had she conveniently died? Perhaps he had poisoned her? My mind ran amok with weird and wonderful notions of deeds of skulduggery.

I fell asleep to dreams of the mysterious Lady Hadleigh returning to haunt the manor, her naked form squatting over Sarah's face to loose her juices in way of punishment, rubbing her gaping slit back and forth over Sarah's pretty face until she let out an eerie moan.

Waking, I knew I was indeed the stud of Royston Manor and should perform my duties to the full. I should not neglect to fuck every hole belonging to every female. Let no nipple go unsucked, or left unhardened, no clitoris unstiffened by my tongue, no mouth without my seed.

Chapter Nine

Belle returned during the early evening, anxious to know if she had been missed. I admitted to being none the wiser, having fallen asleep under the hot sun. But our absence must surely have come to the notice of Lady Sarah. Leaving Belle in the stables, I went off in search of her ladyship, concocting some lie on the way.

Strangely, neither Sarah nor the girls were about the manor house, and the battle-axe could throw no light on their whereabouts. They were probably at Amy's house, Belle and I surmised, perhaps having stopped to take tea.

'So, we are alone on this warm summer evening,' Belle whispered, her big brown eyes afire with passion.

'We are, indeed. Tell me, where have you been that it took you so long?'

'I have been in the wood – walking,' she added, as if by way of an excuse.

'Just walking?' I enquired. 'Then it was a long walk.'

'Why? Should I have been up to something other than walking?'

'I just fancied that you may have been sunning yourself, for your face has caught the sun.'

'I did sun myself, for a while,' she admitted. 'And I

confess to doing so naked, in a small, secluded clearing I discovered.'

Blight of my life! Why was it that I missed so many opportunities? Never to mind, for Belle was with me, and, as she had pointed out, we were alone. Taking her hand, I led her to the field where we had the benefit of the evening sun – and privacy, should Sarah return.

Not a word passed our lips as I unbuttoned her blouse and lifted it from her shoulders. Her breasts appeared firmer than ever and I squeezed and kneaded each one in turn before bending my knees to take her nipple in my mouth, and suckle as would a babe.

'You like them?' she asked, gazing down at me.

'I love them, as I love you!' I replied, reluctantly relinquishing the bud from my lips.

'They are not too large, as yet,' she whispered solemnly.

'But they will grow, Belle, given time, and my attention. They will grow into the finest breasts, with the most wonderful long nipples!'

She seemed pleased by the prospect, smiling and throwing back her head to project her chest. Her nipples lengthened and hardened as I sucked upon them until she could no longer hold back her desire.

'I am hot in my jodhpurs,' she complained, wriggling from them until they were about her ankles.

'Your feet, too, must needs be hot, my love. Allow me to remove your boots.'

Kneeling before her, her pussy aligned to my eyes, I undid the laces of her boots and discarded her clothing. I had hitherto seen her naked only in the stables, where the light was dim. But now, her young, naked body stood before me, in its full glory, lit by the orange rays of the sinking sun. She was even more youthful than I had remembered, and could well have been a boy, save for her slit, plainly visible beneath the sparse hairs of her mound.

Without further ado, I leaned forward and kissed the warmth of her vaginal lips, pulling her buttocks to me as I did so, to press my mouth hard against her. She was extremely wet, I discovered, as my tongue located her little entrance – wetter than she should be from merely having her nipples sucked upon.

'Did you play with yourself whilst in the wood?' I asked.

'Pray, why do you ask such?'

'I know when a cunny has been pleasured by the wetness it imparts, the swell of its lips, and the sweet after-perfume of climax.'

'You know more of a girl's cunny than a girl herself!' she exclaimed, a little coy as I resumed my sucking and licking. Indeed I do, I mused, as my tongue located her little clitoris and began to ripen it.

'Why do you not kneel, for greater comfort?' I suggested as I lay back betwixt her legs in the long grass. Bending her knees, and panting with desire all the while, she set them down either side of my head, her young cunt hovering over me, but still too high.

'Further, my love,' I coaxed. She moved her knees ever wider apart to bring her now gaping slit down to touch upon my mouth. A truly wondrous sight, a young girl's hot, wet, open slit and tender thighs flanking my face!

Wanting even more of her milk, I licked the length of her valley until it yielded more sweet fluid than I had ever dreamed possible. Running down my cheeks, my chin, the nectar flowed as I drank from the very centre of her young being. And heaven it was.

Ray Gordon

By the sound of Belle's quickening breathing and gasps, I soon surmised that her goal was nearing.

I continued to mouth and suckle at her cunt and clitoris as she shuddered above me, grinding her slit back and forth over my mouth, riding me as she would a horse. A young girl's warm juice is the food of the gods, I will swear!

Amidst my delicious musing she came to rest, gently rubbing her throbbing bud over my lips, softly caressing her pink folds against my face. Her hands under my head, pulling me hard against her, she was near senseless with the pleasure emanating from betwixt her slender thighs. Her eyes rolled euphorically and she breathed breaths of gratification as she slowed her motions, finally settling her scarlet bud upon my burning lips.

The red sun, too, was coming to rest in the darkening sky, but our day was not yet over. Presently regaining her composure, Belle eased her drenched slit from my mouth and lay back in the long grass, her legs spread, her hot, crimson cunt asunder. My cock was more then ready to enter the depths of her portal, and I wasted not a moment. In – straight in, it slid, opening the tight walls of her vagina until it pressed gently, but firmly, against the closed end of her tube. Lifting her legs, I held her bent knees to her breast buds to allow deeper penetration and expose the swollen, pouting cunt lips to my gaze.

Her snug tube encompassing my shaft, her fleshy inner lips undulated with each thrust, stroking and lubricating my cock as its fucking motions again brought her towards her summit. Manoeuvring my hips, I steered my shaft into contact with her swollen clitoris, softly caressing the tip to further engorge it. Responding instantaneously, she thrust forward her hips to receive the pleasure and we fucked until she tossed her head as a woman possessed and screamed her joy into the warm, still, evening air. Every drop of my cream did I deposit into the depths of her body; with each savage thrust did I fill her very womb.

Withdrawing my cock, I gazed at her deep pinken lips which dragged, wet and glistening, the length of my sticky shaft. Finally free, they curled slowly, closing, as curtains, to conceal the entrance of lust.

The very sight of my cock withdrawing from her naked body so had hardened it again near to bursting point. Ere I wasted my sperm over her body, I pressed my knob to her mouth. Parting her hungry lips, she sucked me inside and worked with her tongue, round and round, until I shuddered and gripped her head in readiness to fill her. My knees weakening and my knob pumping, I sated her, bloating her cheeks with my hot sperm. She drank feverishly until she had drained the last drop of sperm from my quivering body. Oh, heaven! What delights had I discovered! And what more to come?

'Was that to your liking?' she asked as she sat back on her heels and wiped her mouth, her breasts glowing in the sunlight.

'Indeed it was, my sweet Belle! Indeed it was!' I cried. 'And it will be to my liking if, to show the great love we have for each other, we do it again and again!'

'Should I give myself to you so, again and again, you will no longer require Clara and Elizabeth?'

Promises are not made to be broken, I knew. But, promise I did. It mattered not, though, for had I not already broken my promise to Sarah that I would go nowhere near Belle? Breaking promises, as with lying, grows the more easy with usage. And, as my cousin was wont to say as we played our games in the garden, you may as well be hung for a sheep as a lamb.

Nevertheless, I was troubled. I had been looking forward to Belle, Clara, Elizabeth, and I playing our games in the hayloft. Games of love and lust. If Belle wished me for herself, our games would be no more – perish the thought! Presently, an idea struck me as I lay in the grass next to Belle, gazing at the erect breast buds crowning her firm bumps.

'Of course I will not take Clara or Elizabeth. Not without your presence, that is,' I assured her nonchalantly.

'But you will not need them now that you have me, Tom.'

'Ah, but we are all friends, and, although you and I share love, we cannot exclude our friends. Surely, would it not be most unfair to discard them, simply because we have found love? Imagine your sentiments had I fallen in love with Clara and taken it upon myself to exclude you!'

'I concede your point,' the innocent little thing replied sadly, to my relief. 'But should we not tell them of our love?'

'No, never! For they may become jealous, and we should not wish the deadly emotion of jealousy upon anyone – friend or foe. It is only right that we share our bodies with them – but never our love.'

'You are right, Tom. Our love will remain our secret, and we shall, indeed, share our bodies with the girls, for were I to be the outcast, I should pain most terribly.'

Oh, Belle! Poor, innocent Belle! Guilt pricked my conscience as I took her head in my hands and planted a kiss upon her sweet lips. But she was happy that I had taught her the delights of enjoying a man, rather than a woman. And she was content to have found friends, and love, in the shadow of what I deduced to be a life of misery and loneliness. I consoled myself with the realisation that, should all go wrong for me, should I at some time find myself without Sarah and the girls, there would always be Belle. She would mellow, too – her young breasts would grow into fine specimens, and her body become as alluring as the most sensuous of fillies.

'And now we must wash the remnants of our lovemaking from our bodies,' I said, breaking my reverie. 'Lady Sarah and the girls will return ere long, I am sure, and we cannot be caught, naked and wet, yet with the products of our love.'

'Before we go, Tom,' she interjected, rising to her feet. 'May I ask, do you find my body attractive? Is it of femininity enough for your liking?'

Why is it, at the summit of the mountain, we look back and question our footing? Why is it that the heights of success may yield the greatest insecurities? Particularly in the case of women! Poor, vulnerable Belle was concerned for the merits of her frame at the very time it had afforded me the most exquisite moments of my life! Boyish in figure she may have been, but youthful and innocent in a way that excited me beyond belief.

'Your body is from heaven, my love,' I reassured her.

'Then, you do not find me almost as a virgin?'

'Indeed I do, and that is what makes you so very perfect! Oh, Belle, you know not what a man sees through his eyes, for it is so different to that of a woman's view. I see you naked and yes, innocent. But, to my eyes, a man's eyes, that is the epitome of sexuality, of sweet naivety – of femininity. Do you not see that?'

'I understand such as you say. But the hair betwixt my

legs will grow, my breasts will bloom, and then you will love me even the more, will you not, Tom?'

'Would that the flora of your sweet mound might wither, to complete the perfect picture!' I retorted, pondering on the joy of beholding her barren slit, its delights fully open to view.

'Then, if it is your wish, I shall remove the hair,' she whispered, tugging on her wet curls.

'Will you, Belle? Will you truly do that for me? Oh, what great joy it would bring me to behold you naked betwixt your soft thighs!'

'I will do it tonight – I will shave for you, Tom, I promise!'

Trickery and lies, they were becoming a banal way of life. But how cheered was I at the prospect of encountering a young girl's shaven slit! Would Sarah erase her curls for me? Probably not, I decided. But I *could* tie her down and crop them as she swore and spat and struggled. Ah, delightful dreams!

Dusk fell as we dressed and departed from the whispering field – a fine story it had to tell, too! I reminded Belle of her promise as she wandered into the stables. 'I will do it tonight, Tom,' she assured me as she closed the stable door. I could barely wait to see her intimacy, shaven, hairless – sensual!

I must confess that my feelings for Belle confused me greatly. My love for her body was such that my mind became blurred as to the fact that she was a being with intelligence. That female form, that epitome of sexuality, held a mind within – a thinking, calculating mind of emotion, I told myself. Yet, somehow, I beheld only her shell – her naked flesh, her breasts, her belly, her slit.

Would it not be better if she had no mind, no power of reasoning? Would I not prefer that she comprised only body, that beautiful sculpture so formed of flesh and smooth, warm skin?

I had time just enough to wash in the horse trough before the arrival of Sarah and the girls at the house. At the sound of their carriage, I scurried to my room, for I knew that Sarah would seek me there, and I wished to appear innocent.

'Has all been well in my absence, Tom?' Sarah enquired, peering round the door to find me resting upon my bed.

'Very well, Sarah. I have just this minute finished a hard day's work, and I am fairly whacked.'

'Have you seen Belle?'

'Yes, I have encountered her in my travels.'

'And you have not spoken with her?'

'I have had cause to speak with her, in connection with work, but that is all,' I assured her.

'Then, you have not touched her? And, before you answer, I must tell you that I know when I am being told falsehoods.'

'I swear, inasmuch as you swore that you are Lady Sarah Hadleigh, that I have not laid fingers upon Belle.'

'Why do you mention that?'

'For no particular reason. I was just thinking . . .'

'Then do not think. Now, I am tired. You will not come to my bedchamber this evening for I have had a most rewarding day in that sense – which probably accounts for my fatigue.'

A rewarding day? My stomach churned at the thought of another man taking my Sarah's cunt! Where had she been all the while, and, more to the point, with whom? It was then that I first felt the knife of love pierce my heart. I had thought that I loved her, yes – but I had not fathomed the depth of that love, nor the effect betrayal would have upon me. My time with Belle had been merely lust, I reflected – little more than a beautiful game to while away the time. As with the girls, licking, sucking and fucking had been fun. But Sarah – that was different. Taking Sarah had been so much more than mere fucking. It had been the uniting of two souls, and to imagine her seeking satisfaction with another man, her naked body impaled upon another's cock, pained me deeply.

But is it not true that the dividing line betwixt love and hatred is most fragile? Even as I lay upon my bed, yet newly spurned, that other fire arose in me, as intense as the flame of love. That her ladyship should think only of herself and instruct me not to go to her bedchamber was despicable. Did she imagine that I was to be there, at her beck and call, whenever it took her fancy to be pleasured? Did she, for one minute, imagine that I would stay away from Belle, and be faithful to her only? I was riled, deeply riled, and I swore to avenge myself upon her!

Hearing the girls running across the yard, I decided to discover where they had been all the while, and went out to meet them. 'Why, Tom! How nice to see you!' Clara exclaimed on my approach.

'How nice to see you pretty things, too,' I replied. 'Where have you been?'

'We have been to Amy's house. Her mother was sorely angry with her for walking home without a chaperon! Her father insists that she will be confined to the house for one month!'

So, my much-awaited morning ride was to be in vain! I

had planned, dreamed, and so looked forward to taking the delectable Amy – and now my dreams, my hopes, were dashed! 'You have been there all day?' I asked, my thoughts returning to Sarah.

'Oh, yes. We stayed for lunch, and took afternoon tea.'

'And your mother, she was with you all the while?'

'She sent us off into the grounds for some time. Why?'

'Whose company did she keep whilst you were gone?'

'Lady Miles and her husband – why, Tom?'

'No matter, I just wondered, that is all.'

'You are jealous!' Elizabeth squealed. 'Let me tell you, Tom. She was with the stable lad! That is why we were sent off, but we saw her – doing it with the stable lad! Sitting on his cock, she was, moaning and crying as she rode him!'

I had a good mind to thrash the living daylights out of the little bitch, but remembered my goal – to continue to have each female as often as possible. A maiden so thrashed may not be consenting to the idea with her buttocks yet aglow! And so it was that I wandered off, dejected, forlorn – and very angry. 'I will not have the girls mock my predicament! Sarah will not treat me so!' I swore as I made my way to the house. 'She will *not* treat me so!'

Bursting into her bedchamber, I found her standing naked by her dressing table. 'How dare you come in here uninvited!' she screamed, pulling on her bath robe to cover herself.

'Have you been unfaithful to me?' I raged, grabbing her arm.

'I have no reason to be faithful to you, for we are not man and wife – we are nothing!'

'Just answer my question!'

'Never! I will answer you nothing!'

151

I had it firmly in my mind that she had, indeed, been with another man, and I could not bear the pain she had so caused me. Flinging her across the bed, I rolled her over and disrobed her in one swift action. She knew what was coming and screamed ere I had even laid a finger upon her trembling body. But then I decided that such a punishment would only bring her pleasure; a mere beating was not enough. In a flash of inspiration, the thought struck me that young Belle was the answer.

'You are not worthy of my hand upon your buttocks, even for the sake of punishment,' I scolded. 'I will take my leave of you and go to the hayloft in search of Belle. She is more than worthy of my company – and will enjoy it more so than you!'

'No, Tom! Please! Leave the girl. I have not been unfaithful to you, as you so put it. I have not been with another man since my first time with you, believe me.'

To believe or not to believe – I knew not. A bitch – a shrewd, cold, callous woman – why believe? But believe her I did, and I joined her on the bed. 'What did you mean by your words erstwhile?' I probed.

'To what do you refer?' she sobbed.

'You said that you had had a most rewarding day – in that sense!'

'With you, Tom! I meant with you, this morning!'

A blunder, indeed! Why in God's name did I always rush in, ere knowing the facts? Elizabeth had fired my anguish, and I meant to punish her for her antics, good and proper. A sharp razor to her bush would be apt punishment, indeed! Making my apologies to Sarah, I covered her with the bedclothes, for she was tired – of me, I should not wonder! 'I will see you on the morrow. I shall come to you here, in your room, and love you,' I whispered as she closed her eyes.

'No, Tom! I have had more than enough. Do not come to my bedchamber again. You confuse my mind, you disturb me. Do not shadow me with your presence – ever!'

Damn and curse that little witch Elizabeth for her mischief! Leaving Sarah alone in her bed, I went in search of the fair-haired, blue-eyed beauty who had caused me so much pain, and was, no doubt, shrieking somewhere with her sister at my folly in believing her story. She would be stripped and flogged by my very own hand before the night was out!

I could scarce believe my good fortune as I observed the girl wandering across the yard, alone, in the direction of the stables. 'Where is Clara?' I called as I made my approach.

'I know not nor care not!' came the indignant reply.

'Have you fallen out?'

'Yes, over you, Tom!'

'Pray, what has happened that I make two sisters fall out?'

'She says that you have done things to her that you would never do to me!'

'What things?'

'She would not say. Have you, Tom? Have you done things to her that you would not do to me?'

'Yes, that is true, Elizabeth. There are things that I would never dream of doing to a girl such as you.'

'And, pray, why not?'

'You are far too young, on the first count.'

'I am only younger than she by a year!'

'But you would not wish such delights, I am sure.'

153

'Which delights?'

Which delights, indeed? I had by that time, now two goals in mind. To have the females as and whenever I wanted, I have already divulged. My second aspiration I must confess to pondering on long and hard since that wondrous evening passed in the study with Sarah. Watching her belly jerking and her vacant cunt splayed and gushing forth its juices before me as I took her bottom hole had excited me no end. It was from this lustful union that my second goal – to take all the girls' bottom holes – was born. And what finer opportunity than this, with Elizabeth more or less for the asking?

'I will concede,' I replied at length. 'You are old enough for such delights, and I apologise for thinking otherwise. Let us go to my room now, and I will show you exactly what it is that your indiscreet sister was talking of.'

How Lady Luck did shine upon me, I will swear! As a meek lamb to the slaughter did the sweet Elizabeth follow me to my room whence, with the door securely locked, I proceeded to gently disrobe her. She stood quietly as I deftly removed her dress and her brassiere, her stockings and her knickers, until she was quite naked.

Her young, oh so young skin, glowed in the light of the oil lamp as I laid her upon my bed and softly kissed every inch of her beautiful body. Now, the hour was nigh! Hard and rampant, my cock was more dangerous than ever as my rage mingled with an overwhelming desire to fuck her to death. Rolling her over, I kissed her sweet buttocks, parting them gently to lick and taste her dark crease, her bottom hole. She squirmed with pleasure as my tongue entered that tight little orifice to explore just within. My wanton cock in hand, I covered the knob with spittle ready to slip quickly and easily into her body ere she knew what I was about. Licking her tiny hole until she was wet, I quickly introduced my hard, purple knob to the brown ring, and stabbed.

'No! No! What are you doing?' she cried, her wiggling now a fierce struggle.

'I am only doing to you as I did to your sister! Are you not ready for such delights, after all?'

'No! That will not be delightful, it will hurt! Clara would never have allowed you to do such a thing to her! You lie!'

At this juncture, my knob was squarely aligned with her hole and I could feel the resisting muscles guarding her private portal. All that was required to invade her bottom was a good, hard push – and push I did. Straight in my knob slipped, past her sphincter and into the dark depths of her hot bowels.

'Take it out! Ah, no, no! I hate you!' she screamed. But her protests only served to drive me on.

She wiggled and shrieked as I inched my shaft deeper into her virginal bottom which gripped and spasmed around my intruding cock as it sank in ever the deeper. Ah, tighter than the tightest cunt ever! The very womb of her body, warm, wet, voluptuous, soft flesh, engulfed my knob as even further it slid. Finally, the root of my shaft embraced by her ring, I pressed my belly to her buttocks and rested there, savouring the dark heat that throbbed within.

Poor Elizabeth, how she did struggle and fight to free herself of the intruder that so pillaged her private entrance! But her squirming only served to heighten the wondrous sensations in my now twitching knob and, though I had scarce begun my fucking motion, I sensed that I was about to empty my seed into her bowels. Oh, what joy young Elizabeth's bottom brought me! And what beautiful cries of pain did she emit!

Perchance I was mistaken as to the pain, or else an invisible line betwixt pain and pleasure there must be, for in the next moment she began to tremble and grope desperately betwixt her thighs for her bud. My hand 'neath her bottom, I located her sodden cunt and sank three fingers deep within, opening her soft tube to its limit. She frigging her clitoris deliciously upon my roving hand, all the while my shaft thrusting in and out of her bottom hole, we reached our zeniths in unison. Oh, sheer ecstasy! Her juices gushed from her body, bathing my hand with sticky warmth as I deluged her bowels with my seed. Heaving, panting, gasping, sweating, we fell limp upon the bed, almost senseless with lust and fulfilment. Drained of every droplet of love's juices – of the very life force itself – I was done.

Her face red, her mouth dry, her hair wet with the heat of lust, she slid from beneath me and gathered her clothes. 'You did not once do that to my sister, I will bet my life!' she sobbed.

'No, I did it not the once, but three times, to this day! And she loves it there, in her bottom hole, the more so than in her cunt!'

'You lie!'

Elizabeth banged the door behind her and I heard her footsteps ascending the stairs to her room. Would she tell her sister? I wondered. No, I thought not, for, no doubt, she would be too embarrassed to speak of her ordeal. But I prayed that she would, in time, share her dark secret, so that Clara, too, would come to me and offer her virginal bottom for the taking.

I made a list before retiring – a list of the females in my harem, with columns beside each name where I could place ticks beneath my goals. Elizabeth, bottom hole – tick. Sarah, bottom hole – tick. Clara, blank – as yet. Amy, blank – for the time being. Poor Amy, confined for one whole month! And, poor me!

Sweet dreams I had that eventful night. Sweet dreams of new goals, and more ticks! But nightmares, too – horrendous nightmares of Sarah doing away with me, and burying me alongside the real Lady Sarah Hadleigh.

Chapter Ten

Would Sarah ever speak to me again? Would she force me to expose her dark secret and blackmail her, and break my promise to Harry? Would she be sympathetic to my jealousy, and offer me tea – poisoned tea? Had Belle yet cropped her mound to reveal her little slit to my appreciative gaze? Would Clara invite me to take her bottom hole, to emulate her younger sister? Would Amy be there on the hill? Somehow I sensed that she would escape her parents' grasp and meet me as arranged.

With such thoughts did my mind positively reel as I lay in my bed watching the sun rise in a cloudless sky. I decided to creep from the house and be upon the hill before Sarah rose. She would only dampen my spirits with her ranting and raving and, should Amy be there, I would not wish to burden her with my dull mood.

Belle did not wake as I led Giant from the stable. At least, I presumed her to be sleeping, for I did not ascend the ladder to find out. Giant was quite well behaved that morning, considering I had not ridden him for some time, and he had found an affinity with Belle, who treated him as a brother. But I did detect that he was somewhat disgruntled, for I had not kept my promise and allowed him time with a mare.

The morning air was cool and fresh against my face. It was to be a hot day, I knew, as I galloped across the heath towards the hill. As I neared, I fancied I did perceive a figure seated upon a horse, silhouetted against the low sun, and wondered if it was Amy. Nearer and nearer I came to the form, and I was sure that it was she, sitting upright in her saddle, watching me gallop like a madman across the heath. Or, the terrible thought struck me, could it be her father? Had she been beaten, until obliged to tell of our clandestine meeting? Did he await my arrival – to flog me?

It was, indeed, Amy – four hours early! She could not have expected me to be there at five, surely? 'It is fate that has brought us together, Amy!' I cried excitedly, upon dismounting.

'I could not be here at the appointed hour and hoped, prayed, that you would be riding early today,' she enthused, all flushed as she climbed from her magnificent Arab.

'Your prayers have been answered, my angel, for I could not sleep and the sun appeared inviting through my window.'

We flung our arms around each other's necks as old friends. Then we kissed, passionately, tongue caressing tongue, as lovers. 'You are fired with amour, Amy,' I remarked, taking her hands and standing back to admire her slim figure, so tightly hugged by her jodhpurs and riding jacket. 'It must have been the exhilarating ride that has flushed your cheeks so.'

'No, Thomas. It was the prospect of meeting you that caused me to . . . Well, I must be careful what I say, lest you should think me no more than a trollop.'

'Oh, no! I think nothing of the sort, for you are a fine lady!'

'But a lonely lady, Thomas. My father is strict beyond all comprehension and my mother is as bad, I fear.'

'Then, pray, how is it that you are here? I heard that you were to be confined to the house for one month.'

'Love has brought me here. I should not speak of such, I know, for we are hardly acquainted. But you have been constantly in my thoughts since I first laid eyes upon you. I have neither eaten nor slept.'

'Amy, oh, sweet, pretty Amy! Can you really feel as I do? Is this but a dream? Tell me that we are here, on this hill-top, alone together!'

'We are, indeed. Now, tell me, why are you yet dressed thus in those old breeches – and that worn shirt?'

Damn my rags – and Sarah, for retrieving the fine suit of clothes! Damn my standing as a common employee! Those cruel words of Amy's, uttered in her sweet innocence, haunted me, I will swear!

'I have been . . . I was . . .' I stammered as she laughed.

'It is all right, Tom. I may call you Tom?'

'You may,' I answered, my head hung low.

'Forgive me, for I have laughed at your expense. You see, I know your position at Royston Manor. Clara and Elizabeth . . .'

'They have told you of me? And you do not mind that . . .'

'Yes, they have told me. And, no, I do not mind. I am only pleased that you are a good, kind, attractive, earthly man.'

Curse those girls! But at least I was not obliged to masquerade for a moment longer. And what were those words? Good, kind, attractive – oh, Amy! My list would soon be full of ticks of joy!

As we again embraced, our bodies crumpled onto the soft heath, our lips not parting once until we were lying side by side, entwined, clutching, holding. 'We have but little time, Tom,' she breathed in my ear. 'Do not think bad of me but . . . You see, I have never before been loved.'

'Never?' I repeated in disbelief.

'Never have I had the opportunity. Yet now, I have only minutes, Tom, for my father will rise and find me gone and . . .'

'Calm yourself, my angel. For I will love you, here and now, beneath the warmth of the rising sun, to the sound of the singing birds, I will love you.'

Amy needed no assistance in removing her jodhpurs – nor me, my breeches. Her legs, golden brown from the sun, were smooth, soft and curvaceous, her knees wonderfully rounded. Her riding jacket concealing the tops of her thighs, her bush, I raised it to her navel to expose her sweet intimacy. And what intimacy! Never in my life had I encountered a bush so thick, so hairy, as was spread before my eyes!

Fired by the thicket, and to cover my surprise, I dived straight for my goal. She lay back meekly on the heath and parted her legs as I buried my face within her thick nest and breathed in her warm, wondrous scent. A woman indeed! Her wetness flowed in torrents as I discovered her clitoris and licked and sucked as she moaned and dug her fingernails into my scalp. Oh, how she did cry and force my mouth against her yawning valley as, all too soon, she neared her climax! 'Ah, Tom! Yes, yes! More, more!' Oh, how the words fell from her sweet lips to fill my mind with a raging passion! Her hips wildly gyrating, her cunt hot, she panted and gasped her appreciation until she shuddered and was quickly spent. Whilst she relaxed her trembling frame I licked dry her slit, flicking her clitoris now and then as it withdrew 'neath its pinken hood to rest.

In dire need of relief myself, I freed my aching cock from my linen and presented it to her sopping portal. 'Be careful, Tom! Treat me gently, for I have never before been entered!' she entreated me.

'Do not worry yourself so,' I murmured as my knob tentatively parted her sweet pinken folds. Slowly, gently, I pressed my hardness into her tight tube. She gasped and clung to me and cried a little as I penetrated deeper, through her maidenhead and on toward her womb.

'Be not fearful, my angel, for your horse riding has prepared you well for love,' I promised, as my shaft continued its excavation into her juicy hole, to the very entrance of her womb.

'It is fully in?' she asked, incredulous.

'Fully,' I endorsed, my balls softly caressing her beautiful buttocks. 'It is fully in, my angel.'

Gently, I fucked her until her face reddened, her heart banged within her chest and her cunt tightened and convulsed in delightful jerks around my shaft. Her breasts heaving under her jacket, I undid the buttons to view better their contours. Her blouse, too, I unbuttoned as we fucked, to reveal a lace brassiere which I deftly yanked clear of the firm balloons. Spreading her garments, I gazed at the largeness, squeezed the firmness, and lowered my mouth to suckle upon nipples of such magnitude as I had never before seen!

She gasped as I nibbled and rolled the brown kernels betwixt my burning lips. 'Touch your clitoris, my love, for you will reach your heaven faster that way,' I whispered.

'I know not what you mean,' she panted, to my utter disbelief.

'Then you have never pleasured yourself?'

'I have never tried. I know not how.'

I could scarce believe my ears. My God! What girl of such sensuality, such beauty, has never touched her spot and caressed it to ecstasy? What girl of such ardour knows not what she possesses betwixt her legs – betwixt her full, virginal lips? She had taken her pleasure admirably as I had licked her bud – had she not been aware of its very existence until that wondrous moment?

As my seed neared the head of my cock I caressed her hard bud, whispering instructions all the while for her future reference. 'Like this, softly, but quickly, round and round until . . .'

'Until! Until!' she cried, as my sperm gushed from my bulbous knob and filled her womb. 'Until! Oh, my God! What is happening? Ah, yes, yes! Take me, Tom! Oh, God! I am done!'

Poor Amy near swooned with the ecstasy that erupted betwixt her cunt lips that had swelled as balloons and reddened as cherries. Her nipples, too, had grown even longer, standing erect as I sucked upon them until her climax had subsided and she breathed her cries of grateful appreciation.

'Tom, Tom! That was the most heavenly experience I have ever known! Oh, thank you, thank you, for you are truly perfect! Though it cannot be true, tell me it was the first time for you, too.'

'Indeed, but it was so!' I fibbed to the poor thing.

'But you know so well how to pleasure a girl, I cannot be your first.'

'I have heard and read and learned, my angel, that is how I know. This is, indeed, my first time,' I assured her, withdrawing my limp cock from her tight, dripping cunny.

Damn my lies! Sooner or later, the bitch's daughters would tell Amy of my lecherous ways. But, for now, as I rested my head against her sodden bush, breathing in the heady scent of her spent cunt, the future mattered not. 'I cannot believe that you have never pleasured yourself, Amy,' I whispered, chewing upon the glistening black hairs.

'But it is true! When you kissed me there, I knew not what was happening to me as the pleasure invaded my body and rendered me almost senseless. And when you did fuck me, my stomach swirled and my head swam, and I thought I had died! Oh, Tom, what wonders you have shown me!'

'You will pleasure yourself, now that you know how?' I asked.

'I will, all the while, and I will think of you, my love! Now, I must go, or father will beat me!'

Dressing quickly, she composed herself and smiled sweetly as she kissed me and bid me adieu. I watched her descend the hill and gallop across the fields below until she became but a distant blur. We would meet again, we had promised. But we had arranged our meeting for some weeks hence, for fear that her father should discover her absence and lock her away indefinitely. When her month of punishment was up and her freedom restored, we would meet, on the hill, in the early morning – every morning!

But could I wait that long? I pondered. Knowing that
she was pleasuring herself with her slender fingers, induc-
ing torrents of fluid to flow, and run to waste, could I
endure it? I did not gallop back to the manor in haste.
Instead, I trotted across the heath, reflecting, thinking
upon Amy and her beautiful body and the wonder of her
ignorance of the existence of her clitoris. Had she really
never touched and explored that exquisite location? My
mind could not comprehend such and I relinquished the
thought only as the manor came into view. I did savour one
thought, though – that of Amy, pleasuring herself in her
bed, with thoughts of me!

Belle was up and about looking most anxious as I
approached the yard. 'Where have you been?' she
enquired crossly. 'I have worried myself sick!'

'I am here, Belle. Worry not for me!'

'Giant, you fool! I have been fearful for his safety!' she
cried, snatching the reins from my hand as I climbed down.

'He is safe with me,' I returned.

'Yes, but I knew not of his whereabouts. I thought he
had been stolen!'

Apologising, I left her to rub him down. She thought
more of that animal than of me, I was sure! But kind,
loving Belle – that was her way, and I admired her for it.
'Belle!' I called, turning on my heels and making for the
stable, for I had just remembered something. 'Have you
shaved yourself, as you promised you would, my love?'

'I have, indeed, Tom. And I look like an innocent even
the more now! But you will see later, for I am busy.'

'Just one little peep, please, my love?' I begged.

'No, Tom! You will see all, later! Besides, I am
embarrassed.'

'Oh, I do love you so!' I cried, seizing upon her lovely mouth for a kiss.

'You taste of a strange perfume, Tom. I do detect something upon your clothes, too. Where have you been? And with whom?'

'I have been upon the heath with Giant. There are no girls out there at this time of the day! You are mistaken if you think as much!' I replied, moving away.

She believed me, of course. Who would not believe such an accomplished liar as I? Only Sarah, no doubt, I thought as I washed vigorously in the horse trough to remove any hint of young Amy's love juices.

Sarah summoned me to the house with her hysterical screams as I finished my washing. 'You must leave this house today!' she insisted, her face aglow with anger as she near dragged me into the morning room.

'But, Sarah . . .' I began, knowing full well that I would not be allowed to complete my sentence.

'You will leave now! This instant!'

It was under such duress that, sadly, I was obliged to break my promise to Harry. 'But, *Mary*, I cannot leave,' I said.

Within seconds, her face turned from anger to fear and she looked into my eyes and frowned. 'What did you say?' she questioned, in sheer disbelief.

'I said – Mary, I cannot . . .'

'Why do you call me Mary?' she enquired, her voice low and shaky.

'That is your name, is it not?'

'Have you quite taken leave of your senses? You know full well that I am Sarah! Why do you speak in riddles? I have no time for such nonsense!'

'Lady Sarah Hadleigh is buried in the grounds, is she not? Shall I take you to her makeshift grave and . . .'

'My God! You have gone mad! Completely mad!'

'No, Mary, I am not mad. Now, you were saying that I should leave this instant. Do you still wish me to do so?'

'Of course! Even the more now that you show yourself insane!'

'I trust you will tell Clara of her father's whereabouts? Or, being of foreign extraction, perhaps he has returned to his home country? I take it you are ignorant as to where he is?'

'You are a fool, Tom! You inhabit a strange world of your own, a world of make-believe. Now, be off with you!'

'Poor Elizabeth! Neither does she know of her father. I think it only fair I tell her that, dear though her sister is, she is, in fact, but her half-sister. Do you not agree, Mary?'

Sarah said nothing, collapsing onto the sofa, her mouth hanging open, her eyes wide, her face burning. Leaving her there, I made my way to the yard to partake of some water, for my mouth was parched with fear and anxiety. I felt quite unsettled after what had been, I must confess, the most tricky confrontation of my life, and so wandered into the field to rest and think upon what I had done to Sarah.

The girls giggled and joked as they crossed the yard, calling my name. I remained silent, for I was in no mood for their frivolity. But, alas, they soon discovered me lying in the long grass and settled either side of me. Their skirts high above their knees, they began to tease me and prod around my breeches, enquiring as to whether or not I had relieved myself by hand.

'Be off with you! I am not in the mood!' I snapped.

'Oh, Tom,' Elizabeth began. 'We were so close yester-evening, and now you do not wish to know me. What, pray, have I done to make you feel so?'

'Close?' Clara enquired. 'What did you do that made you close?'

'Nothing that you have not done with Tom, dear sister!' Elizabeth giggled.

'You did not . . . Surely, you did not . . .'

'What we did or did not do is our business!' I hastily interjected, in fear of spoiling my future fun and placing my list in jeopardy. 'Had you been there, you could have participated, but you were not,' I added.

'Oh, this is all so boring!' Clara complained. 'I do wish we could do something to brighten up the day – something naughty, for preference!'

The day would do anything but brighten, I reflected. Sarah, no doubt, would be on the warpath the very minute she had formulated her next move, and I was not looking forward to that! In fact, I was in two minds as whether or not to tell her that I would leave, for I felt bad inside – a feeling that I cannot well explain, other than to say it was surely the accumulative result of lying, tricking and black-mailing, a lifestyle to which I was not accustomed and, at that point, had no desire to become so!

'Tell me, Tom,' Clara said, her legs wide and her knickers noticeably moist with the juice of her cunt. 'Will you not do the same to me as you did to Elizabeth?'

I smiled and my depression lifted slightly as I gazed into her big, dark, expectant eyes.

'I may, I may not,' I replied nonchalantly.

'Oh, Tom! Say you will, please!' she begged, sitting cross-legged before me to display her milk-white thigh tops and drenched knickers which tightly hugged the contour of her young mound.

'But you know not what it was that I did to her!'

'Whatever it was, I am sure that I would like it! Oh, please, Tom. Promise me that you will do it!'

'All right. But only on the condition that you now find your mother, and return to tell me of her mood.'

With that, both girls rose to their feet and bounded through the long grass and round the angle of the stables, giggling and joking all the while. I awaited their return, wondering whether Elizabeth would reveal our secret to Clara. I prayed not, for surely, Clara would not readily agree to her bottom hole being taken! They returned after some ten minutes or so, their faces solemn, without the lines of laughter I had come to love.

'What are your findings?' I asked as they sat beside me.

'She wishes to speak with you,' Clara replied.

'Now, Tom! She wishes to see you now!' Elizabeth rejoined.

'But her mood? Is she of a happy disposition?'

'Hardly, for she has been crying, we know not why,' Clara said dolefully.

Oh, Sarah! What have I done to you? What have you done to me – to yourself? I agonised, as I left the girls and mooched across the yard. But I had to be strong of mind – there would have been little point in blackmailing her so, just to back down the minute her tears flowed.

'You wish to speak with me?' I asked as I entered the morning room.

'I do, Tom,' she sighed despondently. 'Although, I must confess, I know not what to say. I have not left this sofa since your departure, for I have been planning, rehearsing my lines, but now that you are here, I have forgotten them.'

'Then, may I say something?'

'Yes, please do. Although I think that you have already said more than enough!'

'I did not wish to blackmail you, Sarah. But you treated me so badly, yet again, and that kind of treatment I do not deserve. You left me no choice.'

'Why do you wish to know such things about me? What is it that drives you to discover such things, and then blackmail me? If, as you say, I treat you so badly, then why not up and leave? Why is it your heartfelt desire to stay here?'

'Love, perhaps? I know not why I wish to stay, but stay I will! And if you wish to be rid of me, then it will cost you dearly!'

'You talk of love, and in the next breath you talk of your leaving costing me dearly! You have the audacity . . .'

'My audacity is beside the point. Do I stay? Or . . .'

'For the time being, you stay. I need to think, to plan. Yes, for the time being, you stay. But you will not touch Belle or my daughters! Do you understand?'

'There are to be no more conditions, Sarah, for I have had enough of your terms. And now, if you will excuse me.'

'I am not afraid of you, Tom.'

'I am pleased to hear it, Sarah. But, unless you . . .'

'Say no more, please, for I have heard more than enough for one day!'

Surprisingly, the day did brighten, when I heard Sarah and the girls laughing and joking together as they walked through the grounds later that morning. I did not care for

distressing and upsetting Sarah – or anyone, for that
matter – and I consoled myself with the thought that I had
done it with her best interests in mind, for in my heart I
knew that she loved me, when she was not hating me! And
I loved her. The girls, too, loved me, and I, them. As to
poor Belle, though her feelings for me were all too
obvious, I loved her only in a brotherly sort of way –
although my lust for her was anything but brotherly! And
Amy? Amy was an outsider – someone who would, if I
nurtured our relationship and let it grow, become a true
friend. Someone I could turn to, talk with – and love, of
course! Yes, I convinced myself, I had blackmailed Sarah
for the good of all.

I was not sure, at that time, of my ultimate aim. To wed
Sarah? No. To take the hand of one of her delectable
daughters in marriage? I thought not, for to marry the one
would be as good as marrying the both! I am ashamed to
admit that Belle did not figure much in my reflections, save
for one thought – her shaven slit!

I did not further see Sarah or the girls all that day, and I
was happy that we had the time apart. I was sure that the
girls knew nothing of the events that had taken place
between their mother and I. But I was also sure that they
had sensed that something was very wrong. All would be
put to rights when I next saw them, I promised myself.

As the sun fell below the trees, I wandered down to
Harry's to eat, wondering how he was and contemplating
the fact that I had broken my promise to him. I found both
him and Alice high in spirits, for they were to move the
very next day. I took solace in the news for, whilst I had
broken my promise, it was but hours ere that promise
would become null and void. Thus I was able to enjoy a

good meal, and more than enough wine! In fact, I did fairly stagger from the cottage in the early hours, my head spinning and my laughter filling the night air.

Belle ran from the stables to hush me as I danced and sang in the yard. The dear girl helped me climb the ladder to the hayloft where she covered me with a blanket. Though near senseless with liquor, I do recollect her cuddling close to me, admonishing me for my behaviour in one breath, and declaring her great love for me in the next. As the effects of the alcohol subsided I placed my arm around her waist to discover her naked. Running my hand over her soft stomach I was delighted to feel smooth, hairless lips 'neath my caressing fingertips. Fool as I was, I had, in the heat of events, quite forgotten her generous undertaking to me.

'Belle,' I whispered as I sat up. 'Oh Belle, you sweet thing!'

'For you, Tom,' she responded, pulling aside the blanket and spreading her limbs. Casting my eyes down over her breasts, her smooth belly, I gazed at her barren mound, a desert island, lying unashamedly proud and bare. What was it with this entity that so took a hold on my senses? What uncanny, bewitching power possessed this triangle of soft, warm, naked flesh? Clearly defined creases, running from her thigh tops to disappear beneath her buttocks, served to highlight the sacred mound, elevating it above the plateau of her belly. Devoid of its protection, I gazed in wonder at the dividing groove, running from the summit into a valley, deepening as it ran down to the farthest orifice, dark, damp, and sweet with the perfume of her womanhood. The naked feast betwixt those maiden legs aroused a pang of desire so deep within my cock that my balls fairly rolled in anticipation of filling that delicious crack with their fruits.

Fired by a ravenous lust, I lowered my head and kissed the swollen cushions rising either side of the groove, protecting and concealing the intimacy within. As smooth as silk and glowing with youth, they shone wonderfully in the lamplight. Sucking each ballooning lip into my mouth in turn caused them to swell even the more, casting a shadow to accentuate the deepening valley. Opening her thighs further, Belle ran her hands up over her belly and round and round her breast buds as I kissed and sucked until her outer lips lay open, unaided, to allow the pinken inner folds to protrude, inviting my tongue.

But, teasing and tantalising, not once did I allow my tongue to caress the delicate folds as they grew and uncurled and became wet with her milky fluid. My cock, now rampant with lust, strained against my breeches until Belle gave it escape, taking it out, kneading, squeezing and running her fingers around the hard knob.

Stretching her lips apart and up towards her belly, I presently exposed her pleasure centre. Deceptively small for the huge delights it held, its little head protruded, hard, awaiting my attention. Around its base I did run my tongue to gasps of delight from Belle, as all the while she gripped my swollen cock in her tiny hand, bringing it ever nearer to her mouth.

Manoeuvring my hips, I presented my knob to her sweet mouth which ravenously sucked it deep into its warmth, devouring the full shaft. I quivered with delight as she pulled the skin back to expose the purple head to her inquisitive tongue, but still, I touched not her clitoris. My tongue ran down her valley to taste the juices now flowing in torrents from her hole. Her pelvis shuddered as I pushed my way into the wet cavern, exploring round and round, drinking, sucking, flicking her with the tip of my tongue until she pulled my head up to her bud. But still I resisted. Visibly it throbbed and grew as my finger encircled its base. She was near, but I worked her into a frenzy thus until the young bud ripened and swelled to an incredible size and she cried out, pleading for relief.

'Suck it, Tom! Do not tease me so, lick it and suck it!' And lick and suck I did. Engulfing the protrusion, I flicked my tongue over the tip, and she gasped and squirmed and sucked my knob ever deeper into her throat as I allowed her her prize. Thrusting three fingers deep into her cunt to heighten her pleasure, I filled her cheeks with sperm, pulling my knob from her throat to enjoy the caress of her rolling tongue and bathe it with my cream. My fingers were near crushed by the strength of her muscles as I rammed them in and out, causing an emission of juice to bathe my hand and exotically perfume her valley.

We were done – almost. She swallowed several times, loudly, as I spurted on and on until she had drained me – body and soul.

Beautiful Belle! Wet, gasping, she raised her naked, shaven body and stood before me, astride me, opening her cunt to my upward gaze. 'You have taught me how to enjoy this,' she murmured, surveying her splayed, swollen lips. 'You have shown me what this is for, and I thank you from the bottom of my heart, dearest Tom.'

'No, I thank *you*, Belle, for bringing me such pleasure.'

What a terrible thing is guilt! If only she knew that I had taken and loved Sarah, her mistress, in her bed, the study, the stables – and Amy on the hill. If only she knew that I intended to take them again and again, and all the while lie to the sweet little innocent thing. If only she knew that I had sunk my knob – the very knob from whence she had sucked her delicacies – into Elizabeth and Sarah's tight bottom holes! And that I intended to take Clara's and Amy's.

Oh, Belle! The poor girl should never have met one such as I. But met me she had, and happy she was, and happy was I – save for my damn guilt!

Chapter Eleven

Time passes oh, so slowly, when one is waiting. And I was waiting for my delectable Amy to be released from her prison, that she might meet me upon the hill every morning, and roll naked on the soft heather, and love me under the warmth of the early sun. But now, at long last, there were but two more days of pain to endure.

Sarah had barely spoken to me since my humiliating revelation, passing no more than the odd derogatory comment as she handed me my weekly wage. I had not entered the house, having moved my belongings back to the hayloft upon Belle's installation in the cottage. Harry and Alice had not written since their departure, unless – which would not in the least have surprised me – Sarah had chosen to keep their letters from me. Unfortunately, I had missed their leaving, and the opportunity of taking their new address, being otherwise engaged in the entertainment of Belle – with my cock!

For one whole month I had done nothing other than work, eat, sleep – and take Belle in the cottage. I had not, I might add, taken her bottom hole, for she was more inclined to view our relationship as secure and loving than fun and lustful, though the sobriety was not for lack of trying. Many attempts I had made, stabbing betwixt her splayed buttocks and pressing my knob against her brown hole, but she would not yet entertain the idea, despite my attempts to persuade her that such play is but a man's just reward. I do believe, by that time, she was weary of my rewards! Nevertheless, the day would come, I promised myself. I was in no particular hurry to add ticks to my list.

Clara's bottom hole, as Belle's, had remained sadly virginal, and I could not help but wonder why she had not made the effort to seek parity with her sister. Surely, they had discussed our exploits in the course of that long month? Surely, Elizabeth had babbled and told of my knob deep within her bottom? Again, I was in no rush – just a trifle mystified.

Indeed, I had scarce seen the girls at all and suspected that Sarah had deliberately kept them from me, most likely in some futile attempt to raise my sexual urge to such heights that I should beg her for her body. Never! I was happy with Belle and the warmth of her bed, her cooking, her homely cottage. Sarah, no doubt, fondly believed my only form of release to be my hand – how wrong she was! What was *her* relief? I wondered often. I had seen her, on occasion, leaving the cottage in the course of the day, but Belle had vouched that her visits were concerned only with work. About that, too, I wondered often!

It was as I passed a customary cosy evening in the company of sweet Belle that Lady Sarah hammered upon the cottage door. She was not in the habit of visiting during the evenings, and, hastily gathering up all signs of my presence – the extra plate and cup, my boots – Belle bade me hide in the bedchamber.

'He is here, I know!' bellowed Sarah's familiar voice.

'You are mistaken, my lady. I have not seen him this

day,' poor Belle lied unconvincingly. I heard the sound of a scuffle before the bedchamber door flew open and Sarah glared down at me, sitting upon the double bed. 'Come with me!' she ordered threateningly, turning on her heel.

Giving Belle a conciliatory wink on my exit, I complied, more out of intrigue than anything. Four long weeks of near-silence and then she requires that I accompany her – a strange woman indeed! Following her to the house, several yards behind to enable my eyes to feast upon her lovely wiggling bottom, I wondered if she had reached the end of her tether and wished me to pleasure her. I would do no such thing, I decided. Well, probably not, anyway.

Leading me into the study, she sat me down and, to my surprise, poured me a glass of wine. I had sorely missed her, I must confess, and the sight of her slim waist, firm rounded breasts, beautiful cleavage, and the thought of her tight cunny nestling 'neath the velvet of her dress, excited me no end. She, too, I concluded, had missed me, my cock deep within her womb, pumping her full of euphoric delight. In fact, I did behold her gazing at my breeches once or twice as she paced the floor before me, planning, no doubt, the opening lines of her speech.

'I am troubled, Tom,' she began in a tone softer than I had expected. 'You are not as the usual simpletons I employ to work in the stables. You have a brain, and you have used it. I know not to what end, as yet, but you have used it well, it seems. That is one problem that troubles me, and, I admit, I am flummoxed as to the solution – save paying you a large sum of money to be rid of you, but, even so, you may well reappear when it is at an end.'

'And there is another problem?' I asked.

'Yes, indeed, there is. And I know not which problem

troubles me the more. However, Clara is with child and . . .'

'Are you sure?' I near choked, rising to my feet and spilling wine upon my breeches.

'No, not completely sure. But it would appear that way, very much so, I am afraid to say. The child, obviously, is yours, and on account of this most unfortunate turn of events, I have made certain plans.'

Plans! My immediate plans, as my mind ran riot at that moment, were to run! Would Clara and I be married and installed in the cottage? What if Elizabeth, too, were with child? Or Sarah! What thoughts, God forbid! Shocked I was at the news, for I had to admit that such mundane consequences as pregnancy had had no consideration in my mind upon taking those tight little cunnies. With thoughts as these, and my mind racing, I curbed my natural instinct to flee and allowed Sarah to continue, uninterrupted.

'The child will be born: that, we have decided, as it is only right, and, after all, there are no males to carry the Hadleigh name forward, so hopefully . . . Anyway, for the time being, you will return to your room in the manor house, and we shall all be civil towards one another, Tom. Do you agree thus far?' I deemed it right to agree, thus far, rather than lose all hope of a brighter future. But I had also to suppress a snigger at her comments concerning the Hadleigh name!

'The child will be mine, to all intents and purposes. Clara is far too young, and, besides, she is not married. She was to attend finishing school in Switzerland in a few weeks' time but, obviously, that has now changed. We will keep her under wraps until the child is born, when we shall make it known to the world that it is mine.'

'But neither are *you* married,' I pointed out, wondering if I should be asked, or ordered, to make an honest woman of Sarah.

'That is a problem with which I shall deal at some later date. For now, you are to be the man about the house, for we will require help, and Clara will need a father figure. And, being that the case, you will, I dread to say, become part of the family – in a removed kind of way.'

Part of the family! A father figure! This, from the woman who, of late, had barely acknowledged my exist-ence! There was something to be said for advancing my position at the manor, but there were limits, I told myself.

'I am sorry, Sarah,' I replied. 'But I cannot agree to living under your roof as part of the family, "as a father figure, in a removed kind of way," as you presumptuously put it – and yet, in reality, remain nothing more than your employee . . .'

'Think yourself lucky, Tom, for . . .'

'There! You see, you do it again! Why do you not think *yourself* lucky that I am still here? Why do you persist in playing the high-handed lady of the manor when you know full well, I know full well, that you were nothing more than a maid?'

'Are we to discuss this with some civility? Or must we shout and punctuate each sentence with a threat?'

'We will speak in a polite and civil manner if and when you agree to my living here, with you and the girls, as the proper man of the house.'

'As my husband? Is that what you are saying? In my bed?'

'Why not, when, somewhere amidst the hatred you feel

for me, you also have some love? And besides, do not tell
me that you have not missed our intimate times together.'

'I have not missed them, for I have not been alone long
enough to miss them!'

'I talk of our intimate times, Sarah.'

'And so do I! Do you really believe that I have passed all
this month without the company of another in my bed?'

'Oh, you lie! You always lie!'

'Ask Belle, for she is the one with whom I have shared
my body. She may well deny it, but it is true, all the same.'

'You can prove as much by employing but one word to
describe Belle's beautiful little pussy. But one word!'

Sarah looked mystified as she poured herself another
drink. She had not touched Belle, I knew, for she had only
to describe Belle's little cunny as naked to prove her
assertion. She had surely but pleasured herself with her
fingers during our time apart, a poor substitute indeed, I
was sure. Clearly, she had indeed missed my attentions,
for her eyes had rarely left my breeches during our
confrontation.

'Well, what is the word?' I asked with a smirk across my
face. For once, she was lost for words. 'There, you see,
you have never seen her pussy! But I have, most every
night this past month – I have not only seen it, but touched
it, kissed it, licked it, pushed my cock deep inside it – and
fucked it!'

'Stop! Stop! All right, I admit to trying to distress you,
and, it seems, I have succeeded only in distressing myself
by causing you to speak so of Belle. Will you move back
into the Manor House as my . . . as man of the house?'

'Where will I sleep?'

'In your room, of course.'

'No, I will not!'

'Then you will not move into the house at all! I have contemplated taking your life, Tom, for the insurmountable troubles you have caused – bear that in mind, will you not?'

'That surprises me not in the least! Anyway, *I* have contemplated exposing *you*, bear that in mind! Now, where will I sleep, *should* I decide to move into the house?'

'In my room, then.'

'Yes, Sarah. But where, exactly, in your room? I want to hear the words fall from your sweet, pouting lips. Say them, Sarah!'

'In my bed!'

'That pleases me greatly!'

'You are a bastard!'

'Why, yes, I do believe I am. But you love me, do you not?'

'I hate and despise you!'

'You love me, I know it!' I laughed as I took her head and pressed her lips to mine, before departing.

So, I was to be a father! On reflection, what great joy the notion brought me, and what a future I had secured for myself! Sarah's bed – oh, what wonderful nights of love and wanton lust lay before me! But – the thought tarnished my glory – poor Belle! What would she do when she discovered the truth of my meanderings, for the time would surely come when she would have to know. No matter, one step at a time. And Amy? Well, there was nothing to stop me taking an early morning ride across the heath as it took my fancy.

So much was there to consider that my head fairly reeled. A new suit of clothes would be my first priority.

Indeed, so many priorities were there that I near gave myself a headache just thinking about it. Money – ah, money! A most important priority. I would send some to Harry the minute I had word of his address, and the minute I had talked Sarah into opening her purse strings!

The evening drew nigh, and I so looked forward to spending the night with Sarah that I knew not which way to turn. Why I had not discussed the matter further with her, I know not. Should I just arrive at her bedchamber? I wondered. Most likely to be screamed at, but yes! My cock hard and ready for her hot cunny, I would simply walk into her bedchamber and slip into the bed beside her.

As I collected my belongings from the hayloft, Clara and Elizabeth wandered into the stables and enquired what I was about.

'Why should it concern you, for you have both as good as ignored me for this past month?' I snapped.

'You have heard the news, Tom?' Clara asked.

'Yes, indeed. How do you feel?'

'I am not sure, as yet. Mother has told you of her plans?'

'*Her* plans! No, your mother and I have discussed the matter and have agreed, in principle, on *our* plans for the future.'

Clara smiled approvingly. I did perceive that she looked rather pale, though healthy, in the main, whilst poor Elizabeth appeared somewhat put out by the affair, presumably at the prospect of being left out. But left out she would not be, for I had plans for her, too – exciting plans!

My chance in this direction arrived earlier than I could have anticipated when Clara presently left us alone, saying that she had to help her mother with some arrangements in her bedchamber. Ominous, to say the least, I reflected, imagining Sarah lugging a bolster pillow to her bedchamber in order to mark out her territory in the bed.

'I have missed our games,' Elizabeth said solemnly as she lay back in the hay.

'They had barely begun, I am afraid,' I smiled.

'Things will be different now, I know,' she conceded. 'But do tell me that we will play our games again, Tom!'

'Elizabeth, the games shall commence now, and never shall they close, I promise you that!' I assured her, taking her in my arms to kiss her full, hot lips and ravish the dress about her firm breasts.

Her response spoke a million words as she lifted her skirts and slid her knickers down over her ankles to display her bush – the bush I had not laid eyes upon in one whole month! On fire, visibly filled with burning desire, she pulled me down betwixt her thighs and buried my head in her nest. 'I have sorely missed you, Tom,' she breathed as I lost not one second before thrusting my tongue into her wet, oh, so very wet and hungry cunt.

Father figure! The words would not leave my head as I sucked the juice from the girl's writhing body – my step-daughter's writhing body? My sister-in-law's writhing body? Oh, Sarah, what a mess! Oh, Elizabeth, what a lovely cunny! In a matter of months, I had fucked and sucked so many young females, and made one with child, and fucked her mother, and was now to inhabit her mother's bed, and . . . Oh, Tom! How Lady Luck does, indeed, love you!

'Do my bottom hole again, Tom!' Elizabeth cried as her clitoris stiffened 'neath my tongue and her juices flowed in torrents and my cock ached with painful delight. Oh, sweet words, sweet, naughty little girl! 'When I am ready, my love, for I am not yet done with you here,' I murmured through a mouthful of soft flesh, her hot folds encompassing my face.

Opening her cunny lips as wide as was possible without paining the girl, I gazed through her passage to the entrance of her womb. The juices, hot and thick and sticky, clung to the padded walls of inflamed and swollen flesh, ready for the friction of love to ignite the hot depths. Entranced, my tongue involuntarily reached into the cavern to lick upon the soft, pink flesh and entice still more juice to seep from the walls.

Oh, ecstasy! Oh, Elizabeth, how deep your hole – and how meagre my tongue! Further I stretched the portals of her hole, almost tearing the reddening flesh in a desperate attempt to gain access to the depths of the well and drink from the very source. She cried out, I knew not whether with pain or pleasure, or an exhilarating cocktail of both. And so, closing her lips over the fingers now buried deep within her cunt, I worked my tongue around her elongated and most deliciously ripened clitoris.

She cried out in pained pleasure and crushed my fingers as her body convulsed and perspired profusely, soon squirting into my face an involuntary shower of come juice. She was there! At last, she was there, and I continued to work with fury on her cunt, her clitoris, even sinking a finger into her bottom hole to diffuse the pleasure to every orifice, every nerve ending. Long, low moans poured from her pretty mouth as she arched her back and pressed her gaping slit hard against my face. She was done! Her cavern emptied, draining upon my hand as her spent clitoris retreated to its hide to prepare for its next adventure, the protective lips shrinking to embrace their most intimate, secret female parts.

Aroused already near to bursting point, my poor cock did then endure most painful titillation from an unexpected new dimension to our game. For manoeuvring the girl on to her front, and raising her hips to display her pale bum orbs to my hungry eyes I did spy Clara, atop the ladder, sparkling eyes peeping. Yet another tick for my list, I speculated, turning Elizabeth around and parting her buttocks to present the wondrous spectacle to her sister's secret gaze.

'You must become accustomed to doing it in Clara's bottom, Tom, her being with child,' Elizabeth said thoughtfully.

'Indeed, I must,' I agreed. 'For she will dearly love to have her bottom hole fucked, of that I am sure. And now, I will dip my cock into your hot cunny ere I take your bottom, my love. It will lubricate my knob in readiness for penetration.'

'Oh, Tom, be quick, for I fear Clara may return and shame me for allowing your cock in the wrong hole!'

'Did you enjoy the first time I visited you there?' I asked, praying her reply would fire her sister and inspire her to insist that she, too, be taken so.

'It was the most exquisite, heavenly thing ever, I do swear! But I hated you so for doing it! And now, please be quick, ere she returns!'

Her pinken lips sagging open below her bottom, beseeching penetration, I introduced my knob to the wrinkled wings, butting between them to tease her and cause her to plead even the more.

'Put it right up, Tom! Do it now!' she begged in her

frenzy. And so I did, with one almighty shove going in to the hilt. Her cunt was yet hot and wet and gripped me tighter than I had remembered. Rampant as I was with desire after having her with my tongue, I almost lost my seed within its depths as I rammed my shaft in and out of her wriggling body, the little brown hole lying invitingly open before me.

How her little pink inner lips clung to my glistening shaft as I moved back and forth, in one movement sucked with my cock deep within her cunt, in the next expelled with the shaft sliding from her hole. For Clara's excitement, and, I must confess, mine, I allowed my swollen, purple knob to leave her sister's hole to gloat at a good three inches distance betwixt each lunge. The trick seemed to work well indeed, judging by the gasps of delight from the top of the ladder.

As Elizabeth began to murmur and breathe loudly and deeply and raise her hips to meet my thrusts, I knew the appointed time was nigh. Quickly, I withdrew my steaming member from her furnace and presented the slimy knob to her little brown bottom hole. Glancing in Clara's direction, I saw her, still there, still peeping with her wide, expectant eyes as I stabbed at the small hole.

Elizabeth gasped, as did Clara, and indeed I, as the rigid gates yielded and my knob buried itself inside the entrance to her bowels. On Clara's account, I held it there, the bulb rooted, the shaft thick and exposed. And then, to further both girls' delight, I pushed gently, easing the shaft in, deeper and deeper, inch by glorious inch. Again, all three of us gasped as the root of my cock went home, my belly pressed hard against Elizabeth's pale buttocks. How wonderfully constricting was her ring around my intruding member! Shame it was that young Clara could not view the finer detail!

Feeling sorry for the girl, and rather mischievous, I looked to her and beckoned her to come see my cock rooted in her sister's bottom. She hid her face, but then reappeared, grinning, to creep across the hay and take up a stage view of the spectacle. To keep secret my audience, I lifted Elizabeth's skirts over her back so they hung over her head as a curtain to shield her eyes.

'Do it, Tom! Please, fuck my bottom hole ere Clara returns!' Elizabeth cried from 'neath her skirts, her cunny dripping over my balls as they hung, heavy and full with my fruits. Elizabeth's grin broadened with glee and she moved her face within inches of the hole I had well and truly plugged. And then, with all settled and ready, I began. In and out, slowly but firmly, I made my fucking motions to Elizabeth's cries of ecstasy. Her ring tightened even the more as I groped 'neath my balls for her cunny and slid three fingers into its wetness.

Clara, the naughty little thing, not being able to contain herself, did locate her sister's clitoris and frig it until poor Elizabeth screamed with glorious delight. Her entire frame shaking, she gripped my cock as in a vice, crushing the knob until it responded by firing its load deep into her bowels. Her cunt heaved and contracted as Clara worked faster and faster upon the little bud until Elizabeth screamed her pleasure and near caused Giant to bolt from his stable!

Pumping her full to the brim, my joy was enhanced by Clara's free hand kneading my balls as they swung, draining all the while into the little hole so boldly taking its pleasure from my shaft. How sweet are young girls' bottom holes being, as they are, tighter than cunnies, though drier, cooler than mouths, though deeper, with the added joy of being so exquisitely rude!

Ere I had yet finished depositing my sperm in her bottom, Elizabeth shuddered once again and convulsed, yanking my cock from her bowels in her collapse. Thus it was that my last spurt of seed projected through the air to land betwixt the crease of her buttocks, whence it ran to soothe the inflamed and gaping hole, so neatly placed above her dripping cunny. How Clara did shriek with delight at the sight of my cream, causing poor Elizabeth to jump and fight beneath her skirts to free herself. Panic turned to anger as her flushed face emerged to behold her sister, kneeling behind her embarrassingly exposed bottom hole.

'Calm yourself, Elizabeth!' I entreated the girl, who beat wildly upon my chest with her fists. 'For Clara has seen your bottom hole ere now! In fact, has she not licked at your cunt?'

'She has ne'er seen your cock buried in my arse! You are both vile beasts, and I shall never forgive you!'

'Come, Elizabeth,' Clara rejoined. 'You have a lovely bottom, and, after all, I did frig your clitoris for you.'

'You! It was you! Why, you are both more than vile! Tom, you will fuck her bottom hole as I watch! Then we shall be equal!'

Ah, could any other than sweet Elizabeth take the very words from my mouth? Surely, Clara could not deny herself the pleasures she had seen her sister receive? Surely, she would not now turn her back on such delights?

'What do you say, Clara?' I asked, my cock standing erect through the gap in my breeches.

'I think not, for it may hurt me,' she replied sheepishly.

'You *will*, Clara! You*will* have your bottom hole fucked, or I shall never, ever speak to you again!' screeched her impassioned sister.

Much to my pleasure, the two girls began to fight in a blatant affray of stockinged legs, knickers and skirts. Elizabeth, of course, legs wide and high during the scuffle, could not help but display her crack, open and still dripping with her juices. Perchance drawing energy from her recent stimulation, she it was who won the day, pinning poor Clara face down in the hay and ripping her knickers from her bottom.

Moving in quickly, I pulled the knickers over her ankles, and in so doing, observed that they were stained, slightly, with a white cream in the crotch. Ah, wonderful things, cunny holes! And so I told her, 'Your knickers are stained, Clara! Your cunny creamed them as you watched me take your sister!'

'You are vile, both vile!'

'Does your little cunny oft cream your knickers? Do you stick your finger in your cunny to induce the cream?'

'I hate you! Leave me! Let me go!'

'I will have to stick my cock into your hole, as it is so wet and ready for love!'

Straddling her sister's shoulders, Elizabeth managed to raise Clara's hips as I tucked her knees beneath her breasts to expose her bottom hole, and, gaping gloriously just below, her lovely wet cunny. Approaching the pleasurable sight upon my knees, my rod of iron aligned with my target, I slipped the head betwixt her pinken flaps and pushed inside.

'You pigs! You horrible pigs!' Clara cried as I pressed

my knob halfway into her cunny, which Elizabeth had kindly stretched for me by reaching down to her sister's bottom. Upon seeing me fully accommodated, she moved her hands up to Clara's buttocks and splayed them in readiness for my next act. Oh, what more wondrous sight could a man desire than such slender fingers easing apart those virginal buttocks for me?

'You have had not the pleasure for one whole month!' I gasped as my knob withdrew and rammed home again. 'So now you will have the fucking of your life – in both holes!'

'I will not! I hate you both!'

Poor Clara! But despite her perfunctory fight, I could discern by the hot juiciness of her cunt that she eagerly anticipated the change of holes. I made her wait, of course, by taking her cunny slowly, so as not to bring my seed up too soon. Elizabeth, in her wisdom, stuck a finger deep into her sister's bottom which, judging by their squeals, both girls found most stimulating.

'Do her bottom hole now and I will attend her cunny!' Elizabeth ordered excitedly. A better notion I could not have myself devised! No sooner was my cock out of the honeypot than Elizabeth's hand was groping until her fingers sunk between those wondrous swollen lips, deep into the vacant cavern.

'Are you ready for this?' I asked of Clara, butting my slimy knob against her brown hole.

'Never! Never!' came the most rewarding of replies as I pressed hard and the head, of a sudden, popped in. 'Agh! It hurts! Take it out!' she screamed in complaint.

'But Clara, I am only just inside. Your little hole has encompassed only my purple bulb. You cannot say that it hurts! Now, hold tight, my love, for I am going to sink my shaft yet deeper into your secret garden.'

And sink it I did – ah, ecstasy! What a tight little bottom she afforded, far more so than Elizabeth – or Sarah! She cried out and wiggled her hips wildly as Elizabeth stretched open and filled her cunny with her fingers to induce her nectar to flow, and I took her – good and proper!

Without warning, Elizabeth relinquished her fingers and slid from Clara's shoulders, to sit in the hay. I had no time to imagine what she was about before she opened her thighs and moved forward, placing them either side of her sister's head.

'Come, Clara,' she murmured. 'Lift your head and look.'

Clara raised her head to see Elizabeth's cunny spread wide only inches from her pretty face. Without losing a second, Elizabeth shot her hips forward, wedging her cunny beneath her sister's face. With my cock deep in her bottom hole and an open cunny pressed to her mouth, she was truly locked in the most wonderful position I could but dream of! Had Sarah appeared atop the ladder, it would surely have taken her some minutes to resolve just who was doing what to whom.

Neither Elizabeth nor I could hear, or cared, what the poor girl was saying as we pleasured ourselves at each end of her quivering body. But it mattered not, for I rammed her hard until her bottom squeezed my cock in the most delightful manner, bringing my seed almost to its bulging head. Elizabeth worked her hips back and forth and closed her eyes as she cried out and, I imagined, juiced her sister's face freely with the products of her climax.

The time right, I let my sperm gush as Clara shuddered and slurped at her sister's clitoris. All three, heads thrashing, faces afire, bodies locked, shook in unison as we found our release. Ah, to fill a young girl's bottom as she mouths her sister's cunt is the pinnacle of lust, I will swear! My cock refusing to die, even though it had been well drained, on and on I rammed into that tight little orifice, wondering if there could be yet another load in my balls. Alas, there was not, and eventually my shaft shrunk and fell limp, yet held in place by the tight brown ring which oozed with sperm as I finally slid my spent member out.

Elizabeth, meanwhile, had reclined, leaning on her hands, gasping, head thrown back, breasts straining through her dress, and cunny, judging by the wet, sagging, crimson lips, satisfied as never before. But I do believe that Clara it was who enjoyed our entanglement the most, finding, as she did, pleasure either end of her body! Moaning and still writhing a little, she rolled over as if semi-conscious, knees to her breasts, hairy lips swollen beyond belief, face red and wet from her sister's juices, both holes glistening with the fruits of love.

'Pigs! Pigs!' came her gasps, much to our delight. 'Vile, horrible pigs! My bottom hurts, it truly hurts!'

'It will hurt less, next time,' Elizabeth assured.

'There will be no next time – you vile beasts!'

'Oh, but there will, sweet Clara! For your cunny will soon be out of commission, leaving only your pretty mouth and your wondrous bottom hole available for pleasuring,' I whispered, holding her curled, ravished body in my arms.

Lashing out at me feebly with her fists, she arose and adjusted her dress to make her exit. Then, nearing the ladder, she doubled up and crumpled to the floor, moaning and groaning and rolling around in the hay.

'What have we done to you?' I cried. 'Tell me you are all right!'

'Clara!' Elizabeth screamed. 'What ails you? Are you in pain?' Thrashing her head, clutching her belly, eyes rolling, mouth agape, her sister cried out.

'I will fetch the doctor!' I shouted, leaping to the ladder.

'Be quick, Tom!' Elizabeth called, her face stricken with fear.

I was near halfway down the ladder when I heard Clara's words. 'You are both vile pigs! And it serves you right for thinking I was dying, for well I might have been!' Had she not been with child I would have thrashed her there and then. Instead, I climbed the ladder and moved towards her as she giggled and screeched and pointed at me with glee.

'I will take your bottom hole again!' I warned, pulling out my cock which had already hardened at the thought.

'No, no!' she cried as she backed away, her eyes transfixed on the ominous weapon in my hand. 'Not again!'

I did not take her again, but I did make her concede the truth concerning her experience.

'You liked your bottom hole fucked so?' I asked.

'Yes, I did, but it hurt a little at first.'

'It will be easier next time,' Elizabeth rejoined.

'And you liked licking your sister's cunny whilst you were taken so?' I pursued.

'I did – very much.'

'Then we are all agreed that we shall do this again!'

The girls left me to pack my belongings, but just ere they reached the stable door, Clara turned and asked if I knew the location of her bedchamber.

'No, but I will find it, should I need you,' I laughed.

'And mine?' Elizabeth called.

'Yes, and yours, my sweet. I will seek out the both of you, should I be in need of your company during the lonely night!'

Chapter Twelve

How serene my Sarah, eyes closed, hair sweeping the pillow, hands, childlike, each side of her head. Would she awaken as I slipped in beside her? Was she really sleeping? Was she clad in a sensual nightdress – or naked 'neath the bedclothes?

The warm perfume of her body greeted me as I climbed in and moved close to her. She was, indeed, naked, as was I, and I allowed my fingers to explore her curves, her hills and dales, her crevices, so warm and moist. Stirring, she spread her limbs to recline on her back. Now she was open to me, and I caressed the soft down upon her mound and stroked her open valley, causing her entrance to become sodden with the juices of desire.

She did not wake: at least, she did not appear to wake as I slid down the bed, kissing her breasts, her nipples, and her smooth belly. The night was hot and I discarded the bedclothes to reveal the naked beauty awaiting my attention. Was she dreaming? I wondered, nibbling upon her inner thighs. Dreaming of me, deep within her body, filling her very womb with my hot fruit?

Her slit was afire, inflamed, swollen, pouring forth its milky lotion as my tongue found its way betwixt the fleshy folds. Had she embedded her fingers deep inside her cunny hole to elicit such a measure of arousal? Had she frigged her clitoris ere falling asleep? I was truly obsessed with the beautiful body that lay open before me – every delectable inch of it! My mind ran wild with fantasies of the fine lady and her two daughters, all naked and entwined, myself taking centre stage in the tangle of lust.

So to the not less sweeter reality; to taste, to touch, to smell, are senses of love. And to see? To behold every delicate detail of woman's intimacy – the pinken, glistening folds, wet and swollen – surely, above others, fires the flame of love! But alas, in that dim light, I could scarce divine the secrets within my Sarah's magical valley.

Deftly turning up the lamp, I set it upon a chair by the bed. Now I could observe the dewdropped folds in their full glory, the sweet sap trickling from the exotic flora nestled twixt its lush terrain. But the clitoris, that enchanting centre of pleasure, where was she? Ah, there, the blushing bride, hiding in the fullness of her garb, protected by a soft, pinken hood.

Parting the velvety curtains of flesh, I located the crimson bud and pressed around the base to entice it from its hide. Out it popped – how large and hard it grew before my very eyes! Sarah writhed slightly as I tasted the sweetness of her soul but, still, she slept. Her valley now scarlet and yawning, hot and lubricous, I licked, from one end to the other, spreading the sticky milk, swelling the flesh until she opened her thighs further and let out a long, low moan of pleasure. Her hands wandered over her breasts, fingers encircling her nipples as she slept. Oh, what dreams did she conjure? What images filled her mind?

Will she attain her pinnacle as she sleeps? I mused,

sucking upon the bud to make it grow ever the more. As if in answer, she began to breathe heavily, her belly rising and falling in spasms. She was nearing her summit now; round and round I ran my tongue, caressing the magical bud, bringing it all the while nearer to ecstasy until, moaning and throwing her legs asunder, Sarah cried out.

'Oh, what heaven! What divine pleasure does my cunt bring!' Did she speak from her dreams? Was she yet asleep? In wonderment I gazed as her engorged bud throbbed and pulsated and her juices gushed. Grabbing my head, she forced my face betwixt her thighs and ground her clitoris into my mouth as she shuddered and gasped. She had reached her paradise! Taking care not to allow the descent from sexual heights until she was completely spent, satisfied, I continued to flick my tongue over the bud. Barely had it come to rest when, again, it pulsed with ecstasy, causing my sleeping beauty to garrotte me betwixt her hot loins.

Awake or asleep, I knew not her condition, but I continued with my teasing caress until the bud exploded for the third time. Fighting to free herself, she crushed my head and rolled her hips, but my mouth was locked betwixt her fiery lips, her clitoris engulfed and throbbing against my tongue.

Sinking my fingers into her hole I raised her pelvis from the bed with each thrust as she cried out again with pained bliss. 'Fuck me!' she begged, spreading her legs to release my head. Rampant with a pulsating desire, my cock slipped smoothly into her hot depths to be crushed by her wondrous spasms. Only minutes did I last, for I was riding high upon her mound and picturing the girls' bottoms, splayed and open, my knob buried within. My hands beneath her buttocks, I lifted her trembling frame clear of the bed and thrust my fruits deep into her luscious pot until she was full, and I drained. A true woman indeed, arching her back and spreading her legs to suck me deep inside as together we descended to earth, gasping, delirious, genitals locked in lust.

Arranging the dishevelled bedclothes upon our exhausted bodies, I lay my head upon the pillow and closed my eyes, my arm around my Sarah, warm, satisfied, and yet wondering if she had left her sleep.

The pillow beside me was cold in the morning, for Sarah had gone. I quickly dressed and made my way downstairs in search of her, only to be told by the battle-axe that she had taken a ride an hour before. The girls were nowhere to be found, but apparently they had not accompanied their mother.

Being ravenous, I asked the battle-axe, in the most polite and friendly manner possible, if she would be kind enough to make me breakfast. She replied that she would not, and, in my anger, I told her that she should leave the house immediately as I was now master.

'I takes me orders only from 'er!' returned the bastion. 'And I don't like doin' even that, but I 'as no choice!'

'You will take them from me, too, my good woman, or . . .'

'I ain't your good woman!'

I was in total despair. Why would not the old woman be civil, at least? It was not that she disliked the notion of my being master – no, it was her dislike of me, I surmised. 'We both have to live here,' I began. 'And, I would be most appreciative if we all . . .'

I broke off and followed her gaze to Sarah, standing in the kitchen doorway. Oh, how those tight jodhpurs, waisted riding jacket and leather boots excited me, though I was barely awake! And her tresses, bunched up 'neath her hat – a lady, indeed!

'What problem do we have now?' she demanded of the battle-axe, keeping one eye on me whilst slapping her thigh with her riding crop.

'No problem, me lady. I was just tellin' this young man 'ere that I ain't takin' no orders from 'im.'

'And what orders did he give you?'

'To cook 'im breakfast, me lady.'

'A word, please, Tom, if you will,' Sarah decreed, turning on her heels and leaving the room.

I followed her to the morning room where she sat down and bade me do the same. 'You are not master of this house, Tom. And I will not have the cook upset, do you hear?'

'But I only asked if I might have breakfast,' I replied.

'Make it yourself. And, Tom, I should be grateful if you would sleep in Lord Hadleigh's room. I am not accustomed to sleeping with another in my bed, and I cannot, I will not, become used to the idea! I need my sleep.'

Standing open-mouthed, I watched the woman I had fucked to the soul but a few hours earlier flounce from the room. I had penetrated her very core; together, we had made love, walked in paradise, yet still she treated me as a servant! 'Damn you, woman!' I cursed as I paced the floor, wondering if our night of passion had meant anything at all to her. Perchance she had slept through it? If this were so, my lovemaking was sadly lacking in something! No, she was simply a bitch! She had enjoyed every lustful minute of our union, but, for reasons unknown to me, would not, could not, allow herself to love me.

Blackmail, I surmised, was not conducive to love. One couldn't put a gun to a lady's head and demand love! I concluded that I had been deceiving myself all the while, and that she, beautiful though she was, had no love for me whatsoever – merely moments of unbridled lust. Pondering the situation, I decided that the battle-axe might know something and wandered back to the kitchen. She liked no-one, she had said previously. But, it seemed to me, she did not care much for Sarah, either, and I did not for the life of me know why.

'Tell me, what is it about Lady Sarah that disturbs you so?' I probed, closing the kitchen door behind me.

'Ain't nothin' 'bout 'er,' she replied, without so much as raising her eyes.

'Is it that you know about Lord Hadleigh?' I enquired, wondering if she knew more than Harry or I about his past.

That ammunition had the desired effect. Dropping the mixing bowl she had been cleaning, she looked me hard in the eye. 'What did you say?' she demanded, moving round the table as if preparing to attack me.

'Lord Hadleigh,' I repeated, knowing that I had hit upon something.

'Disgraceful, that's what it is!' bellowed the ox, pointing her finger threateningly at me. 'And now you come 'ere and move in like you own the place! Disgraceful!'

'What is so disgraceful about my living here?'

'You won't last long, I tell yer! But I ain't bothered 'bout the likes of you! It's 'er and 'er wicked ways what bothers me!'

At least she was talking to me, which was more than she had ever done before. Now I was determined to coax her gently and discover exactly what it was that she knew. But in order to do that, I would have to bluff her.

'I know all about Lord Hadleigh,' I ventured. 'And, yes, I agree with you, it is, indeed, terrible.'

'Then why you botherin' with the likes of 'er? You look like a decent young man, why bother with 'er and 'er ways of incest?'

'Incest? Oh, you mean . . .'

'I mean incest! A spade's a spade – that's what it is, sleeping with 'er father!'

'Lord Hadleigh?'

'Who'd yer think I mean? Yer knew, didn't yer?'

'Yes, yes, of course I knew,' I replied, taking my leave ere she should notice my expression of utter amazement.

Old man Hadleigh her father! I could scarce believe my ears and my mind reeled with the most weird and wonderful notions. The girls, I remembered, had mentioned watching their mother sucking the old man. My God, what kind of family was this?

I do believe that at that moment my love for Sarah died. I cannot say that I hated her, for I knew not my true feelings at that time. My mind swam with incoherent thoughts and for a while I could barely breathe or stand upright. To say that I was stunned would be an understatement indeed. Rather I was shaken to my very soul!

Wandering into the stable to climb the ladder to the hayloft, I recalled Harry's words. He had claimed that the old man, Lord Hadleigh, had done away with his wife for the substitution of the maid, Mary. So he knew only the half of it! I thanked God that Sarah had not borne the old devil's child. God alone knew what such an obscene union would spawn!

My heart hung heavy, for I had lost Sarah. No matter

what her explanation, her excuse, if ever she took it upon herself to offer an excuse, there was now no denying her vile, wanton incest. Perhaps she had been ignorant of the knowledge that the old man was her father, I mused, in hope of making sense of the affair. But no, I was clutching at straws in an effort to excuse her. For surely he knew – as did she. Harry had obviously known only a few facts, and had assumed the rest. I could not blame him for his assumptions, for at the time they had made sense even to me.

Belle led Giant into the stable and tethered him. I watched her for some time, my guilt rising, for I had treated her so badly, feeding her untruths and taking Sarah and the girls while the poor thing imagined that I was desperately in love with her. If she knew that Clara was pregnant with my child! Happily, for the time being, she did not and my thoughts turned to the future – with Belle.

'Belle!' I called from my perch in the hayloft. She turned, her face lighting up with delight.

'Tom! Where have you been? I have missed you so much. Are you all right? Did you sleep up there? I waited up for you till the early hours!'

Poor Belle. Her questions I could not answer, not truthfully, anyway. I bade her join me and took her in my arms the minute she fell onto the hay beside me.

'I did sleep up here,' I lied. 'I became tired and fell asleep and I . . . well, no matter.'

'I worried, Tom. I thought you were in trouble or, worse still, that you had taken up with the girls for the night!'

'Calm yourself, Belle. I slept here, I told you so. Now, I must go to the house as there is so much to do and the time is running on.'

'You will come to the cottage later?' she asked anxiously, her big brown eyes tearful.

'Yes, yes. This evening, I promise. Now go!'

I walked across the field, across the heath, and sat upon the hill in the very spot where Amy had so willingly surrendered her virginity to me. There I contemplated, slept a little, and wondered why on earth I did not just pack my belongings and leave Royston Manor. So much, it seemed, had gone wrong for me. I had enjoyed my time, yes, but the lies, the deceit, the blackmail – all seemed to be going so terribly wrong.

Returning at dusk, I crept up to the hayloft. I did not go to the cottage that evening, I am afraid to say, but slept, badly, haunted by nightmares of hordes of pregnant females chasing me, until the sun rose. Ere Belle could catch me and ask too many questions causing me to lie yet again, I took Giant up to the hill, for the month was up! My spirits were high and I left the manor and all my problems behind me as I galloped with much haste across the heath.

To my great relief and pleasure, Amy was there. I near fell from Giant in my effort to get to her and hold her and love her. Wearing not her jodhpurs but a beautiful, flowing gown of velvet and lace, her face afire with passion, she was the epitome of femininity.

With Amy full of talk of our long month apart, I barely listened to her sweet voice as I lifted her skirts and removed her knickers to kiss her warm bush. She responded immediately, lying back on the heath, her eyes closed as I parted her fleshy lips and licked at her wondrous nectar as it flowed from her body in a deluge of love.

'I'll have you horse-whipped, young man!' a woman's voice screamed of a sudden, as if from nowhere. 'And you, you young harlot, you will be beaten until you bleed!'

'Mother!' Amy cried, her bush and swollen, crimson pussy lips in full view. 'I was just . . .'

'Get home this instant!'

Poor Amy mounted her horse and raced off with tears streaming down her face as her mother turned to me. My heart beat hard as I awaited the inevitable lecture. She was roughly the same age as Sarah, although not so pretty by far, and a notion suddenly betook me.

'Lay one finger on Amy, and I will tell the world that her father was no more than a passing foreigner – and her half-sister none other than Clara Hadleigh!'

It was clear that my intuition had paid off as the woman turned pale and crumpled upon the heath. Oft had I wondered at the uncanny similarity between Clara and Amy, but until that lucky moment, the true reason had eluded me. On regaining her senses, the woman looked up at me and near swooned again.

'You wicked man!' she scorned.

'And you wicked woman!' I returned.

'You will never see Amy again! Do you hear?'

'Oh, but I will! You see, I do believe that I have fallen in love with your beautiful daughter and I am considering taking her hand in marriage.'

'But you – you are nothing!'

'And what are you? Other than a strumpet! You are on good terms with Lady Sarah, I believe. I will go to her now and tell her that you enlightened me as to . . .'

'She knows, you fool!'

'Yes, but she knows not that I know! Neither does

Clara, I'll be bound – nor Amy! And I should imagine your husband . . .'

'Pray, what do you want?'

What did I want indeed? A good question, for I knew not. Money? Amy? I had no notion! I had wanted Sarah, but no more. What indeed?

'Information!' I replied on a whim, wondering how much she knew.

'Information as to what?' she asked evenly, rising to her feet.

'Lord and Lady Cranfield, for a start.'

'I know nothing of them. What do you mean?'

'They are not of the aristocracy, are they?'

Again, she took on such pallor that I suggested she sit down for fear I shock her the more. Composing herself, she told me that Lord Cranfield had indeed been born of commoners and that, aided by blackmail, no less, he had managed to secure ownership of the manor and assume the title on the mysterious disappearance of the genuine lord. He had then married, hence Lady Cranfield. Of the details, she professed to know nothing, and I believed her. Just how the so-called Lord Cranfield had managed such a feat of deceit was beyond me and, to be honest, was of no consequence. But, I decided, I would pay a visit to the gentleman, just to let him know that I was aware of his skulduggery.

'Amy will meet me here as and when it is her wish to do so,' I declared to her shocked mother, returning to immediate business. 'If she fails to arrive on the morrow, then your secret shall be a secret no more!' With that, I mounted Giant and left the wretched woman deep in thought. As to myself, I enjoyed then a certain pride. Being inept at figures, my father had deemed me useless, but with new insight I perceived that I did, indeed, own a brain, and one that I knew how to use well to my advantage!

Without too much trouble I located the Cranfields' manor from directions given by a farm worker. I was fortunate to be met by Lord Cranfield himself as I arrived at the manor steps. He was older than I had imagined him to be, his grey hair some eight inches long on one side, sweeping over his head to conceal his baldness. His eyes, too, were grey, and deep set. Initially, he charged me to be on my way, presumably thinking I was a ruffian, but changed his mind on my hinting that I knew of his past.

'You are from Royston Manor, are you not?' he enquired as he led me into the hall.

'I am, indeed, Sir,' I replied, wondering how he knew such, for I had not seen him at Sarah's dinner.

'And what is it, exactly, that you wish to speak of?'

At that moment a young girl of eighteen or so entered the hall – deliciously blonde, tall, and slim.

'I am busy, child!' Cranfield yelled as she beat her retreat. Could this beauty be his daughter? I wondered. A girl so young, his daughter? Or had some virile young farm hand taken the girl's mother? More than likely, I imagined, for, it seemed, the local farm hands of some eighteen years previously had sown their wild seeds in every nook and cranny they could find! Perforce I could blackmail Lady Cranfield, I mused, turning to face the old man.

'I want to know how you did it,' I said firmly.

'Did what?' bellowed the old fraud.

'Became lord of this manor.'

'I do believe that you are mad!' he yelled. 'My father . . .'

'No, no, not your father. You mean the *real* Lord Cranfield.'

Old though Cranfield was, he near threw me from the house and in the warm morning air I mounted Giant, swearing that I would see the old devil again. Fortunate it was that I turned to cast my anger to the manor house, for peeping from the window, her pretty face smiling sweetly, was the young blonde maiden. Speculatively, I winked and nodded in the hope that one fine day I might have the opportunity of taking her delightful young body!

I deemed my visit not wasted for, apart from making such a sweet new acquaintanceship, I was now armed with more than enough information to blackmail the local so-called aristocracy and accrue a small fortune. 'A mockery!' I laughed as I rode home. 'A complete sham!'

It was during my return journey that I realised what it was that I wanted from my life. To take the girls and Belle and Amy at my whim, yes. But security, too. During my time at Royston Manor, I had been constantly reminded that I was nothing more than an employee. What I desired, fervently, was to become its Lord!

Pursuing Lord Cranfield would only prove futile, I knew. He was too old to care about the likes of me, and, probably, anyone else, for that matter. As far as I was concerned, he had but one thing to offer – his wonderful daughter! Nevertheless, it is always useful to know one or two things about people, as with Amy's mother, for would not Amy have been beaten and locked away until her death had I not had recourse to blackmail?

Sarah was searching for me when I finally returned. Her eyes were saddened slightly, and I did perceive that she was for some reason in fear of my return. 'What is it?' I asked her as Belle took Giant.

'I have some bad news for you, Tom. It is Harry . . . He . . .'

'He has gone?'

'He has. I have just received word . . .'

'Had you allowed him to stay here! Had you offered a little money! Shown some compassion, at least! But, no. It is not within you, is it? You know nothing of love, compassion! You know only of lies, deceit, ince—'

I cut myself, for, although deeply saddened and angry, I did not want to use my trump card unnecessarily. My love for Sarah, if it had ever been love, had, indeed, turned to hatred. Leaving her in the yard, I wandered down the track to the cottage to think.

Belle joined me, much to my displeasure, and began her questioning, on and on until she wore me down and I exploded.

'Be off with you!' I yelled.

'But, Tom . . .'

'Leave me, leave this place, for it is engulfed with lies, deceit, and evil deeds! Save yourself ere you become entangled in the dreadful web!'

'I will stay with you, Tom, no matter what has happened. I will love only you – always!'

Uncharacteristically, or, I believe, by that time, all too characteristically, I removed her clothes, hurriedly, and threw her across the bed, determined to take her bottom hole. I know not why I desired such a thing at that sad time: I can only assume that a medley of pain, love, hatred and the presence of the devil himself had changed me.

Belle enjoyed my attentions, initially, removing my breeches, kissing me and laughing all the while. But the minute I turned her lovely young body over, she knew what I had in mind.

'Tom, you will not . . .' she began.

'Hold still, my lovely, I will not pain you.'

Elevating her hips, I was delighted to see her intimacy fully exposed to my lustful stare. Just below her bottom hole, her cunny lips were bulging – hairless, wet, crimson either side of her glistening opening. Quickly taking my cock in my hand, I rammed it home into the hot wetness of her tight little cunt. As a man possessed, I held her hips and thrust into her tube, filling and stretching the flesh as she cried out and began to fight. Then, withdrawing my weapon, I yanked her buttocks apart and slid my knob into her bottom hole. It yielded, far more easily than I had expected, and, without mercy, I pressed the length of my shaft home until my belly flanked her buttocks. 'I hate you!' she cried as I allowed my shaft to soak in the dank heat of her bowels. 'I will kill you, I swear!'

'Do not talk such utter rot!' I admonished. 'Now, hold still and take my cock!'

Ah, sheer ecstasy! Another tick for my ever-increasing list of achievements! Scream her protests she did and thrash her hips wildly, unknowingly serving only to heighten my pleasure. I took her as an animal, I must confess. But I was driven by rage, anger, sorrow, hurt – by the very devil himself!

Filling her bottom with my sperm, I allowed my cock to shrink within the tightness of her hole ere releasing her and allowing her to collapse across the bed, her last vestige of virginity gone forever. As she cried and swore that she hated me, I laughed and told her that I knew of the great pleasure it had brought her, and that when she wanted more, all she had to do was plead on her bended knees. I know not why I treated her so, for she had shown me only love. I had become hard and cruel, no doubt as a result of Sarah's influence.

'I have been with Lady Sarah!' Belle screamed as she turned to face me, clutching her buttocks.

'You lie! You think you can rile me with such lies?'

'I have been in her bed, and she in mine, and we have loved! I tried with you, but men are pigs! I prefer women, as I told you in the first instance!'

'Then, tell me of her cunny! Describe it, as there is something in particular about it that you will know of – if you speak the truth, that is!'

Wiping her tears and composing herself, little Belle smiled as if in triumph. 'She has a tiny mole on her inner thigh, her left thigh, high up in the crease of her leg. And she has another, just below her belly.'

She was right! But why had Sarah not told me of Belle's shaven mound when I had asked her to describe the young girl's cunny?

'For how long have you been loving each other, as you put it?'

'For some time now, during the day, whilst you are out working. Almost from the day I started here, we have been loving each other. Why do you think I am in this cottage? Why do you think you were told to keep away from me?' She fell to the floor as, mad with rage, I struck her face ere taking my leave.

Sarah was in the study talking with the girls when I burst in.

'You wish to see me, Tom?' she asked coolly.

'Yes – alone!'

'Run along, girls, while I talk with Tom,' she ordered. Giggling, they closed the door behind them. I had no doubt that they were listening outside, but that did not concern me.

'So, you have been with Belle! You have taken her to your bed and . . .'

'I have done nothing of the sort! We have been through this before, Tom. What is it that you think you have discovered this time?'

'Belle has told me, Sarah. Oh, do not flatter yourself by imagining for one moment that I am jealous, for I am not! I do not want you any more than I want her. You are both no more than tarts, whores, strumpets – lesbians! I suppose you lick at your daughters' little cunny holes, too?'

'You disgust me! You are vile, debased of mind!'

'Do you like fingering your daughters' cunts – does it please you to have them suckle on your clitoris?'

'Get out! You have blackmailed me, tried your utmost to destroy me, treated me with contempt, you . . .'

'I was talking with Lady Miles this morning. She told me one or two home truths concerning you and your so-called family.'

Sarah seated herself upon the window seat and stared blankly at me. I was in two minds as to whether I should tell her all I knew or not; but no, I would save that for the kill! A tear fell from her eye and trickled down her cheek as she looked up to me.

'I have been alone in this life,' she began quietly. 'The nights have been long and lonely. I thought that . . . Well, I did have some love for you, but your continuous blackmail threats left me cold. Belle gave me . . . love, I suppose. Undemanding, unquestioning love. My daughters? No, of course I have not touched them! They are fine girls, and I hope, one day . . . or, rather, I *hoped*, for Clara is now with child . . . Anyway, what is it that you want, Tom? Tell me, what can I do to rid you from my life – once and for all?'

'From what Lady Miles tells me . . .'

'I care not what lies that woman . . .'

'No, not lies, Sarah. Not lies.'

'Whatever, I care not what she has or has not told you. What is it that you want? In God's name, tell me!'

To become Lord of the Manor! But I dared not tell her such at that point. Leaving her with her tears, I made my way to the field behind the stables, for the sun was bright in the sky and I was tired, my head aching, and, I must confess, my heart broken. Oh, Sarah, why could not things have been different? Why could we not have lived, and loved, without the confusion, the pain, the lies, the deceit – the whole sad and sorry mess?

Chapter Thirteen

Piercing shrieks emanating from the direction of the cottage woke me at dusk. Initially, I had no concern, for I was too troubled myself to worry about other people's affairs. But the cries continued to fill the evening air and I was duly moved to discover what poor maiden was in such distress.

Nearing the cottage, it became apparent to me that the screams came from inside the cottage itself. Peering in through the bedchamber window, I beheld Sarah beating Belle with a long, thin cane. The poor girl was tied over the end of the bedstead, totally naked, with her legs spread wide. How Sarah had managed to secure her in such a position, I had no idea. I could only assume that it was part of some bizarre game they played.

'You dare to tell Tom of our relationship!' Sarah screamed. 'You dare! Did I not tell you that he is dangerous? Did I not say that he is up to no good and endeavouring to damage us all?'

'I said only . . .'

'Never *only* say anything! I put on a good show of tears and, hopefully, I have appealed to his weak nature, for weak he is! I placed you in this cottage because I was led to believe that your loyalties lay with me! Yet all you have done is let me down. You were supposed to discover the nature of his game – not tell him of mine! I thought you loved me!'

Oh, Sarah! How could you hope to hold secrets when you loosed your tongue so in anger? I only wished she would say more as she continued the beating in silence. Poor Belle! Her body tethered so, displaying her bottom-hole and her lovely cunny! I pressed my face to the windowglass for a better view of the glorious scenario. The scene aroused my cock, I must confess, and I longed to join them in their wickedness!

At length, Sarah dropped the cane and removed her clothing, falling to her knees to tend Belle's weals. Tenderly kissing her crimsoned buttocks, she opened the girl's red, pouting cunny lips, pushing at least three fingers deep inside the pretty little cunette and, for good measure, pressing her thumb into the little brown hole, whilst with her free hand she frigged Belle's clitoris until the girl cried out in unchecked sexual ecstasy.

As I watched in a delirium of excitement, Belle relaxed, her climax over, whilst Sarah licked the length of her open crease. From her cunny, over her bottom hole, to the small of her back she licked feverishly, all the while attending the girl's clitoris with her deft little fingers.

My cock straining and near bursting through my breeches, it was then that the idea came to me. Taking a length of rope from a nearby farm cart, I stole through the rear entrance of the cottage and edged open the bed-chamber door. Belle was whimpering and approaching yet another shuddering climax, but Sarah heard me and turned her head. Without further ado, I grabbed her from behind, bent her over the bedstead beside Belle, and tied her good and fast.

What a wondrous sight! The two glorious pairs of tight, pale buttocks lay spread before me, ready for my every whim. Sarah screamed and swore to kill me, but I was not in the least deterred by her futile threats – indeed, if anything, they drove me on! Belle begged me not to thrash her, and by the condition of her glowing orbs, I surmised that she could probably take no more.

'You may turn your face to Sarah's and watch her wince and listen to her cries for mercy,' I told her, tapping the cane across Sarah's tightening buttocks. 'Now, Sarah, this is what I do to young women who cheat and lie and interfere with young girls' cunnies!' Her buttocks tightened involuntarily, pulling themselves sharply together with every gruelling slap of the cane. Oh, to watch them twitch, to hear her pleas!

'I will do anything, Tom! Please, anything!'

'But you are in no position to do anything!' I laughed mercilessly, whacking her once again for good measure.

Standing betwixt my beauties, I fondled Belle's cunny with my left hand, and Sarah's with my right. Ah, what pleasure can two wet caverns bring a man! 'The time has come, my Lady Sarah, to take your bottom-hole!' I cried as if possessed, ripping my cock from my breeches. First, I entered her cunt to lubricate my knob with her juices, which were by then flowing down her inner thighs in torrents. How profound the penetration when taking a cunny from behind! To the very depths of her pelvis I drove my rod, she gasping and me near-delirious with the sheer ecstasy.

She reached her climax quickly, for she was excited from attending Belle so intimately. Crying out her expletives in one gasp whilst breathing her gratitude in the next, her cunt tightened around my cock to suck the sperm from my heavy balls; but I held back, for my precious load was not to be wasted in her cunny! Ah, how she did relish a good fucking! But she had more pleasures to come – as did I!

Slipping my knob from her cavern, I ran the head up an inch or so and pressed it hard against her bottom-hole. Wiggle and curse me as she did, I knew only too well that she loved it! Thus in it slipped, inch after wondrous inch disappearing into the dank heat of her accommodating bottom. Not wishing to loose my seed too soon, I withdrew and pushed my weapon next deep into Belle's cunny where I allowed it to rest a while, thoughtfully easing a bunch of fingers into Sarah's hot cunny and one into her bottom-hole to afford her some pleasure as I took her chargeling.

Belle was nearing her climax and I allowed her a little pleasure by gently easing my cock in and out of her tube. The poor girl, she cared not for me or my cock, especially when it was inside her bottom! But she breathed her gasps of sexual gratification as I fucked her – punctuated with pleas. 'Not my bottom, Tom! Please, not my bottom!'

'Oh yes, your bottom, my love. My beautiful Belle, deep into your lovely bottom-hole I will delve!'

'I shall never again speak with you if you put it in there!' she swore. No matter, for I was not overly interested in her speaking with me anyway. Slipping out my steaming cock, I inched it up her crease to her bottom-hole where I let it rest awhile to increase her state of anticipation. A woman should not be taken too hastily, I find, for the longer she awaits the inevitable pleasure, the more she desires and enjoys it.

Much to my surprise, and joy, Belle did indeed desire it, begging me to slip my rampant cock deep into her bottom!

'What brings this change of heart?' I whispered into her ear, but she said nothing, and I was left to imagine it was that she could not contain herself a moment longer with the thought of my cock in her bottom arousing her, wetting her cunt and swelling her clitoris.

Taking my fingers from Sarah's trembling body, I gingerly prised Belle's buttocks open, for they were inflamed and sore from the beating. I could scarce believe my ears as, pushing my knob in to cover the head with her brown ring, she gasped her pleasure and begged me to frig her clitoris. With Sarah all the while threatening the poor girl with all manner of punishment should she enjoy the experience one little bit, I excited the bud for all I was worth until it exploded, young Belle shaking and shuddering as I filled her to the brim with my hot cream. Oh, sheer heaven, I will swear! Allowing my cock to soak in the warmth of her bowels for a few minutes, to my utter amazement I felt it grow and once more open the dark, velvet sheath that so lovingly encompassed it.

Sarah turned her head to scoff at the pleasure upon Belle's face as I pumped and pumped until another load filled her young body, seeping out to run down the bulging shaft of my cock to my balls. Lifting her head to mock too at the ecstasy upon my face, I smiled sweetly and promised that, should she be patient, she would receive more pleasure from my cock.

'You will receive no pleasure from the punishment I have planned for you!' she cried.

Somewhere in the distance I heard the girls calling for their mother. What wonderful mischief to show them her predicament! But another idea betook me – to leave young Belle and Sarah tied over the bedstead for some hours while I took my pleasure with the whippets in the house! 'Your pleasure must wait, Sarah, for your daughters call,' I taunted. 'No doubt they wish their bottom-holes to be fucked by my much-accomplished cock!'

'Do not touch them! Do not dream of doing such to my girls!'

'It is no dream for I have already done such!' I laughed as I withdrew my shrivelling member from Belle's hot bottom-hole.

Buttoning my breeches, I bade the ladies farewell. I could hear their screamed expletives as I ran up the track towards the yard where the girls awaited my arrival. For fear of them hearing the cries for help, I ushered them across the yard and quickly into the house ere they had a chance to tell me what they wanted.

'Where have you been, Tom?' Clara asked.

'And where is mother?' Elizabeth enquired.

'I have been working, and your mother, I believe, went off somewhere with Belle – to the village, I think. Now, what was all the calling about?'

'We just wondered where she was, that was all,' Clara said. 'By the way, Tom, did you know that she has removed your belongings to father's room? I fear she must be displeased with your performance in bed!'

Giggling, they ran upstairs to their rooms. I was about to follow and take them both in their very own beds, for I had yet to set eyes upon their bedchambers, when someone called at the front door. The battle-axe answered as I hid behind the drawing-room door and listened.

'I have called to see Lady Hadleigh,' said a pleasant female voice. Hearing the battle-axe almost disrespectful in her reply, I ventured from my hide to see who it was. To my surprise, it was the young blonde lady I had seen at Lord Cranfield's house. Telling the battle-axe to go about her business, to which she mumbled some further rudeness, I asked the delightful thing in and showed her into the drawing room.

'I am Tom, and I am delighted to make your acquaintance,' I said, and kissed her hand.

'I am Rose, and I have called to see the lady of the house.'

Ah, Rose! So exquisitely pretty, so fresh with perfume, and such wondrous huge green eyes! Her cloak concealed her figure, but I knew it would be gorgeous, for are not all girls on the threshold of womanhood so? I was intrigued, for just 'neath her cloak, her frock, did not her cunny lie? What colour the hair of her mound – if any? How thick her sweet pussy lips? And her breasts – how lush the nipples?

'I am sorry to say that the lady is tied up just now. Is there anything I can do for you?' I ventured, dragging my lecherous thoughts and gaze from her body.

'I have come to give her this letter,' she replied, her pretty little mouth smiling sweetly. 'But my father instructed me to give it *only* to Lady Hadleigh. If she is not here, then . . .'

'Worry not, for she will return shortly, and you can trust me implicitly. The letter is obviously of the utmost importance to warrant your father sending you out after dark.'

'But my father will . . .'

'Simply tell him that you did, indeed, pass the letter directly to Lady Hadleigh. She will receive it within the hour, I promise you.'

As the sweet Rose passed me the envelope, I could not but help notice her slender fingers, so smooth and wondrously long, with their neat, painted nails. Where had they been? I wondered. Had they caressed her bud and brought her ecstasy? Had they parted her soft, pink vaginal lips? Had she pushed them, lovingly, desperately, into her tight little cunny hole and used them as she would a man's cock – my cock – thrusting in and out of her hotness until her clitoris demanded them? Had they gripped a man's cock? Guided it deep into her cunt? Had they tasted a man's sperm? Oh Rose, you mysterious, wonderful creature!

As I reluctantly showed the beauty to the front door, she confided that she often walked across the heath and would be delighted if I were to join her on such a walk one fine day. Not only did I agree, but I arranged to meet her the following afternoon at the entrance to the wood. What a wonderful life! How entrancing young females! So it was in uncustomarily high spirits that I carefully prised open the letter and read the contents:

My dear Sarah,

I have been unfortunate enough to have been visited by that young man of yours: Tom, I believe his name to be. He asked me how I came to be a lord! Lady Miles has also spoken to him, or, should I say, he has spoken to her. It would appear that he knows not only about me, but also Lady Miles, and, I suspect, your good self. In view of the circumstances, I am calling a meeting at my house of all those concerned, including those the young man has not yet caught up with.

I will be most grateful to receive you at eleven o'clock

tomorrow morning when, I pray, we can deal with this most urgent matter.

> *Yours sincerely,*
> *Charles Cranfield*

So, I had stirred up the bees' nest! The so-called aristocracy was in a turmoil! I quickly read the letter again. 'Including those the young man has not yet caught up with.' Most interesting! How many were there, I wondered, who were no more than commoners masquerading as lords and ladies?

My initial thought was to destroy the letter. But, no, the meeting would go ahead without Sarah, and her absence would, no doubt, be cause for some concern. Rose would be scolded, and I did not wish that. Besides, I would do well to watch those concerned entering the house for there could well be one or two faces I could put names to.

Resealing the envelope, I suddenly remembered Sarah and Belle. What a delightful thing it would be to send young Clara and Elizabeth to the cottage to discover their mother! But first, there were one or two little adjustments to be made to the scenario, and I made with all haste to the cottage.

On my return, I found Clara and Elizabeth mooching around the yard in the dark. They were bored, it seemed, and still they asked after their mother's whereabouts. 'She is in the cottage with Belle,' I informed them. 'And she wishes to see you both there, this instant.' With that, they bounded off down the track, closely followed by my good self, of course.

From outside the bedchamber window, I watched and waited until the girls discovered their mother. Oh what joy! Their faces were aghast as they entered to behold Sarah and Belle tied over the bedstead – naked! But better still than the starkness was the embellishment; both girls burst into shocked laughter at the sight of those two lovely bottoms, criss-crossed with weals, their tight, brown rings encompassing the biggest carrots I had been able to spirit from the kitchen! Cursing and swearing, Sarah insisted the girls untie them without delay, which they kindly did, after Clara had retrieved the garnish from Belle's bottom, and Elizabeth, from her mother's.

Ere the shouts and screams filled the air, I ran back to the yard and took to the stables. Within minutes, my name could be heard echoing across the countryside. Sarah was, indeed, a most furious lady – and she was on the warpath! I saw fit to allow her some half-hour or so to calm herself ere finding her in the study with the girls. 'A letter, Sarah,' I said, smiling at all three. Her face turned redder than a beetroot as she snatched the envelope from my hand and ordered me to go. 'I believe that you will be wanting to speak with me after you have read the letter,' I whispered mysteriously, whereupon she ordered the girls to leave.

'How I enjoyed our games in the cottage,' I commented as she began to read the letter. 'We really must do it again some day.'

'I will kill you for what you . . .' Stopping in mid-sentence, she moved the letter nearer to her widening eyes.

'What have you been up to now!' she screeched. 'My God! Do you realise what it is that you have done? By provoking Lord Cranfield you have . . .'

She tailed off as her countenance took on an aspect of near terror. Her hands shook and she clutched at her stomach and, for a moment, I thought she would faint.

'What is it?' I asked, moving towards her. 'Are you ill?'

'I can see no way out of this, Tom! You must leave this house with all haste!'

'But I like it here. I love . . .'

'I do not believe you realise the seriousness of the situation! You have discovered one or two things concerning myself, that is problematic, to say the least. But now, it seems, you have discovered, or are trying to discover, things about others. Lord Cranfield is a most influential man, Tom! He will not stand by and allow your questioning to continue.'

'Then, pray, what will he do?'

'Kill you, more than likely!'

'He is too old!'

'He will pay others to do away with you, you fool! You are too young to be involved. You dabble in things of which you have no understanding. You and your stupid games of blackmail, your puerile games . . . you are but eighteen or so, a mere boy, and you have caused so much . . . Oh, you are such a fool!'

It was true that I knew not what I had involved myself in. I had enjoyed the females, the fun and games, and had taken a liking to the lifestyle. But I was no fool for wanting that! Would not anyone in their right mind crave such a lifestyle, where money and plentiful sex with young fillies were no problem?

I told Sarah that I had read the letter, to which she replied again that I should take my leave and never return. 'For your own safety!' she implored, although I could not for the life of me think why, for she had already said that she herself would kill me.

'There must be a way out of this without my having to run?' I enquired.

'Then, tell me of the way out, for I know of no way at all! To be honest, should I know a way, I would not tell you! You have caused so much trouble in so short a time that I . . . Just go, Tom! Go now, while you can!'

Again, being young and foolish, I repaired to see Belle at the cottage. She was most displeased to see me, forcing me to push my way through the door to gain entry. She was tearful and said nothing as I sat down and asked her what she knew of the affair.

'Nothing!' was her only reply.

'May I sleep here tonight?' I asked.

'No!'

'Good, then I shall settle down on the sofa, for I am tired.'

'You will do no such thing!' she yelled, but I took little notice as she retired to her bedchamber and locked the door.

So heavy with worry was my mind that I barely slept that night. I had tried Belle's door several times, hoping to salve my anxieties with the nectar of lust, but, predictably, it had remained locked. As the sun rose, I left the cottage and led Giant from the stable. My thoughts were with Amy, but I was in two minds as to whether or not to go to the hill. I was in no mood for love; or rather, I was apprehensive, if not frightened, at the possibility of several bloodthirsty young farm hands awaiting my arrival! I am sorry to say that this fear prevailed over the prospect of a good fucking with my sweet Amy, and I decided instead to clear my head before Cranfield's assembly with an exhilarating gallop through the woods.

At length, finding myself in a field some half a mile away from Cranfield's manor, I allowed Giant to graze, for he was sweating badly, as was I, in my case in anticipation of the forthcoming event. Eleven o'clock seemed a lifetime away and, in order to kill time, I decided upon a leisurely stroll to the manor.

By nine, I was settled in an appropriate hiding place in the bushes, with the manor clearly in view. Three people, none of whom I recognised, arrived at ten, followed by another half-dozen unknown ladies and gentlemen in the course of the next hour – and then Lady Miles! I had planned to wait until the meeting was over but I was concerned, for Sarah was conspicuous by her absence, and so I returned to Giant with all haste.

Upon my return to the manor, I was mystified to discover that Sarah, the girls and Belle had gone – I knew not where. The battle-axe summoned me to her kitchen, screeching across the yard as I wandered back from the cottage in search of Belle.

'What do you want of me?' I rasped as she closed the kitchen door.

'You find yourself in trouble?'

'It would appear that way,' I replied, eyeing the fresh bread and cheese upon the table.

''Elp yourself,' she said, pushing the bread towards me. I thanked her kindly, for I was most hungry, having missed both the evening meal and breakfast.

'I don't like you,' she continued.

'Why, you astound me! I should not have guessed so!'

'But I know what you're after and, possibly, 'ow you can get it. *Possibly*, mind.'

'Then pray tell me!'

227

'Search in the lady's bedchamber. You'll find a book with no middle in it. And that's all I'm sayin'.'

I did not question the battle-axe further as she had turned her back on me again in her usual manner, no longer even acknowledging my presence. A strange woman, indeed! She had, obviously, never experienced the delights of a man's cock deep within her cunt, if, indeed, she possessed one. Let alone in her bottom-hole.

Without finishing my food, I left the kitchen and dashed to Sarah's bedchamber. After searching through a stack of books, taking pains to replace each one exactly as I had found it, there it was, the very one in question. Inside were some papers, most of which, on inspection, related to the manor. But at the bottom of the small pile of title deeds and the like lay something of real worth – a certificate of birth concerning one Lord James Hadleigh, born of Lord Archibald Hadleigh and Lady Sarah Hadleigh.

I could not for the life of me imagine what relevance the certificate held for me; indeed, I had never even heard of the mysterious James Hadleigh. But there were no other papers of interest whatsoever, and I assumed that the battle-axe must have had the certificate in mind on direct-ing me to the book. But why? I had not a clue, not about this mystery nor what to do with the document itself. 'Shall I take it?' I pondered. 'Or simply tell Sarah that I know of its existence?'

There was no time to answer my own question for a terrible commotion suddenly erupted in the front hall. Stuffing the certificate in my pocket, I fled the room and crept out through the back door. At the front of the house, Sarah was shouting and yelling at the girls, so I took it upon myself to steal through the shrubs in an effort to discover what was afoot. 'You *will* go to finishing school, young lady!' Sarah screeched. 'Just because Clara is indisposed to go, it does not mean to say that you will not!'

At that opportune moment, a carriage drew up and out stepped Lord Cranfield. After she had dismissed the girls, I heard Sarah apologise for her absence at the meeting and enquire of Lord Cranfield as to its outcome.

'Ere we discuss the meeting, I wish to know what this young man is to you, Sarah,' he began.

'He was a stable lad until . . .'

'So, what is he to you now?'

'Tom is . . . shall we say . . .'

To my utter annoyance, Clara came bounding around the angle of the house with Elizabeth in hot pursuit. They did not see me, thank God, but their mother ushered Lord Cranfield into the house to continue their conversation. I was left, not only fuming, but confused and greatly worried!

Once in the hayloft, I contemplated the certificate of birth. Who was Lord James Hadleigh? It appeared he was just a few months older than myself. He must have been Sarah's son, I surmised, for the real Lady Hadleigh could not bear children. Yet the girls had never mentioned having a brother. Should I be able to locate him, he could perforce return to the manor and . . . But, no! He might throw me out! My mind swam with questions. Where was he? He could well be abroad; it then occurred to me that he might not even be living, yet there was no certificate of death.

Amidst the hay, I confused myself greatly with my different computations and answers to the question of the certificate and its relevance to my problems. Yet, happily,

Ray Gordon

I still found space to accommodate thoughts of the enchanting Rose. We would meet near the entrance to the wood, wherein I would entice her to walk to the clearing. There, I would lay her upon the cropped grass and lift her skirts and remove her underclothes and suck the pleasure from her, ere filling her with my joy. Yes, better thoughts by far with which to fill my head.

But first, I had Amy to attend to. My cock rose in sweet anticipation of the ecstasy that lay before me. Reclining in the hay to enjoy my fantasies I curbed my desire to take myself in hand and loose my seed there and then, for was it not in demand by a line of lovely ladies waiting to be filled?

Chapter Fourteen

Amy sat upright upon her horse, her breasts forward, her head high – all the deportment of a fine young lady. She was displeased with me, for I had not honoured my promise to meet her upon the hill the previous morning. But, I detected, she appeared positively fearful rather than just displeased.

'I am sorry I did not . . . I was troubled of mind,' I began.

'I surmised as much,' she replied, her expression anxious and her colour pale.

'What do you know of my troubles?' I asked.

'Mother attended a meeting concerning you, Tom. A fellow guest at the meeting returned home with her, and I overheard them speaking of you.'

'Pray, tell me – what was said?'

'It seems that you have stumbled across some truths that certain people wish you had not. The daughter of Lord and Lady Cranfield is to lure you to a lonely spot in the wood where . . . Well, I know not the details, but you must promise me not to go!'

Looking plainly distressed, the sweet thing broke down and cried as she dismounted and flung her arms around my neck. I had not the heart to impart to her that my meeting with Rose was arranged for that very afternoon, for she was suffering enough already.

Rose, clever Rose! She had planned and lied so well that I could not let her down. I would, indeed, meet her as arranged for our walk. But it would lead us, not through the wood, where, no doubt, my assailants would be lying in wait, but to some other secluded spot, near the edge of the wood perhaps, where she would receive her punishment. For did not such churlish behaviour require chastisement?

As to Sarah – how could she allow me to walk into a trap? Could she simply stand by and do nothing as I took the path to my death? Perhaps she was ignorant of the plan, for she had not attended the assembly. But she must surely have known of the plot, for had not Lord Cranfield visited her to reveal all? Oh Sarah, how sadly wrong things had gone between us!

Amy lay upon her back on the heath and gazed up at me. Taking my place at her side, I asked of her mother.

'Mother has been most pleasant, I do not understand why. Tell me, Tom, what words passed between you after I had gone?'

'Nothing that concerns you, my angel. But I am pleased that she has permitted you to meet me here, knowing full well what we are about!'

'For some reason, it seems that she has no choice, Tom. What *did* you say to her?'

'I will tell you – one fine day. Be happy that we are together.'

True enough, Lady Miles had no choice, for should her husband discover her dreadful secret, he would undoubtedly dismiss her as a whore and view his daughter in a very different light. However, I had it in my mind that Amy's mother might appear at any moment and confiscate my pleasure, so, without further ado, I lifted the girl's skirts to uncover a most welcome surprise – she wore no knickers!

I do declare that the beauteous sight which met my eyes near caused me to swoon with desire, for her dark thicket was now no more than a sparsely vegetated, shadowy mound, revealing in good measure her slit and sweet, pink inner folds of flesh. 'Do you like me thus?' she asked earnestly as I feasted my eyes upon the soft banks each side of her valley.

'You have done a fine job, Amy! What possessed you to take the scissors to yourself thus?'

''Twas done in a moment of great arousal. I was in my room, attending my clitoris, and, I must confess, I desired to do something naughty – this is the result.'

'Then, when you feel naughty again, erase every hair, that I may view your full intimacy!' I urged excitedly.

'I nearly did, Tom, for the notion arouses me greatly. But I was uncertain as to your reaction.'

'My reaction is one of great delight!'

'Then upon my return home I will forthwith remove every last hair!'

So wondrous was the thought of her mound totally naked that my cock refused to rest. It was then I had cause to remember the uncanny length of her nipples and so made haste to free them from the restriction of her clothing. I had just begun to unbutton her dress front, when she took my hand to halt me. 'What is it?' I asked. 'Are we not to love?'

'I wish to be naked, Tom,' she whispered, standing to remove her frock. I lay on the heath, gazing up at the beauty standing over me as she slipped the garment from her curvaceous frame. Her brassiere unclipped, it fell to the ground, her breasts ballooning, silhouetted against the blue sky. Rounded and full, with nipples of such wondrous length, they eclipsed the sun and cast a shadow o'er my eyes. Such breasts I had never seen before and could barely wait to bury my head betwixt them.

Placing her feet either side of my head, she squatted, lowering her slit to within inches of my face. Pulling her down, I sat her upon my open mouth and licked and sucked at the hot flesh. Aroused and wetter than ever, she was; oh, the sheer ecstasy her juices imparted as I drank! Easing her lips apart with my fingers, I sank my tongue into her depths, causing an even more prolific flow of juice to seep from her body and course over my face. Rearranging her hips, she boldly presented her hard, erect clitoris to my sticky mouth.

'I am so happy that my pussy is to your liking, Tom,' she whispered as she rocked to and fro upon my hungry lips.

I could not reply for I was fully engaged in sucking at her clitoris, her pinken folds. Shuddering and moaning, she pressed her drenched cunt all the harder to my face.

'I pleasured myself, as you instructed,' she gasped, pushing herself down the more until I could scarce breathe. Again, I could not respond for my mouth was filled with her folds, her juice of love. 'I did it every day! With my fingers, I took myself to heaven whilst thinking of you!' she rasped, lost in some wondrous fantasy of lust.

I sensed her bud throbbing against my tongue as she began to shake and writhe, still pursuing her recollection. 'I did it in my bed, Tom!' she cried. 'I put my fingers inside my hole and thought of you there, deep inside, and I creamed myself when my eruption came – I creamed

myself and cried out for the most painful pleasure my cunt
brought!'

God, what words! What images did she conjure as she
reached her climax and lost herself within my mouth.
'Cream yourself now!' I pleaded, pulling away momentarily. Her words mumbled and incoherent, she breathed and
gasped and spasmed her muscles.

Ah, how wonderful her flow of come juice as it poured
forth and gushed upon my face! How she threw back her
head, crying her thanks to the goddess of love! Pushing her
buttocks up for a better view, held some ten inches above
my face, I watched the pulsating cunt lips dribbling their
creamy, precious flow onto my eager lips and chin.

Finally, the flow ceased, leaving her cropped hairs
suspending globules of the milky nectar. Pulling her down
again, I licked and sucked at the irrigated mound, preening
and drying it with my lips. Then downwards to the
entrance of her womb, sticky and wet with her milky fluid,
where my lips closed over the hole of love and I sucked
until she was dry there. At length, I licked her full slit;
from her lovely, tight bottom-hole to the end of her valley,
just below her belly, I licked and cleansed her.

Releasing my belt, I pushed my breeches down in
readiness to climb upon the young Amy and slip my cock
betwixt the lips of her cunt. Without a word of instruction,
she slid her open body down over my belly and sat with my
cock splaying her swollen cunny lips as she began to rub
her clitoris back and forth along the length of my shaft. She
was so hot, wetter than ever by that time, and nearing
another climax. Faster and faster she rode my cock until
she began to gasp and claw her nails into my chest. The
moment she began to shake with ecstasy I pushed my cock

deeper into her tunnel, stretching it wide to pump my sperm inside. She gripped me hard and strong with her muscles of lust, squeezing the juices from my balls as she bounced up and down upon my belly, screaming and swearing her undying love for me upon the hill-top – our hill-top.

Done, she slid from my cock and collapsed beside me on the heath, trembling and kissing my knob in appreciation. Taking the end within her virginal mouth, she sucked it clean and caused it to swell again, to press against her tongue. Would she drink my fruits? I wondered, as she undulated her head, using her mouth as she would the tube of her vagina. I could not hold back and spurted my sperm to the back of her throat as she rolled my balls in her hand and moaned softly. Though she coughed and spluttered a little, she took the unaccustomed offering gladly, ere pulling away and licking her wet lips. Then, tenderly, she hoisted up and buttoned my breeches before lying beside me, thanking me no end for the pleasure I had brought her. Her pleasure! Poor Amy, she could not even imagine what joy I had received! But I acknowledged her gratitude, promising ever greater pleasures each time we met upon the hill. I told her, too, that she should continue to pleasure herself in the warmth of her bed and tell me every detail upon our next meeting. To my delight, the sweet Amy promised that she would do even better and write, explicitly, of her times alone in her bed and, after one week, give me her notes in book form for my keeping.

As she dressed, I reminded her of her promise to remove all the growth from betwixt her legs 'that I may see your full beauty, unobliterated.' She promised from the bottom of her heart to please me so, adding that she would do anything for me. Immediately, my thoughts turned to her bottom-hole, but she was now clad. Upon our next meeting, I promised myself, I would take my pleasure there, betwixt her buttocks, deep within her bowels.

Yet another tick to my list, I mused, as she rode off down the hill, her face burning with the pleasures she had received, her bottom bouncing in the saddle and, no doubt, her cunny oozing with my sperm. Her figure grew smaller as she rode across the heath towards her house, to her mother who, I was sure, would be anxiously awaiting her daughter's return. But she would be able to say nothing, to ask not one question about the girl's time with me. Ah, but she could imagine, picture her girl being taken, fucked upon the heath and brought to sexual heights that the miserable woman had long since forgotten – if ever she had known them!

When Amy had disappeared from view, my thoughts turned to the day ahead, to the wicked Rose and the plot to entrap me deep in the wood. How her father could conceive of using his daughter's body to capture me was beyond my comprehension; for was not employing his daughter's body to his own ends what he was about? Pity the man who could consider such! But his plan would fail miserably, though his daughter's body, poor, sweet thing, would, indeed, be used – to my own ends! Ah, a mental note – add Rose to my list of conquests!

Having returned Giant to the stable, unobserved by Belle, I am pleased to say, I washed quickly in the horse trough, for what with the heat of the day, I was by then somewhat high with the sweat of my exertions. I bathed my cock, too, lovingly washing Amy's sticky milk from the knob in readiness to stir Rose's sweet pot.

Creeping off to the wood, I grabbed one or two items on my way, of which I will tell later, in preparation for the great event. It was not yet the appointed hour and I had time to locate a perfectly secluded clearing on the far edge of the wood, well away from the main paths. No doubt Rose would suggest that we take a certain direction for our walk, but I would sidetrack her and, hopefully, confuse her sense of direction – and my own, more than likely!

Atop a high tree, not far from our meeting place, I could see for miles around me. The rolling countryside was so far removed from the stench of London – and the country ladies far more accommodating! My father had done me a great favour by ousting me and I made a note to tell him so, if ever we should meet again.

As I took in the view, I did spy several figures in the distance, one of whom I perceived, on nearing, to be the delectable Rose, accompanied by her father and four young men – farm hands, no doubt, come to do their dirty deed. Leaving Rose, after some discussion, they made their way into the wood as I descended the tree.

'Ah, Rose, I am so pleased you have come,' I greeted her on her approach.

'Good afternoon, Tom,' she smiled, her thin, low-cut summer frock showing off all too well a fine cleavage, no doubt designed to entice me to follow her. What sort of girl could this be? I pondered. So fine, so lady-like, and yet . . . no matter, for was she not to bring me great pleasure?

We commenced our walk, as I had suspected, with Rose leading the way. After some minutes I decided to put my plan into action. 'I must show you something of great interest, Rose,' I told her, taking her elbow and leading her to a small side path.

'No, no! We . . . we must go this way, for . . .'

'It will take but minutes, and then we will go wheresoever you wish!' I assured her. She followed me, rather apprehensively, into the thicket where, after some time, I admitted to being lost.

'The entrance to the wood is that way,' I exclaimed, pointing in the direction of my lair.

'Yes, I do believe you are right!'

No sooner did we enter the small clearing than she lifted her skirts as if in readiness to flee. 'Pray where do you go in such haste?' I enquired, grabbing her arm. 'Have you seen a snake?'

'I must . . . I have to . . .' She looked about her, her wide eyes darting this way and that, then mirroring dismay in the realisation that she had led me not into the clearing where Cranfield's men awaited, but to one some distance away.

Seizing my chance of lechery, I pulled her close and began to kiss her full lips. Fight and bang my chest with her fists and call for her father she did to no avail, for we were too distant to be heard. Pulling her to the ground, I tore the dress from her frenzied body and bared her breasts. 'They are fine nipples!' I laughed, pinching the teats betwixt my fingers and tweaking them skywards to lift her breasts into cones.

'What are you doing?' she screamed as I wrenched off her frilly knickers and cupped her bushy mound in my hand.

'And a fine cunt!' I laughed. 'What a shame your father and his cronies are not here to see such a fine little specimen as you have betwixt your pretty legs! Perhaps I should call them, and they can take you in turn rather than beat me! I am sure I can strike such a deal.'

'I know not of what you speak! I came but to walk with you, and you treat me thus!'

'No, you did believe that you led me into a trap! But, my lovely, *I* have snared *you*!'

Quite a fight she put up, I vouch, but all too soon she lay upon the short grass – naked as the day she was born! From nearby bushes I retrieved the items I had previously secreted and her countenance registered sheer terror as she gazed wide-eyed at my spoils – a length of rope and a riding crop. Lifting her from the grass I held her against the tree; oh, what joy to tether a naked girl to a tree, her soft breasts pressed against the rough bark, her slender legs wrapped around the trunk, and her fleshy buttocks bared! Plead and lie and beg for mercy as she did, nothing could stop me now.

Tapping her buttocks with the crop, I waited with excitement for her fear to rise ere commencing the beating, delighting in her pathetic pleas and promises of money and gifts in return for her freedom. As I landed the first blow, the skin of her twitching, magnificently rounded buttocks instantly reddened, glowing enticingly in the shafts of sunlight falling through the branches overhanging the clearing. I am not ashamed to confess that such a sight filled me with most rampant desire and before you could say John Thomas, I had exchanged the crop in favour of my hard cock. She could not see what I was about, but she soon learned, only too well, when I stabbed at her cunny lips with my rigid knob.

'No, no! Please do not!' she cried.

'Why, are you a virgin? Then you must be broken in, my sweet Rose! And, if not, you will enjoy my cock within your cunt!' Ere she could answer, I pushed my cock home, deep into the hot, tight depths of her heavenly body. 'Ah, you are so tight!' I breathed, nibbling at her shoulders. 'You like my cock in your hole, do you not?'

'I do not! Please, withdraw immediately!'

'But I have not yet filled you with my nectar, my sweet flower! I cannot take it out until you are full to the brim, to the lips that encompass my shaft so tightly!'

In fear of her father's men searching the wood and discovering us, I lost not a minute and fucked her hard against the tree. How she wriggled as I fucked and rammed into her! And how she despised my commentary!

'My knob is right up your hole! And now my finger is in your bottom, deep inside your bottom-hole! Have you ever had a finger up there? Or a cock? Have you? Ah, here comes the nectar to fill you, my petal! Here it comes! The hot, gushing nectar! Argh! How I fuck your lovely cunt!'

Poor Rose, she had well and truly been taken. I had, indeed, filled her vaginal cavern to the brim with my sperm. She sobbed a little as I withdrew and stood back to admire my prey. Her hips were nicely curved and her buttocks well formed and I decided to make the most of my prisoner. Kneeling before her bottom, I splayed her buttocks to reveal her tiny hole.

'No, no!' she pleaded as I pushed a finger inside and massaged the hot flesh within. 'Please! Please, no!'

'Is that not to your liking? Would you prefer that I push my tongue in there?' I taunted, relinquishing my finger and licking at the hole.

'No, please!'

'My cock then?' I pursued, rising to my feet. 'That will be to your liking, I am sure!'

Withdrawing the skin to expose the bulbous, purple knob of my weapon, I pressed it to the ring of tight, brown flesh and drove it home. She cried out, filling the wood with her threats as I rooted myself to the hilt ere beginning the motions of lust. 'And now I fuck your bottom-hole – hard!' I gasped, biting upon her shoulders and gripping her tiny waist.

'Take it out, please! I cannot bear it in there!'

Quickly, I pumped her full of my seed, ramming, pummelling her delicate body with my rigid member until I was fully drained and she oozed my cream from both holes. Withdrawing my flaccid shaft, I buttoned my breeches and sat upon the grass to rest and gaze at the delightful filly, tied and bound to the tree.

'You are now a true woman!' I laughed. 'A virgin no more!'

'And you are a cruel, inhuman beast to violate a young girl's body so! Now, untie me, please!'

Releasing her used, trembling body, I laid her upon the grass. 'I may as well enjoy you, sir, for my father cannot blame me for being taken so,' she whimpered as she extended her hand for me to join her. God! Are fledgling women never to be satisfied? Is their lust truly insatiable? I could scarce believe her words, unlike my trusty cock which, most fortunately, rose in an instant.

'How right you are, my flower. I will fuck you again, for I like you – even though you would see me dead!'

'They were only to beat you – to frighten you away, no more,' she enlightened me, spreading her arms and legs in readiness for lust. How curvaceous her body, how ample her breasts, and how inviting her lovely wet slit! Once more sliding my cock between her swollen cunt lips, I pushed in to the portal of her womb whilst she exclaimed and writhed and pulled on my buttocks to aid penetration with each thrust.

'You have done this before!' I observed.

'Many, many times!' she laughed.

'But that is simply unfair! I thought you were a virgin; prim, proper, and as pure as the driven snow!'

'I am far from a virgin!' she gasped as her cunt gripped tightly around my shaft. 'There is not a hole in my body that has not been filled with a man's seed – time and time over!'

How misguided can a man be? With the curious revelation, I fucked her all the better for knowing that my performance should bear comparisons. For the young Rose would, I hoped, become a regular fuck in the wood, with the achievement of every feasible trick by our second meeting! I would have spent more time with the girl, but, as my sperm flowed into her womb, I discerned shouts coming from the thicket. 'I must make haste!' I panted, pulling my cock from the hotness of her cunny. 'For death stalks ever the nearer!'

'I shall meet you again?' she enquired, pulling on the remnants of her dress.

'You will not be allowed from the house when your father sees your attire so!'

'I will lie. I am a good liar. I will say I slipped and fell down a wooded hillside. Tomorrow, meet me here – please!'

'You will be alone?'

'But of course!'

'Then I shall be here – at the same hour!'

At a suitable distance from the clearing I climbed a tree and awaited the young men whose voices were, by that time, loud and clear. I could see Rose, straightening her hair and her dress as they approached. 'What has he done to you?' her father yelled as he broke through the bushes into the clearing.

'I fell, father! I slipped and fell down a bank!'

'Then, where is he?'

'We were separated, father. He was playing at hiding from me, and we were separated.'

The young Rose was, indeed, an accomplished liar. I prayed that she had not lied to me, and that she would come alone to our meeting on the morrow, for her father's men were ruffians, to say the least!

When the gathering had dispersed, I climbed from the tree and made my way home, to find Sarah beside herself with worry. Pacing the yard like an insane woman, shouting at the girls and Belle, she saw me and came running.

'Are you all right, Tom?'

'Why, yes, I am fine!'

'Where on God's earth have you been?'

'Working in the far field. I suppose you thought that I would be hanging from a tree by now?'

'To be honest with you, I had rather hoped that you had left!'

'Ah, your tune changes with the wind! Do you hate me or love me at this moment?'

'I hate you, for you cause me one worry upon another! What do you mean – hanging from a tree?'

'Your little plan to be rid of me, that is what I talk of! The band of men sent into the wood to disembowel me!'

'You talk in riddles again: have you been out in the midday sun? Or are you deranged? The latter, I suspect!'

'I have not been in the midday sun, nor am I deranged! I am clever, Sarah. More clever than you believe!'

'You are stupid, for you have riled many people! I am not surprised to hear that a band of men, as you put it, has been after you!'

'Can you help me?'

'I cannot help you, for there is nothing I can do to put right your stupidity!'

'Then I will wash and change for dinner. I will be dining with you this evening, will I not?'

'You will go to hell!'

Belle was even less friendly than Sarah, near pushing me through the doorway as I tried to enter the cottage and hurling expletives at me on my polite enquiry as to the possibility of some sort of nourishment.

'I am leaving, Belle, and I have simply come to bid you farewell,' I lied. Quietening down somewhat, she offered to share her meal. 'Where are you going?'

'I know not where. But, as I am not wanted here . . .'

'It is not simply that you are not wanted, Tom. You have upset Sarah, and me – everyone, it seems.'

'Who is "everyone"?'

'Sarah said that you have upset her neighbours. Apparently, you have been asking about titles and . . .'

'Half of them have no titles!'

'Sarah will be sad to see you go.'

'Sarah will be only too pleased to be rid of me!'

'Clara and Elizabeth will be sad, too.'

'No, no. Clara is with child and . . .'

'With child!'

Ah, my big mouth! But no matter, for the time to leave, I felt, really was nigh. All was lost, it seemed. Belle, tearful-eyed, looked down at her plate. I had hurt her deeply, for she truly did love me. But she would recover eventually, I knew, and I took her hand.

'Yes, with my child,' I sighed, and smiled.

'Then you must stay, surely?'

'No, no.'

'Does Sarah know?'

'Yes, of course. But I must go, for I will not be missed. Do not misunderstand me, though. I would love to stay and make amends, but . . . There is no way, it is not possible.'

My charm, or, should I say, my sob story, was working well. I was sure that Sarah had confided in belle, told her of some secret that could enable me to further blackmail her, that she could help me stay without fear of Cranfield. But it seemed not, for Belle knew nothing of a son born to the Hadleighs; not that I broached the question directly, but it was clear that she knew less than I. Thus I cut short my questioning and finished my food ere returning to the manor house in search of Sarah.

I was determined to stay at the manor, to take all the lovely girls in turn and continue with the life I had come to love. And there was only one way, in my mind, at least, to discover more about the certificate of birth which, I was sure, held the key to my problems. To ask Sarah outright could only lead to an argument, so subtlety was the answer. For if all failed, I would have no choice other than to leave. I would be in need of money, and cursing Sarah would not bring me one penny.

The battle-axe hurled one of her looks of despite in my

direction as I passed the kitchen door. She knew the answer I sought, but I would have to near kill her to prise it from her! Not a bad idea, I thought, for she was that miserable a soul, she would probably find more happiness in eternal hell!

Sarah was in the drawing room arranging some flowers, and I spied through the crack in the door ere knocking, for she was in conversation with Clara.

'There is no way that Tom can stay,' Sarah insisted.

'But there must be, mother! I am to have his child: surely there is a way that you can put all to rights?'

'Clara, were there a way, I should not employ it, for he has treated me, all of us, so badly! Many times he has tried to place his feet firmly under the table. Can you but imagine him living here? It would be hell for all concerned!'

'Not for me, mother – I love him.'

'You know not what love is, girl!'

'No less than you, mother!'

Clara rushed from the room sobbing as I pressed myself against the wall in an effort to hide. Fortunately, she did not see me as she fled to her bedchamber. 'Sarah, I am leaving,' I announced on entering the room.

'Leaving? Oh, good, I am pleased that you have come to your senses, at long last!'

'But, ere I go, answer me one question, will you?'

'If I can.'

'Do you love me?'

'Do not be ridiculous!'

'Who is . . .'

'One question, Tom, and one only. Now . . .'

'Who is Lord James Hadleigh?'

Subtlety is not, after all, my strong point, I fear. Sarah's mouth dropped and her face took on an awful greyish colour, as with the dead. She sat down, or rather, near collapsed, upon the sofa.

'There is no such person!' she eventually replied, all too obviously terror-stricken.

'I think that there is!'

'Then your thinking is wrong! Now, leave me, for I feel suddenly ill.'

'You *look* ill, Sarah! Are you dying? If so, from what, I wonder? Guilt?'

I left her sitting there, alone on the sofa, and made my way to the hayloft. She would search the book with no middle and discover that the certificate had gone. But, no matter, for I was at the end of the line. I could do nothing, other than take my leave of Royston Manor. That, or fall into the hands of Lord Cranfield's ruffians.

I did not believe Rose. They meant to kill me, I was sure. Maybe she was ignorant of that; perhaps they had said that they intended only to frighten me off. But I was sure – they were out for my blood.

Chapter Fifteen

My ride to the hill-top early the following morning was solemn, for I had it in mind to say goodbye to young Amy. The time had come, I thought, to take my leave and find work elsewhere, for Royston Manor was now void of my dreams. Sarah hated me and the fulfilment of my ambition to attain squireship seemed more remote than ever. Even should it succeed, I asked myself, would I relish lordship of the manor without the love of Sarah?

Not wishing to speak with her before taking my leave I had decided to return Giant and collect my belongings ere she was risen. The girls, too, would be unaware of my departure until some time during the day. I am not one for goodbyes, particularly when leaving such a flock of young beauties. But Amy, I felt, deserved a farewell, for she had fought her mother to spend time with me. Besides, her shaven slit was not to be wasted!

My crumpled list of achievements was in my pocket and, as I sat upon the heath awaiting her arrival, I unfolded the paper and smiled as I counted the ticks against each maiden's name. Alas, there was one poor girl's bottom-hole that yet remained intact – the sweet Amy's.

At length she arrived, later than usual, leaping from her horse to greet me. 'I am sorry I am late, Tom,' she smiled as she sat beside me. 'I had something to do ere I left.'

'And what was that, pray?'

Lifting her skirts, she opened her legs to proudly display her shaven slit. What a joyous sight! Smooth, naked lips, glowing with passion, little pinken folds protruding as young birds in the nest awaiting food. Quite unable to help myself, I buried my face there to breathe in the warm scent and feel the softness upon my skin. 'You are happy with my bare pussy, then?' she breathed.

'More then happy, for never before have I beheld such femininity, such rare beauty!'

'Then suck me there, Tom. For I have long awaited this moment, and thought much of it whilst pleasuring myself in my bed.'

Lying back, she opened the delectable lips with her slender fingers to allow my tongue access to the delights hidden within. Oh, Amy, bidding farewell to this wonder betwixt your thighs was torture! Why, oh why does life take such cruel turns?

Her clitoris growing larger than ever before, I took it between my lips to elicit its pleasure – for the last time. My sweet Amy writhed and parted her lips so far asunder that I feared the reddening flesh would tear! Her bud throbbed and her cunny oozed its juices as she cried and begged me to pleasure her so every morning till she died.

My cock rigid, the knob swollen, my balls heavy and full, the time had come to fill my angel with love. Rolling her over, I raised her hips to spy her lovely bottom-hole, my rising lust near forcing me to run my shaft straight into that little haven! But, no, her cunny yet awaited my attention. It was necessary to be patient, wait at the doorstep, until such time as she was aroused enough to embrace me inside her sacred portal.

Her cunette was hot and juicy and her shaven lips encircled my shaft with a new, child-like innocence that drove me wild with lust. She worked her hips, round and round, back and forth, taking the fucking with all she had until she shuddered and crushed my shaft, so that it was as much as I could do to reserve my fruits. Once done, she lay prostrate upon her stomach, my cock slipping from its home as she did so, hovering erect over the dark crevice of her bottom.

Kissing her buttocks, I parted them and ran my tongue around the little entrance. Poor, unsuspecting Amy knew not that I made ready for penetration and wiggled with delight as I pushed the tip of my tongue into the brown ring. When she was wet there I raised her middle once more and slipped my cock deep into her cunny. Well-juiced for my mission, I relinquished the glistening shaft from its customary sheath and, without a second's delay, plunged it straight into her bottom.

'What are you doing?' she cried. 'Tom, that is not where . . .'

'Hold tight, my angel, for you will remember this for the rest of your days!' I promised, pushing my length deep inside the heat of her bowels.

'No, no! Do not . . . Ah! Ah! Yes, yes!'

Allowing herself the unknown pleasures of her bottom, she gasped and moaned long, deep sounds of euphoria. 'That is nice, Tom! Oh, that is heavenly!' Her words stiffened my cock until the veins bulged and the head ballooned and ached to explode. But Amy's pleasure was of as much import as mine, and I rested, with just the head of my cock rooted in the stretched hole. As she wriggled her hips gently, round and round her bottom swung, working the pleasure from her hole until she was in such a frenzy that she frigged her clitoris as I pressed my full weapon into her body.

Too soon, the explosion came, my knob pumping and throbbing as I filled her, she screaming with the euphoria her engorged clitoris conjured until we both near died with lust. Gasping, panting, heaving, we quivered together in a state of collapse. Lying across her buttocks I stilled myself, her bottom-hole impaled, her fingers gently caressing the last wave of ecstasy from her bud. We were done.

'You will take me so again on the morrow?' she pleaded through her gasps, her fingers trembling betwixt her cunny lips.

'I will, my angel! I will take you so every day for the rest of my life!' I promised as her muscles twitched and my knob gave one last shudder within her bottom.

Another problem – even in paradise. How could I leave this heaven? Rose expected me that very afternoon for a session of wanton lust in the wood; the girls could not survive without my attention, I was sure, and had I not heard with my own ears Clara informing her mother that she had found love for me? Belle, poor Belle, she, too, could not live without her stud! As to Sarah – she alone was the one who had disrupted and destroyed my life!

'I am still writing my notes, Tom,' Amy whispered, wriggling 'neath my steaming body. I withdrew my spent cock, allowing her bottom-hole to shrink and close. 'I have written of every explicit detail and you shall read all, very soon.'

'I can barely wait, my angel!'

The sun, now higher in the sky, shone upon the puffed

lips of her cunt as she turned to lie upon her back. Gazing at her naked slit, the glistening pinken folds lying open and wet with the juice of our union, I leaned over her soft belly to lap up the sticky nectar as she closed her eyes and sighed deeply. Parting her thighs, she held my head in her lovely hands and moved me up and down, directing my tongue here and there as her fancy took her until she gasped and, yet again, approached euphoria. 'It is coming now, Tom!' she breathed. 'Ah, it comes again and takes me!' Her bare lips folded o'er my mouth, her clitoris pulsating upon my tongue, her thighs crushing my neck and near drowning me in her milk, I deemed I could not leave the delights I had discovered – I would rather die first!

Quickly composing myself, for I had much to do, I kissed her sweet mouth and rose to my feet. With a promise to meet her on the morrow, I mounted Giant and raced across the heath like a madman, leaving the poor girl bewildered, her skirts pulled high over her belly and her wondrous crack bathed in the heat of the sun.

'I must speak with you!' I called, spying Sarah on entering the yard.

'I have nothing to say!' she returned, picking up her skirts and scurrying to the house.

Such was my fury, I near tore the drawing-room door from its hinges as I burst in. 'You have the answer to my predicament!' I raged. 'You can put an end to this farce, and keep those ruffians from me!'

'I can do nothing!' she screeched, moving towards me, her face afire with hatred.

'Where is Lord James Hadleigh? I shall seek him out and return him here to the manor and . . .'

'I have not seen James for eight years or more! We fell

out, and he betook himself to some foreign land – I know not where.'

'Then you admit to having a son?'

'Yes, certainly. But the girls know not of his existence and . . .'

'Why do they not? Surely, he is approximately of the same age? Did they not grow up together?'

'He was away during his childhood. His father, Lord Hadleigh, was not . . .'

'Was not what? His real father?'

'Yes, he was his real father – unlike the girls.'

My mind reeled. How could she have participated in a deed so perverse as to bear her own father's child? The poor boy would surely be a cruel freak of nature! What sort of vile people would do such deeds? Unable to contain my rage any longer I threw the hussy to the floor and leapt upon her. Her dress torn away, her breasts bared, I sucked fiercely upon them and bit them until she cried out for mercy. 'The truth! Tell me the truth!' I yelled.

'I have told you! You know the truth!'

I had to hear the words from her own mouth. Something blazing within me demanded that she tell the truth and I ripped asunder her dress, her knickers and her silk stockings until she crawled about the floor naked.

'Lord Hadleigh was your *father*!' I screamed. 'You sucked and fucked your *father* – you filthy, wanton, vile, debased whore! I will kill you for your ways! I will take your life as you took my love, and discard your dirty body as I would a dead rat!'

'Yes, he was my father! He was! Please, allow me to tell you!'

Still shaking with rage, I composed myself and sat upon

the sofa. Sarah made to rise from the floor, but I caught her shoulder with my foot and she fell back. 'You shall speak to me from the dirt of the floor, where you belong!' Nothing but utter disdain did I feel for her as she held her shoulder and winced with the pain. She had lost the battle, and she knew it. Moving towards the hearth she reclined against the fireplace and began her story.

'My mother was a maid at a manor some thirty miles from here; my father was a farm hand who left her when she was pregnant with me. The lord and lady of the manor, from the kindness of their hearts, allowed my mother to remain in their house and, when I was older, I too became their maid. Only on her deathbed did my mother reveal to me the identity of my father, but she was ignorant of his whereabouts. Thus I left to seek him, at length finding him here at Royston Manor. He was Lord Hadleigh! I knew not how he had become a lord, but I cared not, for he had money. Had I knocked upon his front door and told him that I was his daughter, he would surely have had me thrown from the grounds for he was, by all accounts, respectably married.'

'Then why did you suck the seed from his cock, and allow him to fuck you? You knew with whom you fornicated! I put it to you that you are no more than an incestuous strumpet!'

'I was fortunate enough to find employment as a maid at Royston Manor, and my father, not knowing my identity, attempted to interfere with me. He would come to my room and put his hand up my skirts and his finger inside me. My lips were sealed for fear of being dismissed! His wife, the real Lady Sarah Hadleigh, was of an unstable mind and he had no love for her – she was mad. Hence he pursued his lustful ways towards me, and yes, he did take me! He had money, so much money! And I had nothing!'

'And so, for brass, you sucked the seed from your father's cock? The very seed you were born of! Filth, that's what it is – debased filth!'

'His wife died and he buried her, as you know. There was no murder, no plot, she simply passed away one night.'

'No funeral service, no certificate of death. Why?'

'Being of the same age as she, I took her place and became Lady Sarah Hadleigh. At long last, I had money, a position – the station that was rightfully mine!'

'You were born of a maid and a farm hand! Your station was in service, to wait upon the aristocracy, not to join them!'

'My father desperately wanted a son and heir, and I knew it could not be. I syringed every time he . . . that is why I took up with Clara's father. My father thought the child to be his, but still he wanted a son. At length, I took up with Elizabeth's father, but still, no boy! I knew not what to do, for night after night he would take me in his desperation for a son. It was not lust that drove me to one man after another – rather more despair, for I knew not what else to do!'

'But you had a son.'

'James was conceived just prior to my finding employment at Royston Manor. I told my father that the child was his, but he knew it not to be. He sent the child off somewhere, I knew not where. I have not laid eyes upon him for seventeen years.'

'You allowed your own child to be taken away?'

'He knows of my whereabouts, for he has written to me.

He will return, I know it! I had no choice at the time – but he *will* come home, to me, his mother!'

'The choice was yours – your son, or money! There is no blue blood in this family! You, your father, your daughters – all are nothing but red-blooded commoners!'

I left Sarah naked on the floor – crying for her sins, I prayed. I had heard the truths I wanted, but there was no place for me in that house. Sarah held nothing but hatred for me, and I for her. The girls? Yes, a sad loss. My child? Oh, Clara, how I wished to take her away with me! But that was not possible, for I had nothing. The child, at least, would grow and live a full life with all the trappings of the so-called aristocracy. A better life than I could ever provide.

Alas, my promise to meet Amy each morning for lust would now be broken too. As I mooched across the yard, Clara and Elizabeth came running to me. I had it in my mind to tell them of their mother and her wickedness and led them behind the stable to the field where we could talk.

'We have spoken with Rose,' Clara said.

'And what did she have to say?' I asked jovially, not believing the girl.

'She said that her father is after your blood! What have you done, Tom? Have you taken her? Is that how you riled him so?'

'Most certainly not! I do not even know the girl!'

'But you do, Tom!' Elizabeth rejoined.

'I know of her, that is all! Anyway, where did you speak with her?'

'She was down by the cottage, earlier. Walking, she said, but she is too far from her home simply to be walking. We believe she was looking for you!'

Watching the girls giggling and rolling in the long grass, showing knickers that so tightly hugged their little slits, again I wondered at all I would be leaving behind. With Harry dead, and my life seemingly pointless, I wondered to what end was my uncanny knack for attracting young girls. The only one I had genuinely felt for was Sarah, and my love for her was, sadly, dead.

But Rose – was she in the wood somewhere? Awaiting my arrival? She was early by far, but keen, perhaps? I left the girls, much to their displeasure, and made for the wood with much haste. The clearing, our clearing, was quiet. Rose was nowhere in sight and so I sat and awaited her possible arrival.

Contemplating the situation, I pondered upon the mysterious Lord James Hadleigh. When would he return? He had written, Sarah had said, but she had not said when. The minute he showed himself, of course, I would be finished, for he would not allow me to blackmail his mother – or take her as and when it took my fancy! Alas, I had no choice other than to take my leave. But, I told myself, I would enjoy one last time with Rose, for she was a nymph well worth the taking. What had she said? 'There is not one hole in my body that has not been filled with a man's seed!' – or something the same. Some strumpet! How should she emerge in her later years? I cared not, for I would not be around; I was only happy that such a wonderful little whore had chosen me to pleasure herself with in the wood on such a fine summer's day.

The appointed time of our rendezvous approaching, I had some concern in the back of my mind for Cranfield's ruffians. Knowing I could trust no-one, I took it upon myself to climb a tall tree to await the arrival of my sweet

Rose, there, in safe hiding. Not only had she informed me that she was a good liar, but proved the fact by telling her father of her fictitious fall. Who was to say that she had not had second thoughts, and would lead the men to the very clearing in which we were to love?

The lady arrived an hour early and, indeed, was not alone. Much to my bewilderment, she was accompanied not by her father's muscled henchmen, but by young Belle! To my even greater amazement, after seating themselves down upon the soft grass, they began to kiss and fondle each other's breasts – and, I gathered, it was not the first time they had done so. Oh Belle! I thought I had put her right, corrected her ways. But, no; not happy with Sarah's body, it seemed, she was now delighting in young Rose's sweet offerings. How long had such lesbian lust endured? I wondered. I would tell Sarah upon my return to the house and distress her terribly, I decided.

Rose was, indeed, a girl of sensuality, I deemed, as I watched her lie back, lift her skirts, remove her knickers and commence to fondle her slit. Oh, what a magnificent view was I afforded from the very tree under which she lay! Spreading her legs wide, she frigged her clitoris with one hand, deftly reaching the other beneath her thigh to bury her fingers within her cunt, as Belle eagerly looked on.

I could see Belle's excitement growing quickly, as was mine, until, not being able to restrain herself a moment longer, she pushed her face into the girl's bush and began licking and slurping as a cat taking milk. Soon the older girl began to shudder and arch her back and whimper, as Belle took her expertly to her heaven.

'We must do it to each other!' Rose suddenly instructed. 'But let us remove our clothing first.' Losing no time, both girls stood and stripped every item of clothing from their bodies ere lying on the soft grass, their skin aglow in the sunshine, their breasts swollen, nipples ripe, their bellies smooth and creamy. 'Why, you naughty girl, you have shaved!' Rose exclaimed upon eyeing the delicious puffed lips betwixt her companion's thighs.

'I did it for Tom. But he has treated me so badly that I have sworn never to allow him to take me again.'

'Then *I* will take you, and lick betwixt your luscious lips until you are wet enough for me to drink from your hole.'

'And I will drink from yours, Rose, for I care more for girls than men – especially Tom!'

Ah, so I had, indeed, failed. Belle's so-called love for me was no more than infatuation, after all. No man, I suspected, would ever break her preference for girls' cunettes. She was a lesbian at heart, and, no doubt, she would stay as such. But I cared not at that time, for the passion 'neath the tree was rising.

Lying head to toe, their legs parted, the girls began to lick at each other's slits, moaning their delight, hands opening lips, fingering holes, sweet mouths drinking the fruits of lust so produced from their union. My cock bulged neath my breeches as I gazed at the scenario and for a mad moment I had it in my mind to shower them with my seed as they writhed! But no, I would save it, for whom or where I knew not. Belle's cunny? Rose's cunny? Their bottom-holes? It mattered not at that moment where I would sink my cock and loose my sperm – but spurt it somewhere, I would!

The girls rolled over and over upon the grass as their climaxes rocked them, shaking every inch of their bodies. Mouths locked to cunts, they squirmed and writhed and sucked until they came to rest and both lay upon their backs exhausted but, judging by the expressions of serenity on their pretty, wet, glistening faces, satisfied as never before.

I had just pulled out my swollen cock, for I could hold my seed no longer, when the branch upon which I sat snapped, causing me to fall to the branch below. The poor things looked up in horror, covering their young breasts as I clambered down amidst a shower of leaves.

'I am sorry,' I said, dropping to the ground, my cock standing proud from my breeches.

'You have been spying on us!' Belle accused me, ashamed.

'No, no, I fell asleep atop the tree and . . .'

'Why, look at your cock – you were watching us!'

'Yes, I admit as much. But what a wonderful sight!'

'Well, we cannot waste such a heaven-sent opportunity!' shrieked Rose. 'Come, Tom, allow me to attend your cock, for it is in dire need of attention, by the sight of it!'

They pulled me to the ground – Belle, too! – making a grab for my cock. What heaven, the sensation of four pretty little hands around my shaft – but there was paradise in store. Wrenching down my breeches, the harlots held my cock by the root and kissed each other, my swollen knob betwixt their pretty mouths. Two tongues, caressing, licking at my knob, up and down my shaft, I must confess was more than I could bear, and, all too soon, my seed did indeed spurt! On and on it shot, as from a fountain, as they sucked and licked and drank, greedy for an ample share of their reward, until my rigid body shook and I was obliged to pull my aching member from their grasp.

But the teasing pleasure was not yet up, for are not all young girls insatiable? Not yet satisfied by far, one sat upon my legs and the other my chest, as they continued their fondling and licking until my poor knob was obliged to swell once again. 'I want it in my mouth, this time!' Rose begged.

'No, mine! You had more than I last time!' My God, what kind of girls are these, that they argue over a man's sperm? But what fortune of mine to be the organ of dispute!

Belle it was who sat upon my chest and as she leaned forward to take my knob inside her mouth she shifted back and raised her bottom. Ah, what heavenly, swollen, shaven lips! Lifting my head, I did manage to reach her delightful cunt and lick the juices from it as she wriggled and moaned and fought to keep Rose from taking my knob. Excluded from the orgy, Rose moved around to my head where she pushed Belle's bottom away and knelt astride my face. Wetter and hotter even than Belle's was her slit as she ground it into my mouth with such fervour that I was barely able to breathe.

In such a stance, she commenced to come very soon; I say commenced, for her climax indeed seemed interminable. Her juices pouring over my face, my neck, but most heavenly of all, into my mouth, her clitoris, hard as a button, rubbing against my lips, she screamed and quivered and groaned and shuddered until she finally relinquished her joy. I, too, found my paradise, loosing simultaneously my seed into Belle's mouth as she tongued around my prick. My knob in a girl's mouth, my mouth in another's cunt – what heaven indeed!

At length, bent on exploiting to the full my body, and

theirs, they knelt astride my head, breasts pressed firmly together, nipple to nipple. Embracing and kissing, their slits hovering o'er my face, they leaned back on their hands, bellies together, and lowered themselves onto my mouth. Two fine, hot, wet slits, awaiting my tongue! What delight, to lick one slit and continue along its length to the other, transferring the milky juices from hole to hole! Ah, two slits pressed together is surely a sight rarely seen, two cunny holes, pinken lips hanging open either side, dripping the juices of love into my thirsty mouth!

Sadly, their clitorises were hidden from view, but not out of reach! Pushing my finger up betwixt the two valleys, cushioned by four swollen lips, I managed to locate the little buds. Up and down I pushed my finger as if in a cunny hole, rubbing both clitties simultaneously. The girls shuddered and kissed and pressed their nipples together as I fingered them until a cocktail of their warm, sticky juices deluged o'er my face as they neared their paradise. What a sight to behold, what taste to savour! Who would first attain their goal? I found myself wondering as I frantically worked my finger.

There was no single winner, for they came in unison. Gasping, hands groping, fingering each other's bottom-holes, they pressed their slits upon my face and rocked until they collapsed onto the grass each side of me – done! I pandered to their exhausted bodies, kissing, licking their legs, thighs, bellies, breasts, necks, worshipping every inch of their spent bodies, ere attending their slits. And then to my prize – first one, and then the other, I licked up and down their hot slits, poking my tongue into their holes in passing, slurping at their juices, sucking the inner lips into my mouth until they were both again fired with passion.

Was their lust truly insatiable? Indeed it seemed so, for they were soon about my face again, in turn moving their open valleys back and forth o'er my mouth, ere moving aside for the other. They were kissing again, and whispering in gasps, but I was in no position to discern their words.

'Is your cock yet again ready?' Rose asked as they climbed from my face.

'It is!' I replied, looking down at the rod of iron pointing skyward. 'Indeed it is!' More whispering, and I wondered what further delights they were planning. I had not long to wait as Rose, dog-like upon all fours, displayed her bottom-hole to my hungry gaze as Belle, being the lighter of the two, mounted her. Four wondrous buttocks! Two bottom-holes! Two cunettes! What was I to do? Which haven should I first honour?

'Take your pick, Tom,' Rose offered. 'But be sure to sow your seed fairly betwixt our cunnies!'

'I will, I will!' Homing in first to Rose's sweet honey-pot, I plunged in my stinger well and truly to the root as it throbbed, and she squeezed. Ah, sheer delight! And then out and into Belle's cunny; tighter, wetter, and heavenly! And so back to Rose and then to . . . On and on I fucked, first one and then the other, until it was time for further adventure. Pressing my knob to Belle's bottom-hole, I pushed my length right in. Ah, how she did wiggle and shriek as I fucked her there!

And then out, straight into the other tight ring. My seed nearing the bulbous, throbbing head of my cock, I withdrew to plunge it into the cosier confines of sweet Rose's cunny which I furnished with three good spurts. Being a man of my word, I withdrew my rod, still pumping, to drive it niftily into Belle's little pot, affording her her fair share of my fruits. Homing from one hole to the other until my cock fell flaccid, I pleasured both girls equally, as they had demanded.

As I rested on the grass, totally exhausted, the girls lay head to toe, sucking and licking the sperm from each other's slits and holes until, yet again, they yielded up their spirits. Ten men could not bring those insatiable young lesbians the measures of gratification they sought, I will swear! Indeed, I do not believe that they did find complete satisfaction, for as they dressed, they spoke of how their next meeting in the clearing would be of lengthier duration, that they could truly enjoy themselves! Indeed, such was their dalliance, embracing, kissing and sucking of nipples, that I was obliged to take my leave alone.

A strange thought struck me as I walked back through the wood. I wondered if my father would take me back into the firm, for I now had a damn good head for figures! But, alas, not only would he not take me back, I could not go. I could not return to such a life – not now I had discovered the delights of living in the country.

Should I have to leave, should I be forced by those ruffians to flee the manor, then, I decided, it would only be right to take the delectable Sarah once again. And to take her with such fervour that her screams of pleasure would be heard o'er the entire county! Perforce taking her to such sexual heights could rekindle her love for me? One never knew, particularly with the mysterious Sarah.

Chapter Sixteen

The afternoon had been long and hot and most rewarding, but my mind was deeply troubled. The time had come, I knew, to make one final stand. I was not prepared to depart the life I had come to love without a fight, though preferably not with the ruffians. Sarah alone held the key to my staying at the Manor House; she was my only hope, albeit a hope in hell.

I found her tending herbs in the kitchen garden behind the house. My inspired surmise concerning Lord James Hadleigh was really no more than a wild guess, but I deemed it worth a try, for I was at the end of my tether. 'Sarah!' I called. Looking up, she quickly returned her gaze to the herbs, upon seeing it was I. 'I wish to speak with you, Sarah!'

'There is nothing to speak about, Tom! I am surprised that you are still here!' she replied, glancing only briefly in my direction.

'I will always be here – always!'

'Then it will be in spirit only, for you will die ere long, that is certain.'

Why was she so? Had the little love she had once felt for me really turned to such hatred? Had she so soon forgotten our passionate encounters – or simply dismissed them?

Handsome she was to behold in her summer dress of pink cotton. Would I ever again encounter a woman of such rare beauty? I doubted very much that I would. I knew also that I would never again meet a woman of such determination, such damn stubbornness! My efforts to blackmail her, to change her mind and win her love, would prove useless, I was sure. But I was determined to try.

'Lord James Hadleigh was born of your vile union with your father, was he not?' I asked accusingly. She said nothing, not even raising her eyes from the parsley and thyme she was picking. 'He was your father's son, your son, and he must have been a poorly thing, for interbreeding is not conducive to fine, healthy offspring.'

Still she did not raise her eyes. Damn the woman! Was I so very wrong in my surmise? 'He is dead, is he not? Buried, more than likely, alongside Lady Sarah Hadleigh!'

'You are incorrect, I am pleased to say. So far from the truth, in fact, that you prove yourself to be nothing more than an imbecile. Why not take a room in the village? As the village idiot!'

'And you are nothing more than an incestuous harlot! Why do *you* not take a room in the village? As a tart!'

'I am finished with you, Tom. There is nothing you can say to distress me, nothing to rile me, for I am finished with you. There, you see, I raise not even my voice in anger, for I feel none – only pity for the weak, impotent, cowardly object you have proved yourself to be. I have told you in the past, you were nothing more to me than a toy, a plaything – and the novelty wore off. As a child discards a boring toy, I have discarded you.'

Curse the woman! If she were not riled, I certainly was! A toy – a plaything! How dare she treat me with such contempt? 'I will see you dead ere I leave this house!' I swore. 'Your debased body hanging in the wind as a lesson to all those who dare even think to use their bodies to their own vile ends!'

'You used me, Tom. You took me and used me for your pleasure. And my daughters – and Belle.'

'You know not the half of it! I have taken Rose, the daughter of the man who masquerades as Lord Cranfield. And Amy, the daughter of Lord and Lady Miles.'

'Then you confirm my suspicions. In trying to play the part of Romeo, you have sullied Shakespeare! You are an impotent Casanova!'

Enough was enough! I was about to drag her to the ground and beat her when the battle-axe called through the kitchen window. Leaving me fuming in the garden, her ladyship repaired into the house. 'You in trouble again, young man?' the battle-axe enquired through the open window.

'I am, indeed!' I replied.

'The boy, James, 'e was 'er father's son, you got that bit right. But 'is mother was the real Lady Sarah 'adleigh. She died a few months after 'aving 'im and old 'adleigh could not cope with the child alone. The boy died when 'e was but a babe, 'e did.'

'The boy died? How do you know of this?' I asked.

'I know, that's all! Tell 'er that you know 'is body is in the grounds. Buried alongside 'is mother.'

With that, she slammed shut the window. Words of great revelation, indeed, but still I had no proof. Mere words did not antagonise Sarah, let alone elicit the truth or subdue her to my threats of blackmail. Besides, for what use was the information? The Hadleighs' son had died, but

I did not see how that could benefit me. Unless . . . in a flash, I understood the significance of the certificate of birth to which the battle-axe had led me. Suddenly, the key to the manor was within my grasp – oh, what a joyous life was mine to be!

'You are still here, Tom,' Sarah remarked coldly on returning to the garden.

'I am indeed, Sarah. And I have great news for you. I will stay on at the manor, after all, for I have discovered the perfect way!'

'You will do no such thing – unless you wish that only your corpse remain here! I spoke with Lord Cranfield earlier today. He will be here, with his men, first thing in the morning – to remove you, Tom. What they will do with you once you are off my land, I know not – and care not!'

'But I have the answer, Sarah! I am to be your son, Lord James Hadleigh – I have the certificate of birth to prove my title!'

'You have the certificate of birth belonging to James. The boy will return home to me, his mother, ere long.'

'He is buried in the grounds – alongside his real mother! Come, Sarah, give up your futile fight and accept me as your long lost, loving son!'

'I will do no such thing! You are worse than an imbecile, you are completely mad! Dead? Buried in the grounds alongside his real mother? I have never heard such nonsense! From whence do you draw such idiotic notions? Your deranged mind, I should not wonder! Go ere the morning, Tom – for your own good!'

'I will not! I shall locate the grave and dig up the child's remains! But not before calling on a police officer to witness the act. You will be thrown into jail, my Lady Sarah, where you belong! And I will be free – to live here with the girls as Lord James Hadleigh.'

Sarah's hands were trembling and her pallor had greyed somewhat. Though visibly shaken, she did her utmost to hide the fact. As she traipsed into the house wearing an expression of great worry, I sat on a nearby garden chair and contemplated the future. Lord Cranfield did indeed present a problem, but if Sarah could be persuaded to tell him that I was, indeed, her long lost son, he would not only call off his ruffians, but welcome me into his house – Rose's house! But, alas, I knew that Sarah would not do as much for me.

Short of locating the grave, there was nothing I could do. But where to start? Acres of land and the passing of some sixteen or so years – more easy to find a needle in a haystack! I could beat the whereabouts of the grave out of Sarah. But no; better still to fuck it out of her! Yes, in the wood, the clearing, tie her to the tree, as I had Rose, and fuck her to her innermost secret. After all, had I not promised myself one last ride with the lady?

Belle had enjoyed our games in the wood, and she seemed to have forgiven me for beating her. She would help me, I was sure, and I made for her cottage with all haste. 'Belle!' I panted. 'You must help me, my angel!'

'How can I help you, Tom? Besides, I am not sure that I *should* help you, for . . .'

'Entice Sarah to the wood, to the clearing. Will you do it?'

'No, I will not! Anyway, to what ends, pray?'

'I am to take my leave of Royston Manor, as you know, but I do not wish to leave. I have but one chance, Belle.

But one last chance to remain here – and you must help me!'

'When and how shall I entice her?'

'How? Why, naturally, by dint of your voluptuous body! And when? Now! This very instant, for dusk will soon be upon us, and I am hard pushed for time.'

'Time for what, Tom? What do you intend to do, once she is there, in the clearing?'

'I cannot explain now. You must . . .'

'If your plan is to harm her, then . . .'

'My intention is not to harm her. Will you do it?'

'I can but try. But I doubt very much that she will accompany me. It is a fair walk and, as you say, dusk will soon be upon us.'

'She will go with you, Belle – she must!'

Making for the wood, I remembered that I had left the very rope with which I had tethered poor Rose hidden under a bush on the edge of the clearing – with the riding crop! My plan roughly formulated, I made with all haste to the clearing to await the lovely Sarah.

Voices emanated from the thicket only a half-hour after I had taken to the tree above the clearing. Ah, Belle! That she should honour her infidel stud! Sarah, with a cotton jacket upon her summer dress, entered the clearing and sat beneath the tree. 'So, Belle,' she said softly. 'What is it that you wish me to see? Or have you brought me here merely because you desire my body, yet again?'

'I desire your body greatly, Sarah. But I also wish to speak with you. You see, I am gravely concerned for Tom.'

'Tom will be gone by the morning, Belle, so do not concern yourself with him! Now, allow me to remove your jodhpurs, my little one, for you must be awfully hot.'

Removing her boots and lifting her buttocks from the grass, the girl allowed Sarah to pull her jodhpurs down her lovely legs and over her ankles. She wore no knickers, and Sarah wasted not one second ere burying her face betwixt Belle's tender thighs. 'Belle,' she breathed. 'I do believe you have touched yourself today, and not so long ago, for you are most wet and sticky.'

'I did, Sarah. Thinking only of you, I did touch myself.'

'Then I must clean your pretty little slit thus.' With that, she did lick at Belle's wonderful slit as the girl reclined and spread her legs. Belle caught my eye in the tree as she looked up, and smiled. From my heart, I returned her smile and winked, for she was my true ally.

From my vantage, I did perceive Sarah to become more aroused than Belle as she licked and sucked and pulled asunder the fleshy lips to expose the young bud, growing 'neath its pinken hood. Then briefly separating her full mouth from those sweet, naked vaginal lips, she removed her jacket and dress, leaving only her lace brassiere, tight and full with her heaving breasts, and her white, silken knickers to cover her beautiful body from my candid gaze.

Turning round, Belle reached up to ease down Sarah's knickers o'er her ankles and began to kiss her slit, as she had Rose's. The lady of the house and the stable girl entwined together in oral lust! Would that Sarah's aristocratic friends could see the woman she really was! They would surely have enough gossip to endure a hundred dinner parties or more.

With both beauties ere long writhing in mutual ecstasy, I watched and waited, for my time was almost nigh. Belle had been clever, for knowing that she would have to flee she had not allowed Sarah to remove her jacket and blouse. Only her boots and jodhpurs would she need to grab ere taking flight. But I had not yet formulated the exact plan and regretted not having plotted the event with Belle in detail beforehand. I did not wish for Sarah to know that she had been set up by the girl, for she would surely punish her and, more than likely, throw her out of the cottage.

Thus, there, perched in the tree, I came upon an idea that I prayed Belle would comprehend. Quietly twisting a branch from the tree, I planned to throw it, causing a rustling in the bushes across the clearing. Fortunately, Belle looked up at me at the opportune moment and I brandished the branch in the hope that she would realise my intention. Grabbing her clothes whilst yet mouthing at Sarah's vaginal lips, she indicated her readiness with a wave of the hand. I hurled the stick and it crashed into the bushes with the desired effect.

Leaving her startled lover to gather her senses, and her clothes, Belle upped and ran as I dropped, silently, from the tree, landing behind Sarah who, seeing it was I upon turning to flee, gasped a sigh of relief, and then, within the same breath, flew into a rage. 'What are you doing, Tom?' she shrieked, making to don her knickers.

'I followed you and Belle here, to this lonely spot of yours, and I have been watching you, my lovely. And now, is it not my turn to take you, for I take my leave on the morrow, do I not?'

Sarah gazed at me thoughtfully, her rage gone – at the prospect of a fucking, no doubt. She said nothing as she dropped her clothes, and, in her obvious arousal, turned to me with a faint smile upon her pretty lips. I guessed that she, too, had speculated upon one last fuck with me ere my departure. My eyes darted from the rope, just visible under the bush, to her firm breasts and upstanding nipples. 'Well, Tom. How are you going to bid me farewell? Not simply by standing there, surely?'

Ah, she was ready for lust as never before, my pretty Belle having prepared her so! I kissed her sweet mouth and squeezed her long, hard nipples as I gently manoeuvred her towards the tree. My timing and my actions had to be perfect, for I had no wish to fight with her. Her back to the tree, I knelt before her downy bush and parted her already wet and swollen lips with my tongue, reaching for the rope as she moaned and looked up to the green leaves of the tree.

Oh, Sarah, sweet Sarah, she knew not what I was about as I stood before her and sucked her nipples until she begged me to attend again her clitoris. Turning her curvaceous frame to face the tree, I swung the rope around the trunk and tied it fast behind her back. Ere she could even speak, I had tied her hands, too, and she stood, hugging the tree, her nipples caressing the rough bark, her buttocks bared.

'What are you about, Tom?' she cried. 'What are your intentions?'

'I am going to whip you, for a start! And then I am going to fuck your bottom-hole until you agree to my staying on at the manor house.'

'Never! Never! I would sooner die than see you living in the house – *my* house!'

'Then you may well have to die, my lovely, for I intend to live in your house, no matter what it may take to do so!'

The riding crop felt wonderful within my hand as I swished it through the air and landed it across her tightening buttocks. Lash after lash reddened her pale crescents until they shone crimson and she cried pathetically for mercy. 'Will you accept me as your son?' I enquired.

'Never!'

'Will you?'

'Never!'

Poor Sarah did take her punishment well, I must confess, and I was fairly worn out after thirty or so thrashings. As I checked my grip on the crop I did notice the carved rosewood handle, ideally shaped for inserting into a lady's neat little bottom-hole! Kneeling behind her, I kissed the weals criss-crossing her glowing buttocks, and pressed the crop handle to her brown ring. 'What is that?' she cried.

'The riding crop handle, Sarah. It will enter far deeper into your hot bowels than my cock.'

'No, no! You are a bastard!'

'Will you accept me as . . .'

'Never!'

'Then, hold tight, for here it comes!'

I felt rather sorry for her as the handle sank into her bowels, deeper and deeper, until it was in no further than a cock could penetrate. I did not wish to damage her, but to my advantage, she was unaware of that fact. 'My God!' I cried. 'A good twelve inches buried deep within your bottom-hole!'

'Take it out, you will kill me!'

'A good idea, do you not agree? Perhaps another six inches . . .'

'No, no!'

'Accept me!'

'Never!'

She was a damn stubborn woman – either that, or plain stupid! But no, she was not stupid, for she knew only too well that I should not harm her. Damn my good nature! Almost she knew me better than I knew myself. I was not to achieve a submission with my present mode of torture, I was sure of that. Slowly withdrawing the riding crop, I discarded it and eased my hard cock from my breeches. 'You will enjoy this, Sarah,' I assured her, pressing my length into her hot body.

Enjoy it she did, sadly, and so did I, filling her with my sperm within minutes; for I had had it in my mind to fuck her until she screamed and agreed to my terms.

'You win, Sarah!' I gasped presently, sliding my shaft from her warm, creamy depths. 'You win, but I will leave you here, all night, in the dark.'

'No, please, you cannot! I will give you some money. Take me to the house, I will give you money for . . .'

'No, I think not, for I will go to the house and take your money, anyway. I will also take Clara and Elizabeth and Belle ere my departure!'

'No, pray leave the girls be! You must release me, for you know not where the money is hidden.'

'I will find it, and, no doubt, the girls and Belle will find you – tomorrow, perhaps, or the day after, for I shall tell them that you are staying with Lord and Lady Miles for a few days.'

'Belle knows that I am here.'

'That is as may be, but she will believe me when I tell her . . . Besides, I may well leave her tied to her bedstead. And your daughters, perhaps I should secure them somewhere, after I have fucked them both, that is.'

'Listen! James was Lady Sarah's son and he is dead, I will admit, but you cannot, you will not take his place!'

'I am finished with this idle chit-chat – goodbye, Sarah!'

Her cries and screams echoed through the wood, fading as I distanced myself from the clearing. The poor darling must have been terrified, I reflected – tied naked to a tree, the dusk falling, the wild beasts roaming! I laughed as I walked on, but stopped dead on hearing someone nearing me.

'My God, Belle! What do you do, creeping upon me so?'

'You were cruel to her, Tom! You cannot leave her there all night. She will die of fright! And you will *not* tie me to my bedstead!'

'Of course I will not, for you have helped me. Sarah will come to no harm, and besides, why should I care if she does?'

'Because you love her.'

Damn all women, for are they not all so clever, so shrewd, so intuitive? Belle was right, my love for Sarah had not died, as I had once thought. I only wished that it had, for life would have been far easier. On reflection, I realised that my love for Sarah had grown, painfully, for she felt only hatred for me.

'She loves you, Tom, in her own, strange way,' Belle informed me.

'Rubbish! Rot! What causes you to speak so? For if she had but one ounce of feeling for me, other than hatred, she would agree to my living in the house with her.'

'Why should she agree to demands made with black-mail? You beat her, punish her, treat her with contempt – and then wonder why she will not allow you in her house!'

'I have nothing more to say on the matter, Belle. I am returning to the manor now, to take her money ere I leave.'

Belle followed me to the house, where the girls enquired of their mother's whereabouts. At first, I ignored them, glaring at Belle ere she opened her mouth.

'Where is she, Tom?' Clara asked fearfully. 'We have not seen her for some while, and it is almost dark.'

'She will be home when she is good and ready, no doubt!' I returned as I made my way to Sarah's bed-chamber.

Having ransacked the room, and found nothing, I sat upon the bed and pondered my next move. 'Why do you not sleep here for the night, Tom?' Belle asked, leaning upon the door frame.

'For one last night, that may well be a good idea,' I replied, for I was dead on my feet and, worse, had no money. Belle closed the door as I lay upon the bed, exhausted of body and mind, and closed my eyes. Ere the crack of dawn I would be up and away, with or without money. Giant? Yes, I would take Giant with me, I decided.

The dawn broke all too soon, and I slept on. It was eight of the clock ere I opened my eyes and wondered where I was. Then it all came back to me, as a bad dream. But the sound of a coach-and-four pulling up outside the house was certainly no dream. In a state of panic, I peered through the window. Lord Cranfield and his ruffians! I was surely doomed. My mind wild with terror, I fought to direct my thoughts. The back way, through a window – no, better to hide in the house until they had gone!

Halfway down the stairs, I stopped dead in my tracks, for Lord Cranfield was standing at the bottom. My time had indeed come – but what was this, some trickery? For he was alone – at least, his men were not in the house. But they would be outside, waiting for me with sticks, whips and guns, I knew.

Sarah had kept to her word. I had always believed that, somewhere within, she held some love for me. But I was sadly wrong, it seemed. Nevertheless, love or no love, I had not really expected her to have me dealt with by ruffians. Where was she? I wondered as I descended the stairs towards Cranfield. Was she still in the wood, tied to the tree? Or hiding with the girls somewhere in the house, waiting for the execution of the dirty deed?

As I stood face to face with Cranfield, he smiled. 'Good morning, Lord Hadleigh,' he said warmly. Lord Hadleigh? What on earth was his game?

'Good morning, Lord Cranfield,' I replied shakily. 'I was just about to . . .'

'I am having guests for dinner this evening and I would be honoured if you and your mother, Lady Sarah, will join me.'

'Yes, yes, of course – we would be delighted,' I replied, somewhat confused, to say the least!

'Until this evening, then – at seven of the clock.'

I stood on the steps and watched his coach follow the sweep of the drive and disappear from view. Mystified, I turned to enter the house to see Clara, Elizabeth and Belle standing as pretty maids in a row.

'Good morning, Lord Hadleigh,' they greeted me impishly, in unison.

'Good morning, ladies. Now, pray, what is this about?'

'We spoke with mother, after releasing her from the tree, that is,' Clara said.

'I told her that, if you were to take your leave of the manor, then I would leave also,' Belle rejoined.

'We all told her, Tom. Told her that we want you here, with us!' Elizabeth cried, flinging her arms around my neck and kissing me.

The three beauties scampered off as Sarah approached from the hall.

'You have won, it seems,' she conceded, with the slightest hint of a smile.

'Indeed, I have! But Lord Cranfield, I thought . . .'

'I spoke with him, this morning ere you woke. I was under great duress, I might add, from your admirers. Even Cook took me aside and begged that I allow you to stay, as my son. I have to say that I am displeased, Tom, most displeased! But I have had little or no choice in the matter. Now, will you join us for breakfast in the morning room?'

Oh, the sun shone for me and the angels sang that day, I will swear! I was Lord James Hadleigh – Lord of the Manor! Surrounded by my beauties, Rose, Belle, Amy, Clara, Elizabeth, my future held an abundance of pleasure and love. And Sarah.

Sarah was not happy, I knew. And I suppose I was not completely happy, masquerading as her son. But the masquerade was for the eyes of society only, for by night we lived as husband and wife, sleeping and loving, if it can be called love, in the warmth of her bed.

Even if Sarah's love for me does, in time, shine through, I doubt very much that I will ever be totally happy. For I am no more a lord than was poor Harry. In fact, so few genuine lords and ladies remain that I wonder, with great sadness, where the true, blue-blooded aristocracy has gone. Or if, indeed, it ever really existed. For so long as the true red-blooded male such as I abounds, surely even the bluest blood, thinned and diluted, must, in time, run red.